Let Jenny Oliver be the dusting of icing sugar on the top of your perfect Christmas

Also by
Jenny Oliver

THE VINTAGE SUMMER WEDDING

Jenny Oliver wrote her first book on holiday when she was ten years old. Illustrated with cut-out supermodels from her sister's *Vogue*, it was an epic, sweeping love story not so loosely based on *Dynasty*.

Since then Jenny has gone on to get an English degree, a Master's and a job in publishing that's taught her what it takes to write a novel (without the help of the supermodels). She wrote *The Parisian Christmas Bake Off* on the beach in a sea-soaked, sand-covered notebook. This time the inspiration was her addiction to macaroons, the belief she can cook them and an all-consuming love of Christmas. When the decorations go up in October, that's fine with her! Follow her on Twitter @JenOliverBooks.

The Parisian Christmas Bake Off

To my mum and dad
for always buying the biggest tree

CHAPTER ONE

'Why is Jesus a Buzz Lightyear?'

Rachel came into the school hall carrying two cups of PG Tips, and a packet of chocolate HobNobs that she'd stolen from the staffroom.

'Purely for my own amusement,' said Jackie, sitting back, feet up on a nursery-school chair as she took three biscuits out of the packet. 'And because the arm fell off the normal one and Mrs Norris's husband is fixing it.' She nodded towards the stage. 'The nativity's good this year, isn't it?'

Rachel turned to where fourteen five-year-olds had forgotten the words to 'Away in a Manger' as they rehearsed. 'I'd say it bears a remarkable resemblance to last year's.'

Jackie did a mock gasp of affront. 'Except for the genius addition of the hip hop WyZe men and One Direction's visit to the manger. I think I'll make the school proud.'

'The head's going to kill you.'

'It's just a bit of fun.' Jackie flicked open her ancient laptop as the kids on stage continued to sing a motley assortment of words while dressed in a variety of home-made costumes. 'So fire me. Who else are they going to get to direct this? It's not as if Nettleton has anyone pre-retirement age left—'

'Look,' shouted one of the kids on stage. 'Miss Smithson's here,' he said, breaking off from the song as the others were belting out the second verse.

Rachel waved. 'Hi, Tommy. Keep singing though—you don't want to ruin the song.' She could see the rest of her class starting to get distracted on stage.

'But I don't know the words,' he said, looking as if he was about to cry.

Rachel jogged up to the front of the hall and climbed on the stage, whispering to Tommy as quietly as she could. 'That's OK, I never knew the words—when you don't know them just open and shut your mouth like this.' She did an impression of a goldfish.

Tommy giggled. 'Can I go to the toilet?'

Rachel rolled her eyes. She didn't envy Jackie the task of keeping this lot in order; just her own class were enough for her. 'Yes, Tommy.'

'Miss Smithson?' said Jemima in the back row. 'My wings keep falling off.'

Everyone had stopped singing now.

'OK, I'll have a look.' Rachel tiptoed round in a crouch trying to be as unobtrusive as she could

manage while Jackie tried to cajole them all back into
singing.

'Will you sing with us, Miss Smithson?' Jemima
asked as Rachel tightened her wonky angel wings.

Rachel swallowed, listening as the little voices
had started up again on the fourth verse. 'I erm…'
She found herself caught off guard with no ready
answer, a whole heap of memories suddenly stuck in
her throat.

'Sing with us, please?' Tommy was running back on
stage, tucking his T-shirt into his cords.

'No. I'm just going to watch.' She shook her head,
her voice annoyingly choked as she blocked out images
of being on that stage herself with her parents clapping
wildly from the front row. 'I like listening to you,' she
said quickly, before jumping back off the stage.

Around the hall members of the PTA were building
the nativity set, sewing costumes and making
arrangements for lighting, seating, refreshments etc.
Mostly they stood gossiping in groups, however, while
one or two put together the bulk of the scenery—
checking how well it had fared in the store cupboard
since last year. Mr Swanson, Tommy's father, was
standing by the steps screwing together the roof of the
manger. 'Difficult time of year for you, isn't it?' he said
as Rachel walked away from the stage.

'Oh, it's OK.' Rachel waved a hand. 'I'll get through
it. Great set this year, by the way.'

'It's the same every year.' He laughed, then went on, 'No need for a brave face, you know. We're all here. All of us. Your mum was a great friend of ours and we miss her too.'

'I know—thanks.'

He nodded and went back to changing the bit on his drill. 'I was meaning to say, I thought you did a good job at the bake sale last week. Excellent scones. I've missed them, you know?'

She smiled. 'Well, they're not quite as good as Mum made.'

Mr Swanson thought about it and shrugged. 'Nearly.'

In the background the children continued to sing out of tune as Jackie called instructions, and the parents chattered away, and Rachel found herself wishing, not for the first time this holiday season, that it could all just disappear. Poof. That she could click her fingers and it would be New Year and she wouldn't have to shake her head and say everything was all right when people asked if she was OK, said that they always thought of her mum at this time of year and understood how hard it must be for her, and what was she going to do for Christmas. As Mr Swanson locked the bit in place on his drill, he put his hand on the wonky roof and said, 'You're a good girl.'

Rachel paused and allowed herself to nod as he watched her and smiled. Everyone was just being kind, she reminded herself. The village was like a family— they had all known her since she was tiny and they all wanted to make sure she was OK. Sometimes, though, she just wanted to be on her own. 'Not so much of the girl any more though, Mr Swanson,' she joked, trying to force a lightness into her voice.

'Don't say it.' He shook his head. 'You stay young, I stay young.'

'OK, you're on.' Rachel laughed as she walked back over to where Jackie was stabbing at the keys of the decrepit laptop.

'All right?' Jackie glanced up.

'Fine.' Rachel nodded, looking back at the stage and taking a sip of her tea. She could feel her heart beating just a bit too fast.

Jackie was clearly about to say something more, to really check if Rachel was all right, but paused, the look on Rachel's face making her decide against it, and said instead, 'OK, look at this—' Jackie pointed to the screen '—check this site out.'

Rachel peered forward to see the display. 'What is it?'

'Airbnb. It lets you turn your home into a hotel. Tonya from the hairdresser's has let her flat out with them to a Swedish couple while she's away over Christmas. Two thousand pounds she got for a week and a half. It's amazing. Such a clever idea—your flat actually earns you money.'

'Yeah.' Rachel nodded, uncertain. 'I think I remember one of my dad's friends used it when he went to New York. Said the pictures weren't anything like the place.'

Jackie shook her head. 'Oh, he probably just likes a moan. I think it's amazing. And especially good for someone like you who doesn't care for Christmas. Wouldn't you say?'

'Not really.' Rachel sipped her tea.

'Oh, I think so. It's a good way to make money,' Jackie went on. 'And the perfect opportunity for *that* person to do what *they* might always have wanted to do in life but was too scared to try.'

The kids on stage had changed song, coaxed into 'The Holly and the Ivy' by Miss Ven at the piano.

'Jackie, whatever it is you're driving at, I'm not interested.'

'But let's say—' Jackie rested one hand on the lid of the laptop and waved the other from side to side as she mused '—for example, someone else thought you were interested in doing something different. Making a change. Thought maybe you were hiding away and wasting your life with a good-for-nothing waster, working at a tiny—but, let's not forget, Ofsted highly commended—primary school, which they knew you liked but felt wasn't quite right for you. Thought that you had other talents that you weren't making the best use of. I mean, what then? What if they, for example, secretly took photos of your flat and maybe rented it over Christmas to a lovely retired couple from Australia who were arriving on Sunday. What then?'

'Well, then…' Rachel put the cup down on the table. 'Then I'd kill you. But I don't think you'd dare.'

Jackie's lips drew up in a wry smile as the realisation of what her friend might have done dawned on Rachel.

And as it did, suddenly all the PTA parents popped up from their various positions in the hall where they'd been painting scenery and bitching about the nativity casting, and shouted, 'Surprise!'

'What's going on?' Rachel looked around as the PTA head honcho Mrs Pritchard, alpha-mother of a girl in Jackie's class, handed her an envelope with Eurostar stamped on the front and everyone clapped.

'I kinda dared.' Jackie looked a little sheepish. 'You're going to Paris.'

Rachel took a step back. 'I'm not going to Paris.'

All the parents were nudging one another, nodding excitedly.

'Yeah, you are.' Jackie went on, 'To bake with Henri Salernes.'

Rachel laughed. 'Don't be ridiculous.'

'It's true.' Mrs Pritchard nodded, patting Rachel affectionately on the arm. 'It's an apprentice competition. The infamous Henri wants an apprentice—well, actually we're not convinced he wants, it's possible that it's more just to make money, but the opportunity is still there. It was a competition on *In The Morning*, on ITV. For amateurs to compete to work for him for a month. It coincides with a new book or something, I think. Was it a new book?' She glanced around at the other parents, some of whom nodded, others looked unsure. 'Anyway, it sounds fabulous. And we all just thought it would be a wonderful opportunity for you. Maybe get you back in the swing of it.'

One of the parents came over with a tray of tea and more biscuits and they all raised their chipped mugs in a toast to Rachel's impromptu Christmas trip to France, enthusiasm plastered on their faces.

Her colleague, gym teacher Henry Evans, was the only one looking less than impressed. 'Don't know what we'll do without you, though. Who'll make the cakes for the Christmas Sports Day? And the Village Lights evening?'

'Shut up, Henry.' Mrs Pritchard elbowed him in the ribs while sipping her tea and then telling some of the other parents how she'd been the one to spot the competition on the telly.

Rachel wasn't really listening; she was glaring at Jackie, who was finding the remains of her tea fascinating. 'How could I have got into that competition? How can I be baking for Henri Salernes when he hasn't tasted what I cook? I can't go to Paris, Jackie, this is insane.'

'We pulled some strings.' Jackie shrugged. 'Well, actually, Mr Swanson pulled some strings—he works for the network. It's all very underhand and not above board at all, but we thought the good outweighed the wrongness.' Jackie turned to point at where Mr Swanson was still standing by the manger, drilling the roof and looking a little sheepish. He waved a hand as if she shouldn't have mentioned it and the quieter they kept it all, the better.

'It's not a problem. I cleared it with the team. Not a problem at all,' he said, although he did look a bit shifty and his neck was flushing a similar colour to his Christmas jumper. 'Wouldn't have done it for anyone else, mind.'

'Look, thanks, everyone, it's really sweet of you, but I can't go to Paris. And I certainly can't bake for Henri Salernes. I'm nowhere near good enough. And, Jackie, no one's going to be living in my flat.' Rachel thought of all her things just the way she liked them being picked up and broken by a couple of Australian strangers. She thought of her usual Christmas Day hiding out in her bedroom with the six-hour BBC *Pride and Prejudice* DVD. She thought of the endurance test that went with avoiding the carol concerts, the presents, the festive cheer. Of locking out thoughts and memories of family Christmases that were just too achingly bittersweet to remember. 'I just—there's no way I'm going. I have loads to do here. I can't. Absolutely no way…'

She trailed off when she looked up and saw all the happy little faces of the kids on stage. They'd stopped singing and run off to the wings without her noticing. Now they were holding up a banner saying, 'Good Luck in Paris, Miss Smithson!', smiling expectantly. All watching.

But now their faces were starting to droop, like flowers wilting. Little Tommy had pulled off his angel halo, his bottom lip quivering. It was as if she'd stood in front of them and picked all the decorations off the big Christmas tree at the back and smashed them one by one underfoot.

Jackie raised her eyebrows; Rachel narrowed her eyes back at her. She felt the PTA parents start to murmur and others look away, embarrassed, as if it certainly wasn't meant to go this way. She watched the uncertain faces of her class, who couldn't understand why their favourite teacher wasn't laughing with delight. They'd clearly been prepped to expect some sort of party atmosphere. So as the silence fell around her Rachel did the only thing that she could so as not to disappoint: going against her every instinct, she swallowed, took a shaky breath and forced her best teacher smile.

'Thanks,' she said, waving the envelope of tickets so the kids could see. 'Thanks so much. It's really kind of you all. I can't wait.' Then she pointed at the stage. 'What a fantastic banner.'

Mrs Pritchard took this as an obvious signal to start clapping and as she took the lead the other PTA parents joined in, unsure at first but gathering steam. Mr Swanson put down his drill and punched the air, triumphant. When the kids heard the cheers they tugged the banner as tight as they could so it pulled up high and just their smiling eyes poked out over the top. Then, when Jackie clicked her fingers, they all ran off the stage and swamped Rachel in a hug, so she was trapped in an island of five-year-olds unable to do anything but fake smile so hard her cheeks started to ache.

CHAPTER TWO

No way was she going to Paris. Back at her flat Rachel was stirring coq au vin on the stove with one hand while trying to pull baked potatoes out of the oven with the other. No way. Turning the dial on the oven down, she noted how clean and shiny it was, how she knew which hob worked and which didn't light, how the cupboard to her left sometimes needed an extra shove to get the door to click shut—strangers staying in her flat wouldn't know those things. Would she have to write them a list?

'Do you want wine?' her grandmother shouted from where she was sitting at the table, her big colourful scarf wrapped multiple times round her neck and the bracelets on her arm clacking together as she raised her hand.

'I'm only just here, Gran, no need to shout.' Rachel winced.

'Sorry, was I shouting? I must be such an embarrassment to you.' Her grandmother cocked her head and pulled a tight smile. 'Do you know, Gran is such a terrible term. I'd really rather you called me Julie. What do you think, David?' She turned to Rachel's father, who was sitting quietly opposite her. 'Don't you just hate the term Dad?'

'Sorry, what? I was miles away.' Rachel's dad had been staring into space and blinked himself back into the present.

'Dad!' Julie sighed. 'Don't you think it's a dreadful word? A label. Wouldn't you far rather Rachel called you David?'

'I've never really thought about it,' he said with a shrug.

Julie huffed a great sigh. 'Well, think about it now! For pity's sake, man, it's just an opinion. He's always been like this, darling, used to drive your mother up the wall.'

Rachel swung round too quickly at the mention of her mother, tried too late to shush her gran, and saw her dad visibly shrink back into his cardigan. She'd made it a point never to mention her mother in front of her dad; he always just clammed up immediately. When she caught her grandmother's eye and gave her a 'What did you have to say that for?' look, Julie just shrugged as if she couldn't see what the problem was.

'I'm only talking about names, darling. I would just prefer to be known by my own name, not some generic term that half my bloody generation are known as.'

Rachel sighed, pausing with her hand on her hip to look back at her. 'We've been through this. I can't do it. It just won't happen. When I try to it feels too weird.

You're my grandmother—that's just the way it is.' Julie made a face as Rachel turned away and slid the steaming potatoes from the baking tray into a terracotta bowl and carried them to the table.

Julie took the bowl from her. 'Well, I don't think things should always be the way they are. Who says that's the way it should be? Do you have a mat to put these on? The bowl is very hot.'

Rachel slid a magazine over so her gran could put the bowl of potatoes down without marking the already pretty shabby table and went back to the stove; they had this conversation at least once every six weeks. 'You know I don't know the answer. I just can't call you Julie. It's weird. And...' she paused, ran her tongue over her lips as it finally dawned on her why she clung to the name '...it reminds me that we're related.' She paused.

'Maybe if your mother was still alive you wouldn't mind so much,' Julie said matter-of-factly. Rachel's dad flinched again.

Rachel smacked the wooden spoon down on the counter. 'Can we please talk about something else?'

Her gran narrowed her eyes and watched her for a moment, wondering perhaps whether to push this tiny crack in Rachel's armour so it might widen and they'd all start talking. Rachel had already turned back to the coq au vin. 'So I hear you're off to Paris.'

'Not that. Something other than that.' Oven gloves on, she picked up the Le Creuset bubbling with stew and set it down in the centre of the table. 'And by the way, I'm not going to Paris. It's a ridiculous idea.'

'Just so you know, I've volunteered to keep an eye on the lovely Australian couple.'

'I'm not going.'

'Why are you going to Paris?' her father asked with vague interest.

'I'm not,' Rachel said quickly.

'Oh, you must.' Julie reached forward and grabbed a potato from the dish. 'Gosh, this is hot,' she said, slicing it open, forking up the fluffy insides and slathering it with butter. 'David, she's going to bake. Rachel, you must go,' she said again, her mouth full of boiling potato. 'This tastes divine. Divine as always. Mine are always so hard and the skin all soft and wrinkly— bloody microwave.' She scooped up another forkful before carrying on about the impending trip to Paris. 'Yes, you have to go.' Then she waited a second before adding, 'Your mum would have been so proud.'

It was Rachel's turn to flinch; as she stirred the coq au vin she felt an unwanted lump rising in her throat. She pushed her fringe out of her eyes then redid her ponytail for something to do instead of answering.

She felt her grandmother watching her. 'She would, you know.'

'I didn't think you baked any more,' her father said, as if he'd missed something along the way, something that didn't entirely please him.

'I don't,' said Rachel, emphatically.

'No. That should probably rest with your mother.' Her father crossed his arms over his chest, and she stared at the holes on the cuffs of his shirt, the ones she remembered her mum darning.

'Oh, don't talk such tripe,' Julie scoffed. 'The last thing your mother would have wanted is you sitting around refusing to whisk a bit of flour and butter because she was good at it. For Christ's sake, Rachel, I know you're a very good teacher, but you were an excellent baker. You need to give it a chance. And, David, I'm sorry, but I can only say that your opinion on the matter is absolute bollocks. Rachel, you go to Paris, and, David, you go back to your bloody dream world and stay there. That's the best option as far as I can see.'

'I was only giving an opinion. I was asked for an opinion, Julie.'

Rachel watched her dad as he took his glasses out of his pocket, put them on and picked up the cycling magazine that he'd brought with him—watched him retreat back into his hobby so he wouldn't have to face any more from her grandmother.

As Julie was about to reply Rachel cut in, saying, 'I've forgotten the water glasses. Gran, can you get them for me?'

Julie flumped up the scarf around her neck with a huff, then pushed her chair back and stood up to rummage in the cupboard. As she clattered about

Rachel tried not to think about what her mum would have thought about a trip to Paris to bake with a professional, tried to ignore the fact that her relationship with her father was becoming more and more distant and how his comment just then had affected her. She'd known he might not advocate a baking trip to Paris, but she hadn't expected such obvious disapproval.

'These are very lovely.' Rachel looked up to see her gran holding up three little mottled glasses with maple leaves painted on the sides that she'd picked up from the local antique shop. 'I'd put them somewhere, if I were you, just in case the Australians are clumsy.'

'I don't want people in my flat, and—'

'Nonsense.' Her grandmother plonked the glasses down on the table and then sat back in her chair, folding her arms across her chest, her silver bracelets clicking, her lips pursed. 'Anyway, it'd do you good to get away from that idiot guitar player. Brad? God knows what you see in him. You should go for that reason alone.'

'Who's that you're talking about?' Her dad glanced up from the pages of the magazine. 'Do you have a boyfriend, Rachel?'

'Of course she has a boyfriend. Really, David, sometimes I wonder where you've been. You've met him—that plonker from the band that played in the pub the other night. Wore all black. Remember? You thought it was all terribly loud. Brad.'

Her father shook his head.

'Ben. His name is Ben and you know that.' Rachel tried to take her annoyance out on her potato, sawing into it with her knife but having to pull back as she burnt her fingers on the crispy skin. 'And he plays the drums, not the guitar.'

Julie made a face as if it made no difference.

'And he's fine. It's fine between us.' Rachel could feel the frustration boiling up inside her as her grandmother raised a brow sardonically, clearly questioning that statement. 'And I'm not going to Paris.' Rachel huffed as she shoved some potato into her mouth, burning her tongue but trying to pretend that she hadn't.

There was another pause as Julie shook out her napkin, then held up her hands as if she'd say no more about it. 'Well, come on, then.' She nodded at the casserole dish. 'Are you going to serve this thing or not?'

As Rachel ladled out the rich, thick stew Julie took a mouthful and sighed. 'I'm going to miss my dinners here while you're in France.'

At four a.m. the doorbell went, followed by the usual tap on the door. Rachel, had been lying in bed staring at the ceiling while her mind whirred with images of Paris, Christmas, her mother in the hospital bed—a limp garland of tinsel wrapped around the bedstead—Henri Salernes' face on the flyleaf of the well-thumbed cook book she had on her shelf. She pulled on her dressing gown and tried to do something vaguely decent with her hair as the tapping got louder and louder. She checked her reflection in the mirror by the door, refusing to think about the fact she'd purposely slept in her make-up on the off chance this visit would happen.

'Rach, honey, darling, beautiful…' Ben bounded in off the step like a Labrador high on the adoration of his fans. Shaggy black hair, crack-addict cheekbones and eyes that crinkled as if they always knew a secret— her on-again off-again boyfriend was gorgeous and he knew it. He would also baulk at the term boyfriend but if she admitted the transience of their relationship in comparison to the time she'd dedicated to it, it would be too depressing.

'Hi,' she said coyly as he twisted her hair round his hand and pulled her head back for a kiss that tasted of cigarettes and beer and the toothpaste she'd just swallowed while running down the stairs.

'Let's get rid of this horrible thing, shall we?' He smirked, pushing her old towelling dressing gown off and sliding his hands round her waist to her arse, then, leaning forward, whispered, 'Go on, make me something nice to eat. I'm starving.'

As she stood open mouthed at his audacity he patted her on the bum with a wink and a heartbreaking smile and steered her in the direction of the kitchen.

Five minutes later Rachel was standing in her nightie, her banned robe still on the floor in the hallway, whipping up the perfect, smooth, yellow hollandaise and checking the timer for the poached eggs while she watched Ben as he sat back, feet up on the table, flicking through her *Grazia* magazine.

'Do you want to sleep here tonight?' She didn't know why she said it; she hadn't said it for months but she suddenly felt the overwhelming need to push the point. He peered over the pages he was holding and watched her for a second before his mouth quirked into its infamous grin.

'Honey, you know I can't sleep here. I need my—'

'Own bed.' She finished before he could and turned her back to him, scooping out the poached eggs. In the last year she'd woken up next to him once, and that was because he'd accidentally taken a sleeping tablet rather than a paracetamol for a headache when rooting through her bathroom cabinet. He claimed that he couldn't sleep anywhere other than his bed and alone, and she'd always gone along with it, not wanting to rock the boat. After a moment or two of silence he came over and wrapped his hands around her, pressing himself close against her back. The sensation felt less fuzzy and cosy than normal, more as if he was locking her into place.

'You smell awesome.'

She turned around in his arms and handed him the plate of Eggs Benedict, trying to ignore the sense of being released when he let her go and took the plate. Her grandmother's quirk of a brow flashed into her mind. This wasn't a healthy relationship, one side of her mind said, while the other just stared at his pretty face and argued that it most definitely was.

'And this—' Ben took the plate from her '—looks awesome.'

As he cut into it, the golden yolk oozing out into the toasted muffin she'd found at the bottom of the freezer and the silky hollandaise dripping from his fork, he paused before putting the first bite into his mouth, as if preparing himself for the bliss.

When he did eat it, gobbling greedily with his eyes shut, he hit the table twice with his fist. 'Fucking amazing. A-mazing. God, it's better than being on stage. Well—maybe not but it's fucking good.'

Rachel couldn't help smiling. Leaning back against the counter, she watched him, enjoying the sight of him eating the food that she had made giving him so much pleasure. Feeling almost proud.

'You—' He pointed at her, mouth full. 'You are going to make someone a great wife one day.'

She paused for a moment, turning to pick up the mug of tea she'd made herself and taking a sip. *Let it go...* she told herself. *Let it go and it'll all just carry on as normal. Life can just carry on as normal.* But then she found herself asking, 'Not you?'

Ben laughed into his cup of coffee.

'I'm serious,' she said, running a hand through her hair and, feeling suddenly hot, holding her fringe back from her forehead.

'Hun, come on, it's too early for this.'

'We've kind of seen each other for nearly a year.'

He made a face. 'I meant in the morning. It's fucking four a.m.'

'Yeah, I know.' She nodded, glancing down at her haphazard appearance as if to show him just how aware she was of the time.

'Babe.' He didn't get up, but took another slurp of coffee. 'No one gets married any more. What we've got... It's good. Don't—' He shook his head, dark hair flopping over one eye, his brows drawing slightly together as if he was on the cusp of getting annoyed. 'Don't spoil it. Just let a man eat. Yeah?'

Rachel opened her mouth to say something but then closed it again.

'And I don't know that it's been a year. I mean, not exclusively,' he added, his eyes focused back on the plate of eggs, shaking his head as he carried on eating.

Oh, my God, she thought. *Oh, my God, what have I been doing?*

Who was he? Who was it that she had been seeing all this time? What had she seriously expected from him?

As she watched him eat, chewing furiously, it was as if the fog lifted and she suddenly saw what everyone else saw. A black hole at her table where her life disappeared.

'OK, babe?' He glanced up, checking that she was still there, still waiting for him to finish. He gave her a quick cheeky grin, as if to gloss over anything that might have gone before.

She nodded, her mouth frozen into place.

He pushed his plate away and stretched his arms high to the ceiling. 'Awesome. Totally awesome, as always. Bed?'

'I erm…' But it felt as if her mind had slipped all the way through her body into a pool on the floor. And instead of saying anything else she let him lead her up to her bedroom, where she was suddenly ashamed that she'd changed the sheets because she'd had an inkling he was coming and had put the winter roses her gran had brought for her in a vase by the bed and sprayed Dark Amber Zara Home room spray to make it smell all moody and sexy.

When the front door clicked shut forty minutes later, she lay staring up at the ceiling and wondered what had become of Rachel Smithson, because right now she felt completely hollow from the neck down.

CHAPTER THREE

King's Cross at Christmas was a nightmare. Giant sleighs and reindeer had been rigged up to float above the platforms from the metal rafters, while Christmas music played on a loop in every shop. Pret a Manger had a queue that snaked out onto the concourse and all the sandwich shelves were picked clean; WHSmith had run out of water, and she'd forgotten her moisturiser but Kiehl's had sold out of her favourite. Everything seemed to be reinforcing the notion that going to Paris was a bad idea.

With just a lukewarm coffee in hand, Rachel forced herself through the crowds, thinking about how, in the end, she'd finally made the decision to go to Paris purely so she never slept with Ben again. It was heartbreakingly good-looking-boyfriend cold turkey— maybe that should have been Pret's seasonal sandwich. She squeezed past kissing couples and hugging relatives to track down her train. The platform was packed; the corridor to the train was even worse, blocked with suitcases and big paper bags of presents.

God, she hated Christmas. She could just about admit, only to herself, that it had become like a phobia. And being on this train felt like when they locked someone with a fear of spiders into the boot of a car crawling with them.

'Erm, excuse me, I think that's my seat.' On the train she pointed to the number on the luggage rack above the seat and showed the young blonde girl who had taken her place her ticket.

The carriage was hot and stuffy and smelt of McDonald's and cheese and onion crisps. Rachel's boots already pinched and all she wanted to do was sit down and wallow in her bad decision but the blonde wasn't budging. 'I really want to sit with my boyfriend,' was all she said back.

'Oh.' Rachel bit her lip. 'Well—' Someone pushed past her and she had to hold the table to steady herself.

'My seat's fifty-seven,' said the girl, shrugging before turning back to talk to the guy next to her.

Rachel nodded, wishing her legs might overrule her brain and walk straight off the train, but then she remembered that she had nowhere to live if she did go home—the Australians would be arriving around about now.

She pushed through the people and luggage in the aisle to her new seat. As she lifted her bag onto the overhead shelf and sat herself down a little boy wearing reindeer ears across the aisle started screaming as his sister ate his flapjack.

'We're off to Euro Disney. Patrick, stop that,' said the woman next to her when Rachel glanced across, watching the boy hit his sister on the head. 'Leila's going to be a princess. Aren't you, honey?' The mother reached over to break up the fight. 'We always go to Disney at Christmas. It's so magical.'

Rachel nodded but then turned away to stare out of the window as the train pulled out of the station, wrapping her scarf up round her head like a cocoon to block them all out. But the reflection of the excited kids in the window forced back memories of being little at Christmas—jumping on her parents' bed and opening her stocking. Hot tea and buttered toast with home-made jam. Her dad always surprised by the stocking her mum had done for him. Rachel's feet dangling over the bed, unable to touch the floor as she ate chocolate coins and a satsuma and looked at Rudolph's half-chewed carrot by the fireplace and the signed card from Santa.

She hadn't thought about that for years.

As the train sped up through the countryside the reflection in the window changed to the memory of the whole village on Christmas morning. Everyone out on the green for a massive snowball fight. Hers flying off at wonky angles because she had such a rubbish throw. Years ago they'd even skated on the pond in their wellies. She vaguely remembered her dad and her winning the prize for best snowman. It had been shaped like a wizard with a pointy hat. There was something about the hat—what had it been made of? It was bark, she thought, curled tree bark her mum had found, and the coat they'd covered in fallen leaves and acorn cups to make the pattern. She saw her dad holding up the prize of a bottle of port, triumphant, then hoisting her up on his shoulders, her wellington boots bashing snow onto his wax jacket.

It was odd to remember her dad with that smile, that buoyancy.

Since her mum had died, he just cycled. Always cycling. A group of them, sixty-five, and cycling. Never smiling. Six months after the funeral he'd gone on a trip and come back with a new bike and all the gear. Kept him busy, he'd said. Out-pedalling the memories, she'd thought. The moment he stopped he'd have to deal with life.

She realised then why she rarely allowed such reminiscences. The thought of them compared to the stark new reality made her eyes well up. She groped in her bag for a tissue; when she couldn't find one she had to ask the woman next to her.

'Of course. I always have a pack. Wet-wipe or Kleenex?'

'Kleenex, please,' Rachel said, trying to cover her face so she couldn't see the tears. 'Winter cold,' she added, while surreptitiously giving her eyes a quick wipe.

The train pulled into Gare du Nord under grey gloomy skies. Paris was freezing. Much colder than England.

People blew into their gloved hands as they queued for a taxi. Rachel wheeled her bag over to the back of the line, rain pouring down in sheets. Her boots were soaked through. People kept cutting into the front of the queue as she was hustled forward, her coat and bag dripping wet. As she waited, rain catching on the hood of her coat and dripping down onto her nose, she clutched the scrap of paper with the road name in her hand, wondering what the place she was staying in would be like.

Jackie had booked her into an Airbnb rental in the centre of Paris. She could have killed her for doing this, Rachel mused as she finally got into a taxi just as the rain fell heavier, like a bucket tipped from the sky. She could actually kill her, she thought while gazing out at a dark, soaked Paris as the taxi whizzed through the streets, horn honking at anything that got in its way. Stab her maybe with her new Sabatier kitchen knives that Henri Salernes had demanded each contestant buy pre-course, plus slip-on Crocs and a white apron with her name stitched on the front. Rachel had failed the sewing part of Home Ec at school so she'd got her gran to do the embroidery this time. Julie had added a flower on either side of her name, for good luck, she'd said.

The taxi pulled up at the end of the road after clearly driving her all the way round the city unnecessarily.

'One way,' he said. 'Your house, at the other end. You walk.'

The rain was unceasing. Rachel, imagining crisp snow-white streets, hadn't thought to bring an umbrella.

The driver dumped her bag in a puddle and drove away leaving her alone at the end of the darkened road, the streetlight above her fizzing and flickering in the rain.

She hauled her bag behind her down the street, wiping rain drops from her nose and eyelashes with sodden gloves, stopping finally at number 117—a thick wooden door studded with big black nails and a brass knocker shaped like a lion's head.

Someone buzzed her in with a string of French she didn't understand. The piece of paper said Flat C. Rachel climbed the stairs, bumping her bag up behind her, holding onto the wooden banister. As she passed the ground floor the steps turned from plain concrete to white and blue tiles and wooden panels became richly wallpapered walls in cream, gold and burgundy. The huge double doors of Flat C were freshly painted glossy magnolia.

A woman opened the door almost as soon as Rachel knocked and immediately warm smells of herbs and cooking enveloped her. Looking into the flat, she saw glistening chandeliers, expensive chintz curtains draped over large French windows, soft cream furniture and paintings of fruits brimming over in their bowls. Wow. It was like looking into the pages of *House & Garden* magazine. She took a step forward. Maybe she wouldn't kill Jackie just yet.

'*Je suis* Rachel Smithson,' she said to the woman in the grey uniform and apron. '*Je reste ici.* Airbnb.'

'Wait,' the housekeeper said. 'I get Madame Charles.'

As Rachel waited she saw in the corner of the living room a Christmas tree that wasn't a real tree but a metal sprig twinkling with white fairy lights and the branches tied with silver ribbons. It was the type of decoration that could be up all year round. Nothing, not even the garlands hanging from the mantelpiece, was too overpoweringly Christmas. Rachel was impressed.

On the sofa, two Siamese cats had wound themselves over the arms like matching cushions. Rachel was staring at one of them, trying to ignore the growing chill from her sopping socks and imagining what it was like to live in such luxury, when a tall immaculate woman, who must have been Madame Charles, appeared in the doorway.

'Eer been bee,' said the housekeeper. Madame Charles looked puzzled, as if she had no idea what she was talking about, and tapped ash from her cigarette in its gold holder into the tray by the door.

The woman was a vision in beige: floor-length oatmeal cashmere cardigan, white hair impeccably styled, wide cream trousers and beige turtleneck with a gold Chanel necklace. She was someone who might adopt Rachel and put her to bed in crisp Egyptian cotton sheets with a decaf espresso and a brioche. Someone, Rachel thought, who she might ignore Christmas with and eat oysters with and drink champagne.

'Airbnb,' repeated Rachel. *'Dans le Internet.* From England. *Je loue the chambre.* For a week. *Pour une semaine.'* Christ, her French was bad. 'Till Christmas,' she added, pointing to the silver branch in the background.

'Ah. Airbnb.' As it finally dawned on Madame Charles what was going on she disappeared back into the apartment saying, *'Un moment.'* One of the Siamese jumped off the sofa after her.

Rachel hopped from one damp foot to the other waiting to be led inside. But, appearing again with jewelled slippers on, Madame Charles said instead, 'Follow me.' And as she swept past her, closing the door, all three of them headed upstairs.

Rachel wondered if there was a separate entrance up there. Perhaps the bedrooms were accessed this way. Up they went, spiralling into what felt like the turret of a tower. The dark wood walls began to narrow and the tiles on the stairs were replaced by rough wooden floorboards.

'Ah, ici.' Madame Charles unlocked one of four doors at the top of the stairs with a big old dungeon key. Rachel took a breath.

Inside was a small room, separated into two by an alcove. It was grey, bleak and stuffy—as if no one had been in for a century. The housekeeper next to her shivered. Rachel felt her 'oysters and champagne under the silver sprig' dream dribble away as the bare light bulb swayed in front of her.

Madame Charles was unperturbed, her cigarette smoke trailing in wisps behind her. 'This is the kitchen.' A white rusty gas oven and hob with a grill pan at the top, the type her gran swore by. A mini fridge, two cups, two plates, one glass. 'The TV.' Certainly not a flat-screen; Rachel wondered if it even had a remote. 'The sofa.' Dark blue, no cushions. 'And here—' they walked through the alcove '—is the bed.' A metal frame with a grey blanket folded at the end and pale pink sheets. A threadbare mat on the floor and a faded Monet print on the wall. The metal shutter on the only window was pulled closed.

'*Ça va, oui?*' said Madame Charles, breezing through the tiny space. 'This was, how do you say? For the help. The servant. *Oui?*'

Rachel tried to make her mouth move into a smile. Her soaking feet and clothes suddenly freezing cold. '*Merci beaucoup.* It is *très bon.*'

'*De rien.* It is nothing.' Madame Charles smiled. 'There is one *petite* problem. The bathroom, it is outside. In the corridor.'

After checking out the sad-looking shower and toilet in a shared room off the hallway, Rachel let herself back into her flat, sat down on the bed and found she was too tired to cry. Instead she just stared around the grey room, at her coat hanging on a chair dripping onto the floor, the bare walls with cracks up to the ceiling, a fly buzzing round the empty light bulb. What was she doing here? Why had she even considered coming? She didn't really bake any more; she didn't want to be someone's apprentice. She wanted to be at home, enclosed by the safe walls of her flat and surrounded by her stuff and, at the very least, central heating.

She watched the fly weave a path from the light to the top of the oven, to the closed shutters and back again.

Standing up, she opened the shutters and shooed it towards the window with a tea towel, where it finally disappeared into the blackness.

It was only as she was closing the window that she saw the view. The trees lining the Champs Élysées glistening with a million lights strung from trunk to tip, hundreds of them shining a dazzling path that stretched on till the Arc de Triomphe, which glowed a warm yellow in the night sky. She pressed her nose to the glass and stared till the steam of her breath covered the view and then she opened the window again and stuck her head out into the rain and stared some more. Hate Christmas as she might, Rachel had to admit that, even in the pouring rain, this was breathtaking.

CHAPTER FOUR

'OK, class, these are the rules: one, I don't want an apprentice; two, you do everything I say; three, if you are shit, you leave.'

Henri Salernes glowered at them and then turned away and disappeared into a side room at the back of the kitchen as if that was him done for the day.

He'd aged considerably since the photograph on her cook book, Rachel had thought when she'd seen him. Thick blond hair was now receding, his skin was rougher and horn-rimmed glasses seemed to make his eyes meaner. She glanced warily around the room. She'd arrived last and missed most of the introductions so immediately felt like the outsider. There were eight of them in total all vying for the coveted apprentice position. She wondered what they had had to do to be selected and felt a flicker of guilt about how she'd got her place. From the moment he'd walked into the room Henri had treated them like irritants he'd rather not have to deal with, and clearly the competition had been dreamed up by his publishers rather than his own desire to share his talent.

As they stood like lemons waiting for him to come back Rachel had another look at the competition. At the back was Tony, tall and dapper, who'd already sliced his hand open getting his new knives out. He looked taken aback by Chef's abruptness and was shaking his head at the red-headed woman next to him, Cheryl, saying, 'That was all a bit unnecessary.'

Everyone knew Henri Salernes had a fierce reputation. Once highly regarded in the industry, he was now a virtual baking recluse. Rachel had expected a bit of moodiness from him but not a complete lack of interest in them. As PTA Mrs Pritchard had said when she'd handed her the ticket, it was all for the money.

In the next row was Abby, who was all red lipstick and huge boobs; she was sighing and tapping her nails on the counter. When she saw Rachel looking at her she rolled her eyes as if to show she had no time at all for Chef's behaviour. Next to Abby was Ali, who had introduced himself saying he 'liked to experiment with flavour combinations' and Rachel had had to stifle a snort. He was currently holding in a nervous giggle and looking about to see what everyone else's reactions were. Marcel, a shockingly handsome Frenchman who had immediately caught Rachel's attention, was raising one brow in disdain at Ali and allowing a sneer to play on his lips. And then there was George: old, bald with a white moustache, he put his hands on the counter in front of him and said, 'Well, what do you think of that?' But no one replied. The fierce-looking woman on Rachel's far right, Lacey, who hadn't told them anything about herself, shushed him. The only thing Rachel knew about her was from a phone conversation she'd overheard outside where Lacey was telling whoever was on the other end of the line that she didn't need to be there. She was just brushing up on her pastry skills. She had a Culinary Arts degree.

They all fell silent as soon as Chef strode back in and Rachel stopped looking around and did what everyone else was doing: she rolled out her knives, checked her utensils, peered at the buttons on the oven and pulled on her new apron—the one her gran had embroidered her name on along with the sweet little flowers—fumbling the strings at the back with clammy hands.

Chef was up at the front shaking flour over his bench, which was double the size of theirs and wooden where their little tables were stainless steel. Next to him the walls were lined with bowls and trays and stocked like a greengrocer's, fresh fruit and veg tumbling out of wooden crates, and huge sacks of flour and sugar leaned against the skirting board like fat men taking a rest.

It had taken Rachel ages to find the place; it was tucked down a side street and someone had graffitied over the road name. On the bottom floor was an unassuming pâtisserie that belonged to Henri and next to it a white door that opened onto a thin carpeted staircase that smelt of air freshener. The school was on the first floor up, a small room with two windows and packed full of work stations. Above it seemed to be another two or three floors of offices; she'd seen people in suits coming and going past the glass wall of their room.

Chef looked up when he was ready. 'You have your aprons?' He nodded when he saw them all, named like food on a shelf. Putting his arms behind his back, he strolled between them, peering at the stitching and reading the names aloud, then paused when he got to Rachel.

'What the fuck is this flower? You think this is the kind of course for flowers?' He glared at her, his thick eyebrows drawn together behind the rims of his glasses. 'A sweet course? You think this is British Fucking Bake Off?'

'No, Chef.' Rachel swallowed.

'You think you are Mary Berry?'

'No, Chef.'

'Get rid of those fucking flowers. Your name. The name is there so I don't have to remember your fucking name. *Comprende?*' She could feel his dislike emanating from him and immediately wanted to roll up her knives and run out of the building.

'*Oui, Chef.*'

He cocked his head. 'Don't mock me.'

'I-I wasn't. I promise,' she stammered.

'I'm watching you, Rachel.' He narrowed his eyes, leaning close so she could see the faint stubble over his jaw and the lines across his brow. Handsomely terrifying, a journalist had once described him, and she knew then exactly why. 'Flower Girl,' he said and stormed back up to the front.

Rachel glanced around, blinking away moisture in her eyes, and saw seven faces pretending not to look at her. George gave her a wink. As she swung back to the front she caught a look from Marcel on her left. Scruffy dark brown hair and wearing a woolly Lacoste jumper, he had bright blue eyes like a wolf's that were watching her with either disdain or sympathy, it was hard to tell.

'Flower Girl. This way!' Chef shouted. 'You're here to learn, not look at the men next to you. *Oui.*'

Blushing scarlet, Rachel fixed her eyes on Chef's table. He'd put out rows of pâtisseries—fluffy shell-shaped madeleines, rainbow-coloured macaroons, bite-sized lemon cakes, sticky rum babas and teetering piles of profiteroles.

Rachel loved profiteroles. She'd make them for Ben. He would say they were the best he'd ever tasted. Crème pâtisserie piped into the centre of perfect choux-pastry balls drizzled with the darkest melted chocolate she could buy in Nettleton. If Chef was going to say that they had to make profiteroles today then God or the Angel Gabriel was looking down on her. Chef wouldn't call her Flower Girl after today, she mused as he summoned them up to the front. She'd be Profiterole Girl. Star Baker Numero Uno.

They gathered round the battered wooden bench, jostling to find a place where they could see exactly what was happening, and watched as Chef started to whisk together eggs and sugar. As he started to talk about all his little tricks of the trade everyone around her pulled out their notebooks and scribbled as he spoke.

Rachel felt herself begin to panic. No one had told her that she needed to bring a notebook.

'Can I borrow some paper?' she whispered to Lacey when she couldn't stand it any longer, but Lacey pretended not to hear.

'What is that? Who is talking while I talk?' Chef looked up from his tray of madeleine moulds.

'I needed some paper.'

'Ah, you think you know everything, Flower Girl? You think you don't need to write it down?'

'No, it's just—' Rachel started but he'd gone back to his mixture, shaking his head as he spread it into the silver shells.

As she felt her face go red and nausea rising in her throat Abby nudged her on the shoulder and tore off some paper and George gave her a chewed pencil stump while Lacey shook her head and sighed.

It was a long day watching Chef work his magic. Rachel was exhausted; every inch of her scrap of paper was filled with notes. Then at the end of the afternoon he told them to make something from the day's demonstration—something that best showed off their skills—and she found herself breathing a sigh of relief. He'd take her seriously after he tasted her famous profiteroles and Lacey could wipe that smug smile off her face.

But two and a half hours later the scene was not quite as she had imagined. Instead of savouring the flavour of her delicate creations, Chef was hurling her choux-pastry balls one by one out of the window, sneering, 'These look shit.'

Rachel fled as soon as she could, stalking down the road, head down, humiliated, hat pulled low, and her coat, still damp from the night before, clutched tight. Her scarf was covering all her face except her streaming eyes. How had her pastry gone so wrong? In retrospect she realised she should have remade her pâtisserie cream because she'd known at the time it wasn't her best, but she hadn't thought it was that bad. It wasn't that bad. Was it? She was out of her depth and the realisation that she hadn't earned her place, that she wasn't good enough, shouldn't be there, was humiliating.

'Hey, hey—'

She heard Abby call but kept walking. Feet pounding the pavement in her winter boots. Rachel had already decided she was never going back. She didn't want this anyway. What had made anyone even think she had it in her to be a baker?

Saturdays at the counter standing next to her mum didn't mean anything. She hadn't actually baked anything that someone had bought, had she? Just pinched steaming loaves from the rack when no one was looking. Or sifted flour into the bowl for the lightest, softest croissants and whipped the egg white for the stickiest meringues while standing on an old bread box so she could reach the counter. It was her mum who'd done everything. All Rachel had done was cut the shapes of the biscuits. Bunnies at Easter. Ears of corn at harvest time. Ghosts at Halloween. Reindeer at Christmas; always with a red blob of icing on their noses. She'd watch her mum flick the nozzle of the piping gun so it was a perfect red dot. Then sometimes turn around and, when Rachel wasn't expecting it, dot her on the nose with red. *My little reindeer.*

'Hey, Rachel. Wait up.'

Rachel paused at the corner, wiping her nose with her glove.

'We're having a drink.' Abby was out of breath. 'Round the corner.'

'Oh, no, thanks.'

'No, come on, we need to get to know each other. That way we're stronger against Scrooge in there.'

Abby did an impression of Chef Henri, waving his hands in the air in disgust.

Rachel shook her head. 'There's no point for me. I don't think I'm coming back tomorrow.'

'Oh, you have to. You have to. You can't leave. You were so brave in there. I'd have had to run away if it was me.'

'Thanks, but it's not really how I imagined it. I don't want to work with him. I'm going to go home actually. Get the first train back to London.'

There was a loud laugh behind her. 'You quit, Flower Girl?' Neither of them had seen Chef Henri cycling past on his old bike.

'It's not quitting,' Rachel muttered, her nose tipped up in the air as she tried to look aloof. 'I just don't think it's for me. I've made a mistake.'

He barked a laugh. 'You are scared like a little mouse and running back to England with your tail between your legs. All the same, you English girls. Weak. Babies. It's a little tough and you run home to Mummy. I bet—' He paused. 'I bet you can't even make bread.'

Rachel took a deep breath, affronted and trying to think of something suitably cutting in reply, but he carried on.

'Go on.' He made a shooing action with his hand. 'Run away. Run, run, run. One less person for me to get rid of. This is beautiful.' He laughed and then cycled off, ringing his bell, before she could get out the words that were queuing up in her head.

She stood staring after him, furious. There was definitely a difference between leaving because it wasn't right and quitting, wasn't there?

'Just one drink?' said Abby, sensing weakness.

What was it her mum had said when she'd tried to leave the Brownies, gym club, pony club? *Just give it one more chance, for me.*

'OK, I suppose one drink.'

'Excellent.'

CHAPTER FIVE

Everyone in the bar was so confident in their skills. Ali was sipping a demi pression and half checking out his reflection in the mirror behind them, pushing a hand through his neatly styled black hair that was so heavily waxed it sprang back into the exact same position as before it was touched. 'I've always known about flavour,' he said, tearing his eyes from the mirror and looking at each of his fellow contestants. 'That's my thing. I'm just worried he's too traditional for me. That we won't be able to express ourselves.'

Marcel was feeding coins into the fag machine. 'You must master the basics before you can express yourself properly.'

'You sound like Chef,' snorted Abby.

'There are worse people to sound like.' Marcel shrugged. 'In his time he was the best. The greatest. My family, they had all his books. His restaurant had queues out the door. I ate there once and I've never forgotten it. The food was exquisite. Like nothing I have tasted before. And then—' he blew a raspberry through closed lips '—nothing.'

Ali went on as if he hadn't heard anything else that had been said. 'It's been since uni—I used to be in the Chemistry lab making cherry essence rather than recreating photosynthesis. I'm like a flavour alchemist.'

'And you don't think Chef is?' Marcel rolled his eyes heavenward behind Ali when he didn't even register the comment and leant against the cigarette machine, unwrapping the cellophane on his packet while Ali waffled on a bit more about the chemistry of taste.

'Did you know about Lacey?' said Abby, cutting in.

'No, what?'

Heads crowded together over the table; Cheryl knocked over the sugar shaker. Rachel stayed sitting back and looked away at the posters of famous film stars like Clark Gable and Brigitte Bardot that lined the walls, not wanting to hear that much more. She was finding it all too stressful, the notion of competition and the obvious desire in everyone to win. It had been a long time since she'd put herself in a position where she could be judged and it made her feel more vulnerable than she'd imagined.

'Big businesswoman. Thirty years CEO of a luxury goods company. Jacked it all in for this.'

'Really?' George was shocked.

'Apparently.' Abby nodded.

'Goodness,' said Cheryl, quietly.

'And how about you?' Ali turned to Cheryl, who was pouring more red wine from the carafe on the table as unobtrusively as she could. 'How did you get into this?'

Cheryl blushed, placing the carafe back on the table and toying with the cuffs of her jumper. 'Same as everyone.'

'Oh, no, love,' said George, his accent thick Yorkshire. 'We're all different.'

Cheryl had a neat red bob, perfect, as if it had been cut with a set square. Rachel watched her flick it so it covered more of her face. 'I used to be a bit bigger.'

'I understand.' Abby patted her on the arm.

'How big?' asked George.

Rachel made a face across the table, trying to encourage him to be a bit more tactful with his questions.

'Pretty big,' said Cheryl, blushing again, her hair getting further over her face. 'To lose it I had to relearn about food. Learn to cook.'

'But all them cakes—aren't you tempted?'

She shook her head. 'I make them for my family, or for the neighbours. It's the baking that hooks me. I just love it and for some reason I've found that if I make it, I don't eat it.' She laughed for the first time.

Everyone smiled but Rachel saw Ali do a little eye-roll behind his beer to himself. As if Cheryl was easy pickings.

'I've got to go,' she whispered to Abby.

'Really? No. Don't go. We're getting to know each other.'

The last thing Rachel needed was these probing, nosy questions and people sizing her up as competition. 'Yeah, I really should go.'

'Will we see you tomorrow?'

'No.' She shook her head. 'I don't think so.'

Rachel walked to the bus stop and when the bus didn't come she walked back all the way to her dingy flat. There was thin drizzle in the night air, the droplets flecking in the beam of the overhead lights. All the narrow streets were lit with Christmas stars that had been twined up the lampposts and tinsel hung from windows and around doors. Outside the churches little nativity scenes glowed bright, but she barely noticed.

When she got to her building she stopped and looked up—at the blazing light from Madame Charles's and then to the dark shutters in the roof—and thought of her lovely flat at home. Everything arranged just as she liked it. No surprises. All warm and cosy and hers.

Trudging up the stairs, she wished she were back home—sitting on her lumpy sofa, marking homework with smiley faces, secretly weeping at *The X Factor*—rather than here, in this draughty loft, baking with a load of strangers.

Inside she boiled up water on the rusty stove-top kettle and sat on the chair thinking about Chef laughing and cycling away. How could she have been so bad? It was gutting. And he was so cruel. She could make bread, for God's sake. OK, she hadn't baked it for years, but that wasn't to say she couldn't.

Bread was the one thing her hands simply refused to make, as if the dough held too much power in its smells, its texture, its taste—just the simple process of kneading and rolling was like her own personal Pandora's Box. But she'd always been good at it. Her gran could often be heard lamenting Rachel's refusal to make her a batch of rolls or a wholemeal. As she thought about it she wondered if Ali, with his flavour combinations, could make a decent loaf.

Damn Chef. He must have weaknesses. No one had come into the workshop and giggled at his past failures, had they?

She leant forward and turned on the oven, watched the flames roar to life through the glass and turned it off again. Then she found herself on her feet taking flour from the shelf, butter she'd got from the Carrefour out of the fridge and breaking eggs into a chipped mixing bowl. Before she knew it she was flouring the worktop and kneading and stretching her dough as if she were on autopilot. Not thinking, just doing. When she looked down and saw the little round blob of dough it almost took her by surprise. She was glad to be able to leave it to prove on the table and got as far away from it as she could, going to the window to stare out at the Champs Élysées view.

She gazed at the perfect strands of fairy lights on the beautifully trimmed trees. It was dazzling—not a blown bulb or twig out of place. But combined with the sweet, sticky smell of raw dough in the air, it all made her suddenly feel quite homesick. Made her think of the monstrous great big tree that they hauled into the centre of Nettleton every year, branches sticking out all over the place. She'd always get needles itching down her back from helping to carry, and Jackie would stand on the church steps, bossing everyone about which side should face front. The great tree would wobble precariously as Mrs Pritchard's handyman, Kenneth, secured the base and her son tied the top with rope to a lamppost and the old King's Head sign. She sniggered at the memory of the year they'd forgotten to tie the top and it had crashed through the upstairs pub window at two in the morning almost skewering a pair of sleeping ramblers.

Compared to these Champs Élysées trees, theirs was like the giant at the top of the beanstalk. Too big, hugely ugly and draped with a ramshackle selection of lights that the village had accumulated over the years. Some were big coloured light bulbs, others small maniacally flashing fairy lights that Jackie's grandmother claimed had given her a funny turn. Around the lower branches the kids hung the snowflake decorations they made at school, all in a big cluster. And on the top was an angel that her gran could remember as a child. It was a disastrous beast. These perfect, beautiful French trees would turn their backs on it in disgust. They would shun the pride and joy of Nettleton.

Rachel had a sudden urge to ask Jackie to text her a photo of it, but stopped mid-message, not wanting her to think she was a pathetic, needy idiot.

Instead the alarm on her phone went off to tell her the dough was ready. In the past she would have plaited plump strands into individual little loaves but this time she just wanted it out of sight and hurled it into the oven, like a hot potato, where it sat off-centre on the baking tray.

There was a knock on the door as she was still staring into the oven trying to work out how there was bread baking in there after so many years of her steering well clear. Surprised, she ran over, oven gloves still on, and pulled it open.

Madame Charles's housekeeper was standing on the landing, a big basket clutched in front of her paisley-patterned housecoat.

'*Bonsoir, Mademoiselle.*'

'*Bonsoir—*' Rachel paused.

'Chantal.'

'*Bonsoir, Chantal.*'

There was silence. Rachel leant by the door unsure whether to invite her in or if she was just about to be told that she'd done something wrong. She wondered whether she should tell Chantal now that she was leaving tomorrow.

'I bring you some things.' Chantal held up the basket, then peered round Rachel into the flat. 'For your room.'

'Oh.' Rachel didn't know what to say. 'I think I have everything I need. Actually I'm leav—'

Chantal cut her off. 'Things to make it—*je ne sais pas*—happy?'

'Happy?' Rachel looked down at the bag as Chantal squeezed past her and put it down on the table.

As Rachel closed the door Chantal pulled out two red cushions, a little frayed around the edges, and went and rested them on the sofa, plumping them up with both hands and then pulling the corners straight so they sat beautifully, as they might have once done in Madame Charles's flat. Coming back to her bag, she took out a strip of thick aquamarine wool and, shaking it out, draped it over the ratty armchair in the corner, tucking it in neatly around the edges of the cushioned seat. Then she stood back, arms pointing to the objects, as if highlighting to Rachel what she was trying to do.

'Happy,' she said again.

Slightly perplexed, Rachel watched her go back to her Mary Poppins basket and pull out a mirror with pink china flowers across the top. Pointing to a chip, Chantal rolled her eyes and said, 'That Madame Charles throws away.'

Next came a spider plant that she carried through the alcove and sat on the window sill alongside a tiny snow-globe of the Eiffel Tower; this she shook and held out to Rachel.

'I buy this for you.'

Crossing the room, Rachel picked the ball of plastic out of Chantal's hands, lost for words. When she shook it she noticed her hands were shaking as she watched the snow fall gently round the spire—twisting and swirling round the miniature statue.

'You shouldn't have,' Rachel said, transfixed by the globe and the kindness of the gesture.

Chantal shrugged. 'I think of you up here alone in this—' she glanced around '—this place and I think that it is not comfortable, especially at Christmas. My daughter, she is about your age and if she was here I would want someone to make her comfortable.' Chantal folded her arms across her chest.

'Does she live in Paris?' Rachel asked, turning the globe upside down again and watching the flakes tumble past the spire of the tower.

'Oh, no.' Chantal shook her head. 'She is in the South. In Nice.'

Rachel looked up. 'I love Nice. I went on holiday there a couple of years ago. Such a beautiful city. How lovely that you can go and visit her there.'

Chantal seemed to hug her arms a little closer round her chest. 'I have not been.'

'Oh,' said Rachel. 'She comes to see you?' she asked and then kicked herself when she realised she'd missed the tension in the comment and should have just changed the subject.

'Non.' Chantal turned to look around the room, and then with a forced casualness said, 'We do not speak any longer.'

'I'm sorry.'

She waved a hand as if it were nothing. 'She has a strong will.'

Rachel nodded, immediately curious as to what had happened.

'Anyway, I think of her when I think of you up here, and I would want her to be comfortable.' The oven timer pinged and Chantal, taking it as a cue to change the subject, wandered over, peered in through the oven door and, smelling the freshly baked bread in the air, she sighed.

Rachel went to place the plastic snow dome on the shelf but changed her mind and kept hold of it as she glanced at Chantal, who seemed suddenly smaller and more alone than she had done when she'd first come in. 'Would you like some bread?' Rachel asked.

'Oh.' Chantal rested her hands across her waist and stood as if this were what she'd been waiting for all along. 'If it is not an intrusion.'

Rachel shook her head. If anything it was something of a relief to have someone there with her and Chantal appeared to feel the same way.

A few minutes later the housekeeper was sitting at the table with a cup of tea, smiling through a mouthful of warm, soft bread. *'C'est très bon. Parfait.'* Tearing off another piece, she said, 'You make very good bread.'

'Thanks.' Rachel hadn't touched hers; she was somewhere else entirely, overwhelmed by the smell of fresh-baked dough, the sadness in Chantal's eyes when she talked about her daughter, and distracted by her snow-globe and the red cushions.

'Yes. It is very good. *Très bon.* Like the *boulangerie* at the end of the road.'

Rachel thought again about what her mum would say if she told her she was going to quit the contest: *One more chance. For me.*

'You compete, *oui*? For the bread? That is the competition.'

'Pretty much. With Henri Salernes.'

'*Oh la la*, Henri Salernes. Very grand. Whatever happened to him? I had his book. Very good, a very clever man. And his brother, yes? The two of them, they had a lot of skill. And their restaurant, it was very famous. And now nothing except the pâtisserie, *oui*? Just a little pâtisserie that no one would know belonged to him. Very sad. Trying to prove too much too young, I think. That is what the papers say if I remember, grew up badly—not a good home, you understand?'

'I don't really know that much about the restaurant. Just that he was an amazing baker once.'

'*Oui*, once. He was the youngest and the most celebrated. He changed the way we bake. And his brother, he change the way we cook. One was the savoury and one the sweet... Then it all goes, pouf, like that. All the money for Henri on the drink and the drugs, I think. It is always on the drink and the drugs. Silly man. He had a lot of talent. But...' she held her arms out wide '...*c'est la vie.*' She popped the rest of her slice of bread in her mouth. 'Well, if I was the judge, you will win already. You do very well.'

Rachel reached forward and tore a little chunk off the loaf and popped it in her mouth. The power of the taste almost made her crumple on the spot. Soft and warm like a blanket.

One more chance. For me.

'Very well. Very good bread.'

For me?

OK, Mum. She nearly said it out loud, nodding and holding tight to the globe.

'You find it better? Yes?' said Chantal, following her gaze from the snow-globe to the rest of the room.

'Yes. Thank you,' Rachel replied. 'I find it much better.'

CHAPTER SIX

Next morning Rachel arrived at the pâtisserie with all the embroidered flowers that he'd made such a fuss about snipped off her apron, determined to prove to Chef Henri he was wrong about her.

Then she might leave.

The pâtisserie itself was one of her favourite bits about the whole competition. On the ground floor, it was small and unassuming but the counters were piled high with some of the most delicate pastries and tarts she'd ever seen. The glaze on the tart au citron shone as if it'd been freshly polished that morning. The sign on the front of the shop was written in gold and inside an old lino floor was scratched and scuffed where customers had stood waiting in line. To the left of the counter were high stools that seemed to seat the same three old men every day, who came in to drink espresso and eat croissants, and behind the counter was a young woman with bright pink lipstick and wild curly hair pulled into a messy plait, who had introduced herself to Rachel as Françoise the day before when Rachel had been completely lost trying to find the competition kitchen. She'd patted her on the shoulder and wished her good luck in a conspiratorial tone that Rachel hadn't quite understood until she'd come face to face with Chef.

Now, as she walked in and bought herself a *pain au chocolat* for her breakfast, when it came time for her to pay, Françoise raised a brow as if to ask if Rachel now understood her words of luck; Rachel nodded, a silent understanding between them about the tyrant boss. Françoise laughed and told her that he didn't get any better the longer you knew him.

As Rachel left the pâtisserie through the side door that led into the corridor she'd just started to take the stairs up to the kitchen when she came across a man in a suit, who flattened himself against the wall to let her pass.

'*Merci beaucoup,*' she said, not really paying attention, caught up in thoughts about what Chef would say about the fact she hadn't run back home to England.

'It is my pleasure,' he replied as she passed. His perfect English made her glance back. Short, neat black hair, sharp, tailor-made slate-grey cashmere suit, thick, dark eyebrows that drew together now over big brown eyes as he watched her looking at him.

'Thanks,' she said again and then felt foolish. 'I er…' she started, pointing up the stairs. She felt her cheeks start to get hot and looked away, embarrassed by her reaction to him. He wasn't good-looking per se, but striking in the kind of way that she just wanted to stare at him for days. Trying to disguise the reddening of her face by pretending she had an itch on her cheek, she turned back and said, 'I'm going up there.' A blatantly obvious statement that she couldn't quite believe she'd just said. She hadn't been so flummoxed in the presence of a stranger ever. *Pull yourself together, Rachel,* she thought.

'So I see,' he replied with a smile twitching on his lips and before she could reply he held two fingers to his forehead in a salute and turned away, clipping down the stairs.

She watched him leave, pulling on a dark-grey woollen coat as he got to the bottom step before yanking open the door into the icy cold. A lingering smell of expensive aftershave and soap made her close her eyes and consider how well groomed the French were. She breathed in again, trying to catch the scent once more, but it was gone. Running her finger along her bottom lip, she did a flash replay of the momentary conversation in her head, shook her head at her own embarrassingly floundering responses, and found that all she could remember was his eyes. They were espresso dark and dancing with confidence—that last little amused look had knocked her totally off kilter.

'He is nice, *non*?' Françoise had stuck her head out of the doorway and was following Rachel's gaze.

'Oh, I wouldn't know,' she said too quickly.

'He is very nice, I am telling you.'

'Well…' Rachel shrugged as if it barely mattered because she would never see him again.

'You are still early, *non*?' Françoise said as she wiped her hands on her apron then looked at the paper bag with the *pain au chocolat* clutched in Rachel's hand. 'You should enjoy your breakfast, eat it at the counter with an espresso, *mais non*?'

'I shouldn't really.'

'Ah, yes, you should. I will have one too. It is quiet. I am bored. I like to have someone to talk to.'

'But—' Rachel glanced up the gloomy staircase to the workshop where everyone would soon be gathered waiting to stab each other in the back or wait for the weak to fail. An offer of plain, simple company from Françoise was too tempting to turn down. 'Go on, then.'

Back inside the pâtisserie, she perched on a stool by the counter as Françoise bashed away with the coffee machine.

'This thing, it is shit,' she muttered as she flicked some switches and the thick black liquid poured out into a small white cup rimmed with gold.

'You sound like Chef.' Rachel laughed.

'Fuck no.' Françoise sneered.

'And again.'

Françoise laughed. 'I have worked with him too long. He is a tyrant.'

'He is, isn't he?' Rachel took the espresso cup and saucer from her and declined the two sachets of sugar.

'No, I am being mean.' Françoise shook her head. 'He is OK. I think he suffers from the past.'

Rachel raised a brow in disbelief. 'I think he's a tyrant.'

Françoise laughed and then turned her back to Rachel and started doing her hair in the mirrored wall behind the counter. 'My boyfriend arrives today. From Bordeaux.'

'Very nice.' Rachel sipped the coffee, wondering if she should say anything else.

'I only see him once in the month. He is very—' She paused, untwisting her lipstick. 'He is like Chef. He has the hot blood.' She turned back round to face her, eyes smiling, her mouth pulled into an O as she slathered it with more Chanel Rouge. 'You just need to learn how to handle the men like Chef. That is all. Do not let them scare you. The anger, the words, it is all air that is hot. Big, hot air.' She laughed. 'Underneath is the mouse.'

Coffee finished, Rachel was second to arrive in the workroom. Lacey was already there; she'd watched her stalking up the stairs, and now she was standing alone, polishing her tabletop.

'Hi,' Rachel said as she unfolded her knives and put her snow-globe on the bottom shelf of her work surface where Chef wouldn't see it.

Lacey didn't reply. Rachel studied her, her loose grey curls pinned into a neat chignon at the nape of her neck, apron covering a three-quarter-length mauve dress with capped sleeves that revealed gym-toned arms. Gold studs in her ears, coral lipstick and glasses hanging on a diamanté chain around her neck.

'Where are you from?' she asked as Lacey continued to wipe.

'London.'

'Oh, whereabouts? I went to uni in London. I'm from a tiny village in Hampshire.'

'Look.' Lacey screwed up her cloth and turned towards her. 'I don't want to be rude but I'm not here to make friends. This is a competition and I just want to keep it professional. No games.'

'Games?' Rachel looked perplexed.

'I saw you yesterday with your little flowers getting all the attention. Some of us are here to work. Hard. So...let's just—' She held her hands up and then went back to polishing her station.

Rachel couldn't believe it. 'I'm not—'

'You came back. Hurray!' Abby bounded in with George, unaware of the tense silence in the room. 'We wondered. We made bets. I said you would.'

'I thought I'd give it one more go,' Rachel said, hesitant after her altercation with Lacey.

'Well, I'm really glad you did. We need to stick together.' Abby patted her on the shoulder and walked over to her bench.

Over the next five minutes all the others trooped in, with Marcel last. He glanced at Rachel and said, with his smooth French accent, 'Looks like I lost my bet.' Then he winked at her just as Chef strode in so she was blushing red as he towered over her station.

'You are still with us? I thought you run back to England? *Non?*'

Rachel shook her head. She tried to think of him as the great baker who had lost everything. Of the boy who had grown up too fast. Of the genius who revolutionised French pâtisserie. Last night she had crept down the stairs and perched on the bottom step outside Madame Charles's flat and, tapping in the code that Chantal had slipped her, had surreptitiously logged into her Internet. There she had spent an hour or so Googling Henri Salernes. The restaurant he had set up with his brother that had taken Paris by storm and made them among the youngest three-Michelin-starred chefs in the country. She'd pored over pages and pages of glowing reviews from even the most hardened critics and pictures of snaking queues out of the door and celebrities huddled in darkened corners sipping champagne.

Then the headlines changed to the shock exit of his brother, who walked away at the height of their fame. And then the steady charting of Henri's epic rise and fall. The temper that had driven away most of his best sous chefs, the arrogance that had banned negative critics from walking through the door and the gradual loss of his Michelin stars, one by one over the years until there were none.

But just as the articles got juicy, she'd heard the click of Madame Charles's heels on the stairs and, slamming her laptop shut, Rachel had backed up into the shadow of the landing and watched as her elegant landlady swept into her apartment, the lights glistening, the warmth emanating, and as the door shut the soft lull of some classical music and the ring of the telephone accompanied by Madame Charles's soft, low voice as she answered the call. Rachel had watched the closed door jealously, reluctant to go back up to her room, especially now she was going back for more of Chef the next day. Wishing instead that the doors to this sumptuous apartment might open up and swallow her whole.

What was it Chantal had said about Chef? *Not a good home.* Rachel had thought of lovely little Tommy back in Nettleton who'd been adopted by Mr Swanson and his wife two years ago. He'd had *not a good home.* As he stood in front of her now she tried to imagine Chef at Tommy's age. Looking up at his stern, miserable face, she tried to picture him as a five-year-old, as one of her sweet little class with trousers too big and jam down his cardigan.

She watched him glance at her apron and take in its absent flowers.

'Well, we'll have to see if you do better today, won't we?' He smirked.

'Yes, Chef.' She nodded. No, it was no good. He just wouldn't shrink to the size of one of her pupils. He had been born a fully fledged pain in the bum, she was sure of it.

'I have my eye on you,' he said as he strode away.

Rachel made the mistake of glancing to her right and saw Lacey raise her brows with disdain.

The day started with pastry. Filo, short, flaky, puff, choux. Savoury and sweet.

'You know nothing about pastry. Everything you think you know, you don't know,' hollered Chef.

All morning they sweated over it. Chef coming over and screwing it into a lump, slapping it across the room to the bin, shouting, 'Too much flour. Start again.'

Abby cried. George had a coughing fit and Tony cut another finger, rendering him useless for the afternoon's challenge.

'After lunch you make me something. I spend the day teaching you, now you give it back to me. I want to see what you have. In here.' Chef bashed his chest with his fist. 'Now leave, it is lunchtime.'

Rachel walked out with Abby, both bundled into their coats and scarfs ready for the wintry cold that had hit last night.

'I've left my family at Christmas for this guy. He's a nightmare,' Abby whispered as they left the room.

'You have kids?'

'Two. Little girl and boy. One year apart. Glutton for punishment, me. I've told them I'm off meeting Santa—we need to discuss how good they've been this year.' Pulling out her purse, she showed Rachel a picture—a passport-photo strip in a plastic wallet of two bright blond children, aged about six or seven, could have been younger, and a fun-looking surfer-type guy holding them on his knee.

'He looks nice.'

'Doesn't he? Jane from number seventeen thought so, too. He left last year, bought a boat, said family wasn't for him, he felt suffocated, and he's sailing round the world now—with her. Have you seen those boats? If anything's suffocating I'd say it's them—can't even stand up half the time. He sends postcards from places like Mauritius and the kids think he's all exciting and glam. Not like boring old Mum.'

'You're cooking in Paris. That's glamorous,' Rachel said, and they both turned to look back up the stairs at the peeling paintwork and blown light bulb and giggled.

Marcel was just jogging down the stairs and gave them a funny look when he passed them laughing. 'It is something about me, no?'

'No, not at all.' Rachel waved a hand to show that it was nothing, that they were laughing at something else.

Marcel shrugged, a lazy grin on his face as he pushed open the door to the street. 'You could give a man a complex,' he said, winking as he strolled out and then lighting a cigarette behind hands cupped against the breeze.

'You could give me anything you want, Marcel,' whispered Abby dreamily. 'He's so pretty, isn't he? Like a model for Gucci.'

Rachel nodded as they watched him disappear up the road. Marcel was chocolate-box handsome; perfect as if he'd been chiselled from marble and on show in a museum.

'I find him very distracting,' Abby mused. 'I have to consciously not look at him during baking, otherwise I'd be all over the place.'

'You have to get a grip—' Rachel leant on the door, letting in a shock of icy air '—or he'll sense your weakness.'

'Please, God.' Abby clasped her gloved hands heavenward. 'Let Marcel sense my weakness.'

Passing the pâtisserie, Rachel saw the guy she'd passed in the corridor earlier standing drumming his fingers lightly on the counter. Same grey woollen coat, same thick dark hair, same instant flutter in her stomach. No one seemed to be serving. She glanced through the window, peering over the gold scrolled lettering that spelt out Salernes on each window, and saw no one except the customer. Where was Françoise? Had her boyfriend arrived already? She glanced from the shop back to Abby and said, 'Do you think I should go and look for Françoise…?'

'No. Absolutely not.' Abby shook her head, pulling her coat round her against the chill and blowing on her hands. 'Stay out of it. Come on, it's freezing out here.'

They walked on a step but Rachel found herself turning back. 'I think I should. Look, he's waiting… And I don't want her to get into trouble,' she added, refusing to acknowledge that her reason for returning had very little to do with Françoise.

Doubling back in through the side entrance of the shop, she checked the two cubbyholes to see why there was no one about. The back door to the patio outside was open, cold air was streaming in along with the raised voices of an argument. She ventured forward and, peering round the door, saw Françoise and a man who must have been the boyfriend from Bordeaux in the middle of an almighty row, arms waving in the air, voices raised, Françoise's hair all loose and wild escaping from her plait and the boyfriend scowling as he flicked cigarette ash angrily onto the paving stones. It certainly didn't look like the romantic reunion Françoise had been dreaming of earlier.

'Françoise,' Rachel whispered, but she didn't turn.

Rachel coughed a couple of times to try and distract her but she was clearly in her stride, yelling and shouting all over the place, her finger stabbing him in the chest as he flicked the fag away and huffed out an exasperated breath, running a hand through his hair.

'Shit,' Rachel said out loud as she stepped back from the doorway and into the cubbyhole.

'Is everything all right?' the man asked, a look of amusement on his face as the insults from out on the patio streamed in through the back door.

'I don't think so.' She shook her head and made a face as she walked forward towards the counter. 'I don't think there'll be anyone to serve you.'

He shrugged. 'Can you?'

'Oh, no, I don't work here.'

He frowned. 'You look like you do.'

Rachel found herself watching, distracted, as his fingers drummed casually on the counter top, mesmerised by his eyes as they glanced over the array of cakes. Then realising she hadn't replied, said quickly, 'The owner would kill me if he found me here.'

The man laughed, his eyes crinkling softly at the sides. 'Well, I wouldn't want that to happen.'

'No,' she said, trying not to stare. He wasn't her type, not at all, yet she wanted him to keep looking at her that way. Maybe it was just because he was French and exotic and she felt far from home. She was usually all about the rough and ready, love 'em and leave 'em types, not the well-groomed, mature alpha males who looked as if they would buy her red roses, talk about current affairs over dinner and shrug unfazed if someone mentioned commitment. 'I er—' She pointed to the door, without taking her eyes from him. 'I er—should be leaving.'

'That is OK.' He cocked his head, not bothering to hide his amusement at how flustered she was becoming as he went back to perusing the rows of pâtisserie.

She started to walk away but then found herself stopping and asking, 'What were you going to have?'

'I don't know. I never know what to choose,' he said, glancing up from the counter. 'I like the eclairs, but I also think maybe the *millefeuille*. Or sometimes the tarte Tatin. There is too much to choose from and my eyes they are, I think I heard the phrase once, bigger than my stomach.' He laughed. 'It is hard, *non*?'

'Oh, I know. I'm like that too.' Rachel found herself bending down on the other side of the counter to look at the array of desserts between them. 'I just want everything,' she said, then, embarrassed by her own enthusiasm, quickly glanced away when she met his laughing eyes through the glass.

There was a pause as she felt him watch her blush, and then she heard him say, 'Who would have thought choosing just one little cake could be so difficult?'

'Well, if it was me…' She gazed over the rows and rows of treats that sat in front of her. Bright marzipan shapes, chocolate twists dusted with sugar, sticky *millefeuille* layers oozing with cream, tarts brimming with frangipani, coffee eclairs lined up like fat fingers, red berries piled high and tumbling off crème pâtisserie tarts. And on the shelf above were piles of glistening chocolates. Dark glossy liqueurs with cherry stalks poking out of the top, dusty truffles and striped caramels, fudge coated in ganache. Strawberry creams shaped like tiny fruits perched next to pralines wrapped like presents in gold.

But sitting perched on the tray to her left were Rachel's all-time favourites. 'I always like a Religieuse,' she said, pointing to the tower of two round eclairs balanced with a ruff of cream piped around the neck. 'They are my first choice whenever I get to come to France.'

'The Religieuse—the little nun,' he said and she watched him laugh through the glass. *'Bon choix,'* he added, before glancing up and meeting her eyes. 'You are here for Christmas?' he asked.

Rachel nodded, caught off guard by the question. He tilted his head, as if processing the fact and mulling over another question, but said nothing more, just went back to studying the cake choices.

Then suddenly a shout from the doorway made her jolt upright, almost banging her head on the top lip of the counter. She heard a loud, angry voice shout, 'What are you doing in my shop? Where is Françoise?' and turned to see Chef standing, hands on hips, in the doorway.

At that moment Françoise came hurrying in, hair all over the place, pale-faced and terrified, mascara streaked down her cheeks.

As Françoise rushed past her Rachel grabbed her arm to hold her back and said to Chef as confidently as she could in the face of his scowl, 'Françoise wasn't feeling well. I said I'd help.'

The cosy warmth of the pâtisserie suddenly felt too hot as Chef looked between the two of them, disbelieving. 'You are ill, Françoise, you come to me. Rachel—out. Françoise, serve the man.'

As Chef narrowed his eyes, waiting for her to leave, Rachel whispered, 'Are you OK?' to Françoise, who'd clearly caught a glimpse of herself in the mirrored wall behind them and started scrubbing the black off her face.

'Yes, yes, it is always the same,' she muttered under her breath as she retied her hair. Then smoothing down her apron and giving Rachel a quick little wink, she added, 'We will make up later.' Rachel rolled her eyes and as she started to leave turned to look apologetically at her customer. 'I'm sorry about this.'

'It's nothing. *Merci beaucoup* for your choice, *mademoiselle*.' He tipped his head to her, his dark eyes crinkling with humour as he surveyed the scene. 'I'm Philippe, by the way.'

'Rachel,' she said. She paused for a moment to smile at him and then, remembering where she was, turned and ducked away past a furious Chef to Abby, who was waiting, one brow raised, her arms folded tightly underneath her cleavage and her breath coming out in white clouds from the cold.

'Even I could have told you that wouldn't go well.'

Back at the workroom everyone was starting to prepare. There was a sense, as they plucked butter from the larder and scooped up flour from the bags, that they weren't pretending any more.

'You have an hour and a half. Everything here, it is for you. Use it. I don't want to see some shitty nothing on a plate. Enjoy. I am here, having coffee.' Chef took his seat at the front and surveyed them like a headmaster.

Rachel looked around; it seemed everyone was going sweet. Lacey was cutting figs and straining pruncs from a jar. She could see a row of tiny moulds ready to be lined with filo. Marcel had told them on the way in that his chocolate tart never failed. The secret was Armagnac from his family's distillery.

Rachel was dithering, her hand hovering over peaches. She watched George pick the fruits for a pear, apple and orange blossom tarte Tatin. Cheryl was asking Abby to confirm ingredient weights for a cherry and date Bakewell. And Ali had decided on a basil and white chocolate vol-au-vent, the idea of which had made Chef snort with disgust.

As she stood panicking, gazing at all the ingredients, her eyes landed on a lump of feta, hard and crumbling into the wooden cheese board on the side, and she had a brainwave. Almost kissed the air and said a prayer of thanks.

When she reached for the cheese she caught Lacey roll her eyes and mutter under her breath, 'Oh, here we go. Trying to be different.'

But she ignored her. She wasn't trying to be different at all. She was trying to do whatever it took not to be at the bottom. Being last wasn't a feeling she was used to. And if she was going to cling on and prove she had some skill, then this recipe was tried and tested. She knew because it wasn't just Ben's taste buds that recommended it, it was generations. A recipe passed down from her Greek great-grandmother to her grandmother, her mother and her.

Tiny filo cheese pies so thin and delicate, brushed with glistening egg yolk and packed full of feta, ricotta, blue cheese and parmesan that cracked and burst on the top like volcanos when cooked. Baked till golden, they were the taste of summers in Greece sitting under vines, Coca-Cola for them, chilled retsina for the adults. Clinking ice cubes, steaming plates of cheese and spinach pies, sizzling prawns, pale pink taramasalata, olives warmed by the sun. Her gran in a hat fussing. Her great-grandmother in a chair, faded blue sundress and Scholl sandals. The waves rolling the pebbles. It was the taste of summer and sunshine and family.

It was the taste of a time that was perfect.

She still made the pies, every now and then, but she didn't go to Greece any more.

As she rolled out her filo, Chef sat up at the front sipping his espresso, Lacey carved her figs into intricate flowers, Marcel dripped chocolate from up high so it would cool into stars on his baking parchment, Ali started whipping his basil with the blender to make a foam, and Tony cut his finger again—Abby said it needed stitches. Chef sighed. Rachel's pies puffed and cracked in the oven.

Time ticked away and she ummed and ahhed about taking them out as she watched Lacey make the finishing touches to her tartlets, dusting icing sugar over a flowered cake stand she'd brought from home.

'Five minutes,' said Chef.

She needed six.

Abby was brushing down her counter. Rachel's was a mess, the sieve poking out from a pan, a baking tray at an angle in the sink, spoonfuls of cheese splattered across the surface.

'One minute,' Chef yelled.

Rachel looked at her pies. Almost. Almost. She heard her great-grandmother: *Patience, Rachel. Patience in the kitchen.* Her timer ticked.

'Fuck it,' she said in the end as the others stood neatly by their creations. Fifteen seconds to go, she yanked open the oven door, her glasses misted with steam, and tipped her pies onto a white plate she'd found under her counter.

When the stopwatch beeped, Chef slowly unfurled himself from his chair and walked from stand to stand perusing the goods. Marcel had supplied a crystal glass of Armagnac, Abby had a model Santa and a sherry to go alongside her mince pies. Lacey's beautiful tarts sat proud and decadent on their tiered platter, as good as anything Rachel had been served for her birthday tea at the Ritz. Slicing a sliver here and a chunk there, Chef announced his verdicts.

'*Délicieux.*' Lacey's tartlets.

'Average.' Abby's pies.

'A waste of good Armagnac.' Marcel's chocolate.

'Intriguing.' George's tarte Tatin.

'Disgusting.' Ali's basil creation.

Then he stopped at Rachel's. She watched as he cast a disapproving eye over her bench. He picked up and dropped her sopping cloth, then prodded her haphazard pile of pies. Their innards were squelching out as they squashed each other without the proper time to cool.

He took one between finger and thumb, holding it as if he found it as distasteful as the dirty cloth. He blew on it, tore it in half and listened for the crack in the filo. Satisfied by the sound, finally he put it in his mouth. Biting, waiting, smelling, biting again, swallowing, pausing.

Her palms were sweating. She couldn't believe how much she wanted to impress him.

'Rachel,' he said. Paused. Seemed to disappear from the moment for just a second. Took another bite. 'Your food, it looks like shit. But it tastes... It tastes not bad.'

CHAPTER SEVEN

'The drinks are on me.' Rachel didn't know if it was happiness or relief but, God, she felt good.

Most of the group was crammed round a booth table in the corner of the bar; a carafe of white wine and a stack of tumblers were in the centre. Dressed in a black shirt and leather jacket, Marcel was loping back in after a smoke and Lacey hadn't come because she didn't like to socialise with the competition. Poor old Tony hadn't fared the pastry test well and was pulled aside at the end and told not to come back.

He was sitting now, head in his bandaged hands, nursing a whisky and soda.

'Bloody hard, wasn't it? I mean, tough competition. Tougher than I expected.' Tony was a proper English gentleman. A deputy head at a private boys' boarding school in Suffolk. 'I'll have to lie to the kids. Can't have them thinking I went out first round. That would never do. I'd never live it down,' he said, taking a large gulp of his drink and shaking his head as the fire hit the back of his throat.

'It's not so bad,' Abby offered.

'And you had hurt your hands,' Cheryl chimed in softly. 'You can't be expected to do your best if you're injured.'

'Yes. Absolutely. You're quite right. That's exactly what the wife said. She arrives this afternoon. I told her someone else already went out yesterday. We'll have a couple of nice days in Paris. Spot of Christmas shopping and all that. Maybe go up the tower. Nice view from the top of the Pompidou, so I'm told.'

'Where are you staying?' asked Rachel, taking a sip of her wine while an image of her depressing little flat popped into her head.

'The Ritz.'

'Oh.'

'And you?' he asked, whisky glass to his lips.

'Not the Ritz.' She laughed.

As more drinks were bought, and tiny bowls of nuts and olives plonked onto the table by a moody waiter, round the table people had started talking about Christmas plans for when they went home.

'I'm flying back on Christmas Eve, straight after the final event. Not that I've a hope after today.' Abby poured more *vin blanc*. 'Hopeless. How can you tell someone their pastry is hopeless? Like a soggy sock, Chef said. Here, taste this—does it taste like a soggy sock?'

Rachel took a bite of the boozy, sugar-encrusted mince pie Abby had handed her and shook her head.

It tasted sweet and delicious to her, of plump sticky raisins, spiced brandy and flaky, buttery puff pastry.

Marcel sat forward, twirling his half-empty glass of rum between his fingers, wolf-eyes locking on Rachel. 'When do you go home?'

'Boxing Day,' she said, glancing away, hoping the conversation would move on.

'Boxing Day?' repeated George. 'You got family here or summat?'

She shook her head. 'No. No family.'

Marcel sat back, swirling his drink in his glass, and she could feel him watching her closely.

'What will you do on Christmas?' Abby asked.

'Sleep probably. I think Christmas Eve will be a big day whether we're in the final two or not.'

'But it's Christmas...' said George, pulling open a packet of crisps and glancing round as some instrumental Christmas music started up as if illustrating his point.

'I know. But really it's just a day like any other.'

Abby looked at her as if that was certainly not the case.

Rachel shrugged.

Marcel leaned forward; the perfection of his features made her want to reach out and trace them. 'So you do not *do* Christmas?' he asked with a quirk of a dark brow.

'*Non.*' She smiled, a touch shyly under his gaze. 'I like Easter.' She laughed.

Abby asked why she didn't like Christmas but Rachel did a Lacey and pretended she hadn't heard.

'Interesting. Well…' Marcel sat back and licked his bottom lip—the look in his eye reminiscent of Ben, and Rachel found herself wondering for a moment what he was up to back in Nettleton, whether he'd found an adoring groupie to visit in the early hours. She felt a shoe brush her foot and pulled away before realising it was Marcel's. Brown hair falling in front of his eye, he pushed it away and went on with a drawl, 'If you get lonely, you are welcome to spend the day with me.'

Rachel giggled and felt her cheeks start to pink. '*Merci*, Marcel.'

Abby shifted in her seat, pushing her boobs a little closer together to enhance her already impressive cleavage and leant a touch closer to Marcel. But Marcel was looking only at Rachel when he replied with a shrug, '*De rien,*' his lips turning up into the hint of a smile.

That night Rachel strolled back from the bus stop; the rain had stopped for now and the sky was completely clear. The shadows of the plane trees speckled the road like puppets in the moonlight and the puddles of water glistened like crystal. Looking up at the few stars above her, she felt a rush of excitement.

'Not bad,' she said out loud. 'They tasted not bad.' And allowed herself a surge of pride.

At her door she found Chantal sitting on the thin wooden bench on the landing, knitting what appeared to be an incredibly long scarf in purple and maroon wool. She was buttoned up in her camel coat and scarf and Rachel wondered how long she'd been there.

'*Bonsoir, ma petite.* What did you cook today?'

Rachel unlocked the door as Chantal packed up her needles and followed her in.

'Cheese pies.'

Rachel stood back as Chantal squeezed past her while taking off her coat and hat, patting her hair into place and peering over the rim of her bifocals. 'Ah, *très bon.* I put the kettle on?'

'OK.' Rachel watched her from the doorway, a little warily, as Chantal made herself at home—filling the kettle, laying out cups and a plate for the pies, then hoisting another huge bag onto the chair.

'I bring more things.'

Rachel unwound her scarf and pulled off her gloves. 'Chantal, you don't have to.'

Chantal looked round as if it was obvious she did. Then began laying out her bounty. Another bedraggled plant. A bright blue frame, a horse ornament with only three legs, a throw for the sofa, a green glass vase with a crack down one side, and a lace doily that she placed in the centre of the table under the teapot. '*Et voilà.*'

Rachel laughed. 'Thank you, Chantal,' she said, thinking of all her minimalist white furniture and key pieces from Anthropologie and Heal's back home.

The flat was coming to life. Splashes of colour and all the little extras beginning to make it more homely. It wasn't her taste but it was certainly better than it had been.

Before she left, full of cheese pies and tea, Chantal threw an orange linen napkin over the sidelight so it cast a soft, warm yellowy glow on the room. She stood back and said with pride, 'It is nearly perfect, yes?'

Rachel nodded, desperate to ask her why she didn't talk to her daughter any longer and—if the way she'd adopted Rachel was anything to go by—wishing that her daughter knew how much Chantal clearly missed her.

Chantal was waiting the next night as well, when Rachel came home with strawberry tarts overfilled with crème pâtisserie so the strawberries wobbled precariously on top and most had slid off into the box.

'Not very pretty.' Chantal laughed. 'But *très bon*,' she said, licking her fingers and depositing a clock, a stripy rug that had begun to unravel and a red and white spotty biscuit tin.

With the tea and cake over she clapped her hands together and beckoned to Rachel. 'Now you come downstairs with me.'

Rachel looked outside; it had started to snow, light flakes frosting up the window. Chantal was wrapping up in her layers.

'Come,' she said again, more forcefully.

Rachel made a face behind her back, as if she really didn't want to, but pulled on her coat and boots and tramped down the stairs after her thinking about how tired she was and how many steps she'd have to trudge back up again.

Outside Chantal beckoned her into the alley alongside the front door.

'Really?' Rachel questioned, thinking this might be some crazy human-trafficking ploy. How well did she actually know Chantal?

When Rachel peered round the corner, Chantal lifted a hand to point and said, *'Et ici!'*

Rachel looked at where she was indicating and there, tied to a lamppost with a chain and padlock, was a rusted old fold-up bike. Chantal slipped her the key.

'It was my daughter's. She didn't want it. She was going to leave it in the road. It has been in *la cave* at my house.'

The bike was turquoise, scratched and rusted with *Mirabelle* written down the side in white bubble writing and a white wicker pannier on the front.

'For your cakes.' Chantal laughed, pointing at the wicker basket on the front, which she had strung with silver tinsel.

'I don't know what to say.' Rachel ran her hand over the handlebars.

'You say nothing.'

'I'm so touched.'

'Ah, you are sweet.' Chantal patted her on the arm and walked over to her 2CV. *'Joyeux Noël.'*

'Chantal…' Rachel called as she watched her heaving open the battered door.

The housekeeper turned, her hat pulled low almost covering her eyes, white curls just poking out around her ears. *'Oui?'*

Rachel wasn't quite sure what she wanted to say, so just asked, 'Are you sure your daughter won't mind?'

Chantal shrugged. 'She did not take it with her. I think she would like someone to have it.'

Rachel nodded. 'Will you thank her from me, you know, if you talk to her this Christmas?'

'We will not talk,' Chantal said, attempting matter of fact but the sharp intake of breath at the end of the statement gave her emotion away. Then she got in the shabby old car and drove away while Rachel stood where she was, one hand still clutching the handlebars, and waved, wanting nothing more than Chantal to talk to her daughter so she wouldn't have to see her look so sad again.

The following day, Rachel cycled to the pâtisserie, the tiny specks of blizzarding snow hitting her cheeks, making her feel alive and excited as she pedalled as fast as she could. Who'd have thought she'd be cycling the streets of Paris like a local?

Locking up her bike, she saw her man from the pâtisserie, Philippe, drive past and she put her head down, unsure why, but the thought of talking to him, of the look in his eyes when he spoke to her—of confident amusement—made her fumble her lock and then drop it in the snow by mistake.

But as she walked round to the front of the shop she saw he was just coming down the street, striding along in a dark cashmere suit, his long grey overcoat unbuttoned, and it was too late to pretend she hadn't seen him.

'*Bonjour.*' He smiled, waving from a couple of metres away. Like hers, his scarf was up over his chin to avoid the pelting snow and when he got close he had to wipe the moisture from his face. 'It is good weather, *non*?'

'Hi. Yes. *Bonjour.*' Rachel nodded, immediately flustered, immediately wanting to check her hair in the pâtisserie window. 'Look, you know, I'm sorry about the other day. With Chef. It was very embarrassing.'

'It's not a problem. I know what he's like.' Philippe shrugged. He was much taller than her, which she wasn't used to, Ben being about five foot seven, and she had to glance up when he spoke. Brushing the snow off the front of his coat, he went on, 'Henri's my brother. We have worked in the same building for a very long time.'

'Your brother? Wow.'

Stepping forward, Philippe opened the door for her. 'I'm not sure wow is quite right, but, yes, he's my brother. He is less…let's just say his bark is worse than his bite.'

'I don't know about that.'

'You take my word for it. He er…' He paused, changed tack. 'He is consumed by it, by the baking. And I think it makes him—' he blew out a breath '—frustrated when it doesn't all go his way. As he would like. He doesn't understand that not everyone is like him. Their brains are different. *Oui?*'

'If you say so.' Rachel raised a brow in disbelief, at the same time as trying to get a peek at the state of her hair in the reflection of the glass in the door.

'Life has never worked out quite how it should for him. He's OK. I promise.'

'OK.' She looked at him dubiously. 'I'll take your word for it.'

As he gestured for her to go inside she hovered by the open door, pointing for him to go first instead, trying to be polite, but he stood firm, hand out to encourage her to go in. She hesitated and then they were suddenly both going through the door together, bashing into each other so their shoulders hit and they concertinaed in like an accordion.

Philippe laughed. She could feel the deep rumble where their bodies touched.

'I'm so sorry,' Rachel muttered.

'It was my fault. Not like a gentleman.' He laughed again and she watched his eyes crinkle up at the corners.

And noticed how his hair, neatly combed to one side, had flopped a little out of place. When he smiled his teeth were perfect and his long aquiline nose with its bump on the bridge seemed suddenly to give him an air of distinction. She hadn't thought of him as good-looking—not in the conventional way like Marcel or Ben—but now, as he smiled in the doorway she realised he was handsome. Like a nineteen-forties movie star.

And she also realised that she'd been staring.

'OK, then. Good. Lovely. *Au revoir.*'

'Hang on a minute,' she said suddenly as he started to walk away, a realisation dawning on her. 'If Henri is your brother, that makes you the other Salernes... You and him, you had the restaurant together. *Oui?*' She smiled at herself, as if she were a regular Columbo, but her expression wasn't reciprocated.

'*Oui,*' he said with a casual shrug but wasn't forthcoming with anything more.

'You're a chef,' Rachel went on. 'You're an amazing chef.' From what she'd Googled, the Salernes brothers had taken the culinary world by storm, and it certainly wasn't all Henri. While he was infamous for inventing mouth-watering desserts that challenged the very physics of pastry, his brother, this man standing in front of her, was responsible for some of the dishes that changed the way people cooked. He brought a simple, affordable casualness to the Michelin-starred nouvelle cuisine that was dominating restaurant fare. He learnt from the masters and then twisted the rules in his own unique way creating a culinary revolution.

'*Au revoir*, Rachel. It was nice to see you again.'

'No, wait. Hang on. You can't leave just yet. I read about you. The other night.'

Philippe cocked his head, a smirk on his lips.

'No, I mean—' She huffed out a breath, half embarrassed, half exasperated. 'I Googled Henri and I read about you. You were amazing. People said you were amazing. I really admire what you did and the boundaries you broke with your restaurant. Especially in a country with such a strong culinary tradition.'

Philippe shrugged. 'I don't cook any more. It is the past. Life, it has many cycles.'

'But you should. People would love to see you cook again. You should do a book or something,' Rachel carried on, moving down a step so she was a little closer to him, hardly able to believe that he could let such talent go to waste.

'But I do not want to do a book.' Philippe unwound his scarf and shrugged off his coat, shaking off the snow and deliberately avoiding eye contact with her. 'You can learn everything you need to know from Henri. I am not interested, not any longer.'

'It's crazy. You have so much talent. You shouldn't waste it. I would totally read a book by you.' Rachel bit her bottom lip and stared down at him, her head shaking slightly.

She watched as he paused, folded the coat neatly over his arm and draped his scarf over the heavy woollen material, then, running a hand over his light smattering of stubble, he looked up, his eyes just a touch narrower than they had been. 'And what about you? What are you hiding?' he asked, taking a step forward, almost invading her space. 'Not many people would come to Paris alone over Christmas, not even to bake.'

Rachel gave a little snort, retreating back into herself quick as a flash, and, stepping backwards up the stairs, muttered, 'Point taken.' Then she swept her fringe out of her eyes and said politely, 'I have to go now. I'm going to be late. If I don't get a move on.'

'Of course.' He stood where he was and watched her as she made to go.

About to hurry up the stairs, she paused with her hand on the banister, torn, wanting to run away but also not wanting to leave it like that between them. She didn't know him well but she'd liked him instantly and was frustrated with herself for prying, for pushing him when, as he said, she had her own issues that held her back that she wouldn't want to air to anyone who asked. 'Did you—?' She turned back to look at him. 'Did you enjoy your Religieuse?'

'Very much.' Philippe smiled, straightening his tie.

'Good.' She nodded, waited to see if he was going to say anything else and when he didn't she turned and flew up the stairs, two at a time, without looking back.

Walking into the workshop, she found she was the last one to arrive. With poor Tony gone it was down to seven of them. Everyone was waiting, standing straight like toy soldiers behind their work stations.

'Today is bread day,' shouted Chef as he marched in the room.

Rachel had known it was coming. Lacey had told Marcel in confidence that bread was Chef's pièce de résistance. It was all he cared about.

'If I could—' he stood at the front, hands on hips, nose in the air '—I would bake nothing. *Nothing* but bread. It is the essence of our existence. The food of generations. It is life. Bread. *Le pain.* Jesus—even Jesus—saw the promise of the loaf of bread.'

Rachel wanted to say that she thought the Feeding of the Five Thousand had another angle more important than the loaf but now certainly wasn't the time. She glanced at Marcel, who rolled his eyes, which caught her off guard and made her burst out in a little laugh.

'You find bread funny? Rachel, tell us what you find so funny about bread.'

'Nothing. I don't find it funny at all.'

Chef walked over and towered over her. 'No. Rachel is the expert, it seems. Today *Rachel*,' he sneered, slamming his hand down on the counter, 'will be teaching us how to make the bread that she finds so funny.'

CHAPTER EIGHT

'No, really. I couldn't p-possibly,' Rachel stammered at the idea of having to demonstrate to everyone.

'Bake,' he ordered.

'Oh, really.' Lacey sighed under her breath as she strutted over to Rachel's counter.

'We will all watch, Rachel.'

Rachel felt her hands shaking. Chef was standing so close in front of her she could feel his breath on her face. Everyone gathered round and stared in uncomfortable silence.

Gathering all her ingredients and a large mixing bowl, she took a deep breath and tried to calm the nerves that were shooting through her, but when she poured out some flour into her scales half of it tipped out into a heap on the counter.

'I'll get it,' said Abby.

'*Non.* It is Rachel's work. Rachel will tidy it.'

Lacey tapped the surface, her diamonds clinking together, her lipstick drawing into the grooves around her pursed lips. Marcel was lounging back. For a second Rachel wondered if he had tried to make her laugh on purpose. She glanced longingly at the door. She'd swap this moment for a thousand Home Ec lessons with their Hitler teacher, Ms Potter, breathing down her neck.

Chef was clicking his fingers for her to get a move on. Ali was writing notes and was about to say something but Abby silenced him.

'I don't think I can—' Rachel started to say as she scooped up the flour she'd wasted. But as she instinctively used it to cover the board for later, she was all of a sudden reminded of her mum doing exactly the same. *Can't waste it. Think of all the work that went into picking and grinding the little sods.*

And it was as if she were there suddenly, pulling up the stool next to her; Rachel could practically smell the Estée Lauder. *Why are you doing that? It'd be easier like this. Don't worry too much about scales, feel how much you need—sense it. Bread should be about you. What flavour do you like?*

Everyone at school has Mighty White.

Well, let's make Mighty White, then. She'd laugh.

Rachel reached for the wheat grains and malt that her mum would add for sweetness and wholemeal to her starchy white bread. She glided through the motions as all the rest of them blurred into a mist beside her. She was aware Chef was talking, but she wasn't listening. All she could hear was her mum, whispering words she'd been blocking out for years—the tone of her voice, her laugh, the touch of her hand on her shoulder, the way she'd brush her hair out of her eyes or sigh at how slow sieving things was. *Shall we just chuck it in? Come on, no one will know.*

It had been much easier to teach little kids their alphabets, Rachel realised, than step back into a bakery.

When she went to put the bread in the drawer to prove, she looked up and was surprised to find all the faces staring at her.

'I'll leave it for an hour,' she said slowly, coming out of her trance.

There was silence for a second or two, where people glanced at one another, as if they'd all been somehow bewitched by Rachel's demonstration. Finally Chef tapped the table and said, '*Bon*. Everyone, please, to the front.' He seemed a littler quieter than usual. Less aggressive. 'I will make soda bread while the dough rises.'

'Was that OK?' Rachel whispered to Abby.

'Well, aside from you completely ignoring his every instruction, I'd say it was bloody marvellous.'

She didn't listen to any of the soda bread instructions, just thought about the fact that twice now she had baked bread when she had been at her lowest point— lonely or afraid—and both times it hadn't been the horror that she had imagined. It had actually been quite comforting. Sort of like a hug.

Out of the oven Rachel's bread was beautiful. Exactly like the fake Mighty White her mum used to make.

'This is delicious,' sighed George with his mouth full.

'Very tasty,' Lacey managed through a tight grimace.

By lunchtime everyone had had quite enough of bread and they were all going to the bar, but Rachel cried off with the excuse that she had some stuff to buy. Instead she sat in the park on her own.

She found an empty bench and brushed off the snow with her glove, then sat on an old Pret a Manger napkin she found in her bag. The air was sparkling like a shower of glitter as the snow fell through the pine trees that loomed above her, big and dark and exotic. Huge pine cones jutted from the branches, white tipped with snow like porcupines, and birds dotted from branch to branch shaking the dusty sleet from their feathers.

All Rachel could think about was bread. To begin with the memories had been beautiful. But now that it was baked and eaten and over, she just felt sad. Drained. Drained by the memories and the emotion. Deflated and vulnerable, stripped of every barrier she had in place. She had felt her mum next to her as she had worked the dough, and, while at the time it had felt precious and perfect, now she felt as if she were back to those horrendous few months after she had died. It was as if she could see the hole in her heart and it was bigger than she'd ever let herself believe.

Christmas lights were twinkling in every tree, glowing stars dangled amongst the branches, and, all along the street, angels were looped across the road by their wings. She watched the people hurrying past on their lunch breaks, the pavement packed, everyone carrying bags of Christmas shopping. She heard carols echo from the nearby church choir practice and thought of her and Jackie singing in stupid voices as teenagers at the school Christmas choir service. Rachel pulled her hat down over her ears.

'Is this seat taken?'

She looked up, surprised, and saw Philippe, his grey woollen overcoat hanging open over his suit, his scarf draped over his shoulders. Rachel shook her head and moved her bag along to make room. 'No, please sit.'

He made a poor effort of brushing off the snow and folded himself down, resting his elbows on his knees and turning his head to look at her.

'My brother is better today?'

'No,' she said with a laugh.

He nodded silently, then stared out ahead of him. 'I wanted to apologise. For earlier. I was rude to you.'

'Oh, no, you weren't at all.' Rachel shook her head, pulling off her woolly hat and trying to straighten her fringe. 'I shouldn't have gone on about you having a book.' She laughed. 'Who'd want a book anyway?'

She saw his lips tilt up ever so slightly at the corners. 'A lot of people I think would like a book.' He glanced over his shoulder at her. 'Just not me, I am afraid.'

Rachel nodded, unconsciously pleating the fabric of her hat in her lap.

'But it is no reason for me to be rude to you,' Philippe went on. 'Why you are here has nothing to do with me, and I should not have made a point of it. Once again, I am not like a gentleman.'

As far as Rachel was concerned no man had ever been quite so gentlemanly with her before. Certainly not Ben and his four a.m. visits and no sleeping over. 'Honestly, it's fine. We were both at fault,' she said.

Rachel watched as he ran a hand over his bottom lip, once more staring straight ahead. She took the moment to study his profile, his wide broad shoulders that seemed to pull on the fabric of his coat, the neat line of his hair at the back of his neck and the smattering of stubble on his jaw. She liked sitting next to him. Liked the feeling of being in the park in the snow with this man on the bench next to her.

'I have a problem,' he said after a second.

'Really?' she asked, intrigued. 'What kind of problem?'

He laughed. 'Nothing serious. I must buy a gift.'

'Ah, I see. What kind of gift?'

'I'm not sure yet. That's my problem. I feel I will only know when I see it.'

'A tricky gift.' She laughed.

'*Mais oui.*' He sat back, stretching one leg across the other, raking a hand through his neatly cropped hair.

'I am on my way to look now. I see you and I think maybe you would like to come? Your taste so far has been...impeccable.' He smiled.

'Oh, no, I can't.'

He nodded and looked forward again, unmoving. 'That is a great shame.'

'I have to go back to class soon. I don't have time.'

'How long do you have?' He checked his watch.

She looked guilty. 'Forty-five minutes.'

He smiled again. 'I understand.'

'No, no, you don't, it's just I feel I need some time. Something happened in class. I just—'

'Come anyway.' He cut her off. 'Come anyway, just because. Maybe just because I really do need some help.'

Rachel fiddled with her gloves, picking a hole in the wool. The snow had started to get heavier, dusting the pavements like icing sugar.

'OK,' she said after a pause. 'OK, why not?'

'*Bon.*' Philippe stood up and held out his hand to help her up; she took it for a second but let it drop as soon as she was standing. As soon as she did she wished that she hadn't.

He put his hands deep in the pockets of his overcoat and they walked together to the row of little shops in the Marais.

'Wait a second—what is this?' Philippe stopped her halfway down the road and then peeled something off the back of her coat. 'It is a new look, yes?'

She blushed as she looked at the tatty, wet napkin he was holding that she'd used to sit on. 'It was to protect my coat,' she said, grabbing it from his hand and scrunching it up in the bin.'How embarrassing. I walked the whole way from the park with it hanging off me.'

He blew out a breath. 'No one will care. They will think it is fashion.'

She raised a brow as if that would never be the case and he laughed as if he completely agreed.

They walked on in the direction of the Marais, their feet leaving a trail of footprints in the light coating of snow as Philippe pointed out landmarks and places she might want to visit some time.

Approaching the network of narrow streets, she saw all the gift shops were bustling, looking warm and inviting, playing classical carols and serving glasses of *vin chaud*.

'So what does your friend like?' Rachel asked.

'I'm not so sure.'

'Great start. Male or female?'

'Female.'

She felt a bolt of jealousy that took her by surprise. Who would be buying her presents this year? Not Ben. She always insisted he shouldn't bother and he never did. Jackie always gave her a bottle of champagne that they drank on Boxing Day. Her dad usually posted her a paperback. And her gran would declare that she was sending a donation to the RSPB or something similar in

Rachel's name—*Birds, darling, I much prefer birds to humans*. Then there was little Tommy from her class; he always gave her something. It was a tradition. She tried not to have favourites but he was so sweet and ever since she'd found him standing alone in the playground complaining of a tummy ache, which after floods of tears he'd said was caused by no one wanting to play with him, she had made it her mission to make sure he wasn't left out again.

She'd put a cushion in the corner of her classroom with a stack of books next to it and a secret packet of chocolate digestives and said if he ever felt lonely he could go and sit there at lunch break. She'd kept an eye on him, encouraging him to pluck up the courage to ask if he could join in with the games the other kids played and finally knew he was OK when she caught them all tucking into the digestives, Tommy beaming that he'd been the one to show them the stash. Since then he'd always made her presents—for her birthday, for end of term and for Christmas. Last year it was a Santa made out of a loo roll, painted red with a cotton-wool beard. She'd left it up all year round.

Philippe paused next to a stall selling herbs and baskets of lavender and she watched as he scooped some dried oregano up and smelt it.

'This is my favourite. I adore it. Here, smell.' He held the little silver scoop out for her to have a sniff.

'No.'

'No?'

'No, it's his stall.' Rachel looked around, embarrassed. 'You can't just smell things.'

'Why, of course you can. It is what it is here for. I think you worry too much about what all these people you don't know think. You are a chef? Why do you not smell?'

Rachel caught the eye of the stall-holder, who nodded as if he couldn't care less what she smelt, and leant forward for a quick sniff. 'Very nice.'

'Ah, *oui*. And this.' He picked up another, crushed rosemary.

'Again very nice.' She did a quick embarrassed smell as he went on to sniff the lavender and the nutmeg and the big bags of ground cinnamon. 'Do you smell everything?'

'Everything,' he said, very seriously, and asked the stall-holder to bag up some cinnamon for him. 'For the *vin chaud*,' he said to Rachel.

After paying they strolled on and Philippe turned to her and said, 'Do you smell nothing?'

'Well, yeah, I smell some stuff but not in the street.'

'I think you are mad. The smell, it is the most sensual of all the senses. Here…' They paused at a fruit and veg shop. 'What about this?' He picked up a fig and held it to his nose. 'It is divine. It is much better than the taste.'

She peered forward, checked the shopkeeper wasn't looking and had a smell of the fig. 'It is very lovely. It reminds me of my holidays in Greece when I was little.'

'*Pas oui*, of course, it is the best memory of them all. It reminds me of the tree we had in our garden. Henri would make me climb up it to get the biggest figs at the top. One day the branch break and I fall to the floor. And Henri he laugh and that makes me laugh, not cry. I was only six. All that from a fig.'

Rachel thought of her dough and her soft, sweet-smelling Mighty White loaf. She was about to say something about how it could sometimes be too powerful, the memory too overwhelming, but she stopped herself and laughed instead, saying, 'You're a crazy smeller.'

'Yes, that is the case. I am. Look at my nose—it is built for the smelling.'

'Mine too.' She laughed, pointing at her own long straight nose that had been the bane of her life.

'I think you have a very nice nose,' he said, looking down at her face.

'I think *you* have a very nice nose.' She laughed.

And then they both looked away, as if they were both equally unsure what to say next.

'I will buy the figs,' Philippe said and disappeared inside as Rachel looked out into the street, at all the stalls selling gifts and trinkets and delicious delicacies, unable to hold in a smile to herself that he'd said he liked her nose.

Philippe came out with three bags and handed two of them to her. 'A gift to say thank you for shopping with me.'

'Oh, thanks, you shouldn't have,' she said, surprised, taking the scrunched brown bags from him and peeking inside. The first glistened like rubies—a bag of hundreds of tiny dried cranberries. The second was bursting with thin strips of candied orange thickly coated with crystals of sugar. They felt like the most perfect presents she'd ever been given.

'These are lovely. Perfect. Thank you.' She glanced up at him, a huge smile on her face that she couldn't hide, but as he watched her his demeanour seemed different. It was probably just her being paranoid but he seemed suddenly to regret buying her the bags of fruit—as if in the giving the gesture had turned into something more than he'd intended. 'They might be good for the baking, you know.' He shrugged distractedly, staring ahead at the snow-covered canopies of the stalls, then he started to walk on and Rachel had to do a little jog to catch up.

'Is everything OK?' she asked, wanting to go back to the ease between them. Wanting to tell him that she knew it was just fruit, nothing more than that, however happy she'd seemed when she'd looked in the little bags.

'*Mais oui.*' He turned to her and smiled. 'It is all fine.'

'OK.' She nodded, shaking off any unease. 'So say again what it is your friend likes.'

'She likes beautiful things,' Philippe said after a moment.

'Don't we all?' Rachel laughed. 'Expensive, beautiful things.'

'Ah, *non*. Not expensive.' He shook his head. 'I don't think expensive is what she'd want.'

'Fair enough.' Rachel stared into the shop window wondering who this perfect woman was. 'How about a scarf?' She nodded to the mannequin in front of them.

'Too plain. She has one already. Too boring.'

'Oh, OK.'

'No, no, don't take it that way. It was a good suggestion. I just think something maybe more like this—' He pointed to a jewelled box in the next window.

'Hideous,' Rachel said before she could stop herself.

He laughed. 'See, this is why I need a second opinion.'

They strolled on in silence. Rachel didn't often do silence—usually chattering away to fill the spaces in her mind—but it felt as if silence was something Philippe was comfortable with. And somehow that started to make her comfortable too.

When they paused at a stall selling roasted chestnuts and bought a bag to share, she was almost reluctant when she said, through a mouthful of burning chestnut, 'You know, I should be getting back.'

'*Mais oui*, of course. I forgot. We can go this way.' He touched her elbow to steer her down a side road and she felt a tiny jolt at the touch.

She thought about Ben saying she'd make someone a good wife one day and she'd known before she asked that it wouldn't be him. She realised then, as she strolled with Philippe, that it hadn't been Ben keeping her at arm's length—well, of course, it had been—but it had been her, too. Who had a relationship that lasted between the hours of four and six in the pre-dawn morning?

Ben was like Tony's jam tart—looked good but no substance. And she realised, as this French stranger steered her down the street, that she had chosen that.

She had chosen tasteless. Bland.

Tasteless was easier than complexity and flavour. Less work. She had had a boring flan when really she should have been holding out for a coffee profiterole or a violet and blackberry macaroon.

'Ah, what about this?'

Philippe had stopped midway down the cobbled street. Rachel turned and was caught by the beauty of the window display before she could summon up her usual disdain for anything Christmas.

It was a Russian shop—the window a scene from a fairy tale. Black lacquered boxes, painted with princesses in chariots pulled by fiery red horses and a wake of golden stars, were lined up like presents under huge frosted trees. A snow-capped forest towered high around a figurine of the Snow Queen, decked out in all her silver finery. And hanging from thick satin ribbons along the window were rows and rows of baubles, from big to tiny. There were diamond shapes and twirls or circles and hearts. Some white, some black, some shocking pink, with fairy-tale scenes intricately painted on each.

'They're beautiful,' she whispered.

He clapped his hands as if decided. '*J'agree. Merci*, Rachel.'

'You found them.'

'Yes, but I wouldn't have done without you.' He started to walk on.

'Aren't you going to get one?'

'Later,' he said. 'You have to get back.'

'Oh, thanks. Yes.' She glanced at her watch, having, in that moment, completely forgotten about the time. 'Yes, I do.'

As they stepped out onto the main street she was checking the traffic to cross the road when her eyes fell on his coat. 'Look,' she said and pointed to where a thousand snowflakes had caught in the wool.

He paused, then picked one off and held it on the tip of his gloved finger. 'It is perfect,' he said, then took her hand and touched it to her glove where it sat tiny and perfect like a gift.

She felt him looking down at her, watching.

After a pause she blew it away, embarrassed by the whole gesture. 'I can never believe that each one is meant to be different.'

'Well, *we* are all different.' He shrugged.

'That's true.'

'Every one of us unique.'

'I know, we could be anyone. I mean, if you think about it, I don't really know you at all, or you me.'

She looked from his white-flecked coat back up to him and he seemed as if he was about to say something but changed his mind. Instead he just smiled and she noticed he had snowflakes on his eyelashes.

They had an hour and a half to make a Christmas-inspired bread.

Marcel was making an apricot, date and nutmeg Panettone. George was muttering about some sort of cherry-brandy yule-log buns. Lacey said nothing, just got to work. Abby looked perplexed—Rachel could see the competition was starting to get to her. She'd cried in the bar last night, weeping that she missed her kids. She'd Skyped them in the morning before class and had come in with red-rimmed, puffy eyes.

As Rachel watched Abby, Cheryl leant across her and picked some coffee grains off the shelf. 'Sorry, hun, didn't mean to push,' she apologised, her cheeks flushing red.

'No, it's fine, I was miles away.' Rachel stared at the ingredients. She thought about Philippe telling her she worried too much about what people thought—she felt it in herself, sticking too much with conventions and not going with her instincts. But her brain was blank. The only thing coming to mind was Easter. Warm hot cross buns that ripped apart like candy floss. She was reminded of the smells in the street today. Of the different spices and the sharp tang as they hit her senses. Of roasting chestnuts, mulled wine packed with star anise, cinnamon and nutmeg, and the brown bags of dried cranberries and candied orange that were stuffed in her jacket pocket.

That was it… Hot Cross Christmas buns. Warm and sticky and sweet. She'd pack them with candied orange zest and slivers of cranberry, raisins, sultanas and glacé cherries. Then glaze them with cinnamon syrup and white icing and when they were opened up she'd have a chocolate and chestnut purée that sank, melting, into the warm, fluffy dough.

They worked in silence, heads down, kneading, flouring, rolling, shaping. As Rachel's dough was rising she tore the skins from her roasted chestnuts, burning her fingers, popping one into her mouth when no one was looking.

Chef was called down to the pâtisserie as she was melting her chocolate and when he left it was as if everyone had been holding their breath and could collectively exhale.

'Oh, my God.' It was Abby who punctured the contented silence.

'What?' Rachel turned.

'I've used salt instead of sugar.'

'No, you can't have done.'

Everyone paused except Lacey, who just carried on silently. Marcel strode over and picked up the container. 'She has. She has used the salt.'

'Shit.' Abby slumped onto her forearms. 'How can this have happened? I don't have time to do more. Oh, God, I'm out. How can I tell my kids that I'm out because of some stupid sodding mistake from being tired? You idiot.' She smacked herself on the forehead. 'I'm just so tired.'

Rachel watched as her friend started to cry. Hot, fat tears falling into her failed dough.

'Don't cry,' she said, walking over to helplessly pat her on the back.

'It's useless. I'm useless. I'm a failure. A failure. A fucking failure with a stupid husband sailing the fucking Caribbean or wherever the hell Mauritius is.'

'It is in the Indian Ocean, off the coast of Africa,' said Marcel.

'Thank you.' Abby wiped her nose on the tissue Rachel gave her.

'Look, just have half of my dough,' Rachel said.

'I can't take your dough.'

'Yes, you can. Just pick the bits out and he'll be none the wiser. You're adding chocolate and vanilla anyway, aren't you?'

'But there won't be enough.'

'There'll be plenty.'

'It's cheating.' Lacey stopped kneading and turned round.

'Who cares? We're all adults. It's not school, Lacey.' Rachel shook her head. 'And you know he'll kick her out and she doesn't deserve to go over a mistake.'

Lacey pursed her lips, tapping the wooden spoon in her hand against her palm.

'I wouldn't do it if I thought she made crap dough. It was a mistake.'

Lacey was silent.

Then Abby said, 'Would you tell, Lacey?'

There was a pause. Rachel watched George and Ali exchange glances, Marcel raised a brow, intrigued at how this would pan out, and Abby looked on with pleading eyes.

'It's none of my business,' Lacey muttered in the end and turned her back to them.

Rachel winked at Abby and went and pulled her dough out of the drawer, tore it in half and the two of them went about picking out all the cranberries and raisins she'd so lovingly folded in half an hour ago.

Chef strode in just as Rachel was running back to her bench, slamming her bowl of dough down hard by mistake. He paused, seemed to smell the air like a lion sensing a change in the atmosphere. Then he walked over to Rachel's bench, reeking of fags, his expression suspicious. 'What's going on?'

'What do you mean?'

'Something happened. And it is usually you.'

'No, Chef. I'm just mixing my chocolate into the puréed chestnuts,' she said without looking up.

He waited, and she could feel him staring at her, as if he knew exactly what was going on. Her heart was starting to quicken as she tried to act as nonchalant as possible.

'Hmm.' He stuck his finger in the mixture and licked it. 'You try to be very calm. You are never calm,' he said, then walked away, not before lifting the tea towel off her dough and scowling at it.

When they came to laying out their breads Rachel had brought in a special box—one that Chantal had given her that Madame Charles had discarded. It was wooden, meant for a small hamper from one of the expensive food shops on the Champs Élysées. The name was embossed on the side in grand, swirling writing. Rachel had lined it with a strip of red wool and piled her soft, squishy but depleted buns inside. Each one had a white star of icing piped on the top. The chestnut and chocolate purée was in a little glass jar nestled in the corner.

Chef peered at it. 'Presentation—better. Could improve.'

Rachel nodded, holding in a smile that she'd at least moved it up a notch.

He spread the thick chocolate on the ripped-open bun that was still warm and steamed in the cool air. He closed his eyes as he ate, savouring the sweet softness. 'Very nice. Clever. I didn't expect... Very nice,' he said again, as if caught off guard, then he nodded and walked on. Rachel nearly punched the air. Abby gave her a thumbs up.

Chef prowled the other benches, tasting, criticising, praising faintly. Marcel's Panettone hadn't risen very much but looked amazing. He muttered that Ali's pumpkin, cider and marzipan buns were too sweet but better than he'd expected. Poor Cheryl's coffee and pistachio tea-loaf had burnt on the top and risen unevenly. The dough inside was undercooked and Chef refused to put it in his mouth.

'This will be the last day for you, Cheryl. You will go home. You understand?' he said, prodding the soft dough with his finger.

George gasped.

Cheryl nodded silently, her hair falling forward so it was hard to see the reddening of her cheeks. When Chef walked away, Rachel watched her dab a tea towel to her eye and hold it there for a second as she took some deep breaths.

George's, Chef thought, was marvellous; he couldn't get enough of it. He even laughed at how he'd managed to make a bread look like a yule log.

'This is very inventive. I like it.'

George was beaming.

Chef came to Abby last. Rachel felt her pulse start to speed up. When he put the chocolate twist in his mouth and paused, she thought she could actually feel the minutes tick by. By the time he swallowed and said, *'Très bon,'* Rachel thought her heart might have leapt out through her chest and run out of the room.

'That is OK.' He nodded. 'A good dough. Some OK flavours. But a little small.'

'Christ,' said Abby as they stumbled out, laughing. 'I thought I was going to die.'

'Me too.' Rachel was clutching her chest.

'Thank God it's over.'

A door slammed above them and then she heard her name being called from behind her. 'Rachel! Stop there.'

They paused and turned to see Chef standing at the top of the stairs. 'A word.'

Abby made a worried face and squeezed her hand before sloping out while Rachel backtracked up a floor.

Chef was waiting, thumbs slung in the string of his apron. Rachel paused on the top step but he beckoned her to come further forward, to stand right in front of him.

She waited, glancing from his weathered face to the slogan of the pâtisserie on his apron, to his polished black shoes.

'You think after twenty years I cannot taste?' he asked.

She looked at the floor. Staring at the patterns in the carpet.

'Let me tell you something,' he sneered. 'All good bakers have a signature. Did you know that?'

Rachel shook her head.

'A cake, a loaf, a tart…it is signed by their own hand. You—' He pointed at her. 'You leave a signature. And I can read it.'

Rachel glanced up.

'Yes, that's right. A big, bold signature.' He almost spat it out.

She was suddenly terrified that he was going to boot her out.

Over the last few days this competition had gone from being a burden to the most important thing in her life. She'd started to find the challenge addictive. While she loved her job in Nettleton, she hadn't realised how much she had missed this—the skill, the craftsmanship, the smells, the textures, the familiarity. The thrill of knowing that she had a talent, however rusty. She would do anything for it not to end now.

'I'm sorry. I'm really sorry. I was just trying to help. I didn't know. I did know. I know it was wrong. Oh, God—'

'I should throw you out the door. You hear me? You waste my time. You make a fool of me.' He waved his hands in the air. 'You throw this away. That is what you have done. This chance that you 'ave to be good and you have thrown it away.' He paused, taking a deep breath.

She glanced up tentatively. Saw a look of confusion and annoyance pass over his face. It felt suddenly as if he wasn't talking to her but that instead the words were ringing truer to himself. She thought of the stories she'd Googled. All that success that he had let slip through his fingers, the crown that he had allowed to topple, the reputation that had ended up in tabloid ridicule. In the moment's pause he seemed to deflate before her eyes, his cheeks less puffed out, his colour less red. She bit her lip and tried to show the depth of her apology in plaintive eyes.

'*Merde*, and I know what it is like. You are stupid.' He took off his glasses and rubbed a hand over his face.

Rachel nodded, sensing something odd was happening between them. That she was teetering on the edge of being on the next train home but something, some emotion flickering over Chef's face, might just be about to save her, throw her a rope and pull her back. 'I'm sorry.'

He exhaled like a bull about to charge and ran his fingers over his stubbled chin. 'I give you one more chance because you have a shred of promise. A shred. I am stupid to do it. But fuck me over again...you have no more chances. *Comprende?*'

She nodded, flooded with relief as if she might collapse into a puddle on the floor, and pleaded with herself not to cry.

'*Comprende?*' he said again.

'Yes, Chef.'

CHAPTER NINE

That night Rachel got so drunk out of relief that she was still in the competition, terror at having been yelled at, and shock at the haunted look in Chef's eyes. Her stupor meant that she didn't pull her foot away from Marcel's when he pushed his against hers under the table. Nor did she look away when he smirked at her across the table, his flirtatious eyes glinting beautifully. He had that familiar predatory nature of Ben that was surprisingly comforting.

When she'd walked into the bar Marcel had singled her out, got up to give her his seat, poured her a glass of wine, complimented her on her bake. He had made it more than clear that he was interested and the attention was intoxicating.

'I think you are the best cook here. Without doubt. Chef, I think he is jealous,' he'd whispered. 'And—' he'd paused '—you're the most beautiful.'

She'd glanced away, blushing, but the words had hit their mark. He was pumping up her deflated ego, as if he knew exactly where her weaknesses lay, and she was lapping it up. Anything to take the attention away from her run-in with Chef.

Women were looking at Marcel from the bar, glancing round to see if he might be interested in them but he wasn't; he was looking at Rachel.

'So what did Chef say, Rachel?' Abby leant forward, her eyes darting to Marcel as if trying to attract his attention, swirling her wine round in her glass.

'Nothing. Just a reminder to work on my presentation.'

'Ooh, special treatment for Rachel.' She whistled, supposedly joking, but Rachel caught a weird look in her eye. 'You and George had it nailed today,' she said, taking a great gulp of red wine and pouring some more.

The air between them all was definitely changing. It was as if this really was a competition and for the first time in Rachel's life she was near the top—not just hovering over average but up there in sight of the prize—and that clearly made enemies.

'Don't be daft.' She laughed, brushing the comment away and reaching for a glass and the carafe to pour herself some wine. 'He just loathes my mess.'

Abby raised a brow, disbelieving, clearly still smarting from her failure, and seemingly pissed off that Marcel wasn't paying her the attention he was Rachel, and downed her drink before holding her glass out for Rachel to top her up.

'A dark horse in the race, Flower Girl,' drawled Marcel and, under the table, she felt his hand scrape her thigh. He had perfect hands, neat blunt nails and a dirty tan as if he'd spent the summer on a yacht in St Tropez and skied all winter. She decided that, in his black cashmere jumper, he actually looked fresh from the slopes of Val d'Isère. Close up she could even make out the remains of sunburn on the tips of his cheekbones.

'Is there something on my face?' he asked and she realised she'd been staring.

'No, no. I was just wondering if you skied. You know, why you had a tan in December…' She cringed at the embarrassment of being caught.

'*Mais oui*, I spend every weekend in the Alps. It is my passion.' He examined his hand to check out his own tan. 'Do you ski?'

Rachel thought about the time when the hill on the edge of Nettleton had been caked in snow and Jackie had strapped her into her snowboard. *You'll be fine, just point it downhill and sit down if it goes too fast.*

It had been a disaster not to be repeated. Rachel had sat down almost straight away and shot down the incline head first, one foot flailing about having popped from the binding and the other dragging the snowboard along with it. She'd waved her arms about in the air with the aim of getting someone to help her; instead the whole village had stopped what they were doing to watch. A photo of her at the bottom of the slope, caked in white like the abominable snowman, legs skew-whiff in the carved-up muddy slush, had appeared on the front page of the *Nettleton News*.

'I snowboard.' She shrugged, as if it were nothing. 'Sometimes.'

A forgotten memory popped up of her and some of her class piled into an old canoe later that same day, winning a downhill race against Jackie and most of 3F on garden sacks, which was much more pleasing and obviously gave her a look of casual confidence that appealed to Marcel.

'We should go together some time. Maybe.'

'Maybe.' She smiled, high on the attention, flirtily trying to tousle her hair.

'Ooh, I'll come,' said Abby. 'I've never been skiing. We could all go—it could be our reunion.'

'*Pas oui*, definitely. The more the merrier. That is the phrase, *oui*?'

When Rachel nodded, Marcel squeezed her leg under the table and whispered, 'I would prefer just the two of us.'

'Me too,' she whispered back, catching her smile with her teeth, relishing the attention, enjoying the haze of the wine and their intimate secret little club of two that was pulling back all the confidence she'd earlier let slip away.

'Would you come, George?' Abby leant forward, her boobs pushing together between her upper arms and, while not having the desired effect on Marcel, working well to get George's attention.

'Where?'

'Skiing.'

George snorted into his beer. 'I don't think so.'

'Oh, come on, it'd be fun. We'd all have to go.'

'I think I'm a bit old to be throwing myself down ski slopes.'

Abby stuck her bottom lip out as if he'd ruined everything and George laughed. 'I'm here, in Paris, isn't that enough?'

She tipped her head from side to side. 'I suppose.' Then took a great gulp of wine and said, 'Where did you learn to bake?'

'Baker's boy in the sixties,' he said, stretching his shoulders back and taking off his glasses. 'Sexual revolution passed me by. I had my head in a bloody oven the whole decade. Pay packet taken by me mum, bugger all I got. Everyone else is having sex left right and centre and I'm shovelling loaves.'

Abby laughed. 'Surely, then, this should be the last thing you want?'

He tapped his nose. 'You may think so, but what we forget is as we get older we find most comfort in the familiar. My wife died ten years ago, my kids have gone—all grown-up. All doctors—the lot of them. And I found myself alone, baking again. Then I had so much I took it round the neighbours and they passed it onto friends and then I had a little business. I made a cart out of builders' crates that I take round offices. Who'd have thought? My neighbour, Jayne, painted it blue with lettering and that's my job. Forty years an accountant, now a baker, just like I was as a boy.' He put his glasses back on and shrugged, took a sip of his half-pint. 'It's a way of making friends. Keeping busier.'

Rachel listened through her wine haze. Comfort in the familiar. She looked at Marcel and he winked at her.

She smiled and kicked his foot under the table. 'And what about you?' she asked.

'Lovely Marcel does it for the women,' Abby slurred.

'Touché.' He smirked, tapping a cigarette from the pack in his pocket. 'I do it because I can. Because it is something I am good at. It has been in my family for generations, from my great-grandfather grinding the wheat. One side of my family, they make the alcohol, the other side the bread. The two staples of life. So this for me is in my blood. I understand it,' he said, tucking the fag behind his ear. 'Like the women.' He grinned, pushing himself from his seat and sloping outside into the falling snow.

Rachel watched the smoke of his cigarette curl up into the overhead light, twining round the glistening flakes.

'He's just so good-looking. It's almost unfair.' Abby had her chin in her hand and was looking out to where Rachel was staring, Marcel's profile just visible through the half-open door.

They turned back to the table when someone else went outside and pushed the door shut behind them, partially blocking off the view.

'It's a shame Cheryl's gone, isn't it? I liked her. Unassuming,' said George.

'I know.' Abby swept her hair back from her face. 'Did you see her crying? It was terrible. I hope it doesn't push her back into eating.'

Rachel bashed her on the shoulder. 'It's not going to do that.'

'Well, you never know,' she said into her wine glass and Rachel rolled her eyes.

There was a pause as Abby tried to formulate her point but had had too much to drink and Rachel went back to watching Marcel. The barman reached up to flick on the stereo and gypsy jazz started to play softly in the background.

'It's a shame someone has to win,' said George into the silence.

Abby snorted.

Surprised, Rachel looked away from the smoke outside and back at George, a man with a bushy white moustache whom she had barely noticed that week, and smiled.

'Yes.' She nodded. 'It is a shame.'

***

Marcel offered to walk her home and, about to say no, Rachel found herself agreeing. The idea of no-strings company in her lonely flat, especially such goddamn good-looking company, seemed like the perfect rebellion from the strictures of the competition. It was like giving into pure, unadulterated temptation. Standing there in his battered leather jacket that shone in the moonlight, his arm draped casually over her shoulder, Marcel made her feel like the centre of the moment. It wasn't buying a present for someone else with Philippe or begging Chef to keep her on or wishing Ben would sleep the whole night in her flat. It was her, singled out and centre of his attention and the feeling was addictive.

When she nodded Abby gave an unsubtle thumbs up that made Marcel smirk.

'It's a long walk,' she warned him.

'I like the challenge.' Marcel shrugged, a cigarette clamped between his teeth.

She unlocked her bike and he took it from her, pushing it along beside them, leaving snake tracks in the snow.

'This is a child's bike.'

'No, it's small because it folds up.' She laughed.

He held it at arm's length, studying the rust. '*Non*. It is for the child,' he said, then clambered on, cycling in wavy lines along the snowy pavement. 'Get on.'

'No way. You'll kill me.'

'Get on, Flower Girl, live a little.' He circled her on the bike, his knees practically up to his ears as he pedalled.

'OK but—' As he slowed Rachel jumped onto the handlebars at the front and yelped as he rode them away along the cobbled backstreets, slipping through piles of grey slush and midway through taking one hand off to light another cigarette.

'Are you smoking as well?' She could barely turn her head, terrified that any minute they would crash into a wall.

'*Mais oui.* It is fun, yes? You are having the fun?' Plumes of smoke mingled with the falling snowflakes as he talked.

Squeezing her eyes tight when he veered from a lamppost, she opened them again to feel the snow dusting her face and her freezing hands clutching tight to the metal handlebars. '*Oui.* I am having the fun.'

'*Bon.*' He laughed and pedalled faster, but then slipped on a muddy puddle of slush and they fell off into a great mountain of snow that had been shovelled to the side of the road.

Rachel was on top of him, the bike halfway across the pavement; she was brushing snow from her mouth while he was leaning back laughing up at the clouds.

'*C'est* fun, *n'est-ce pas?*' He smiled, snow all in his hair, and then tightened his arms around her and rolled them over so he was on top of her and she could feel the freezing snow down her back.

'I am going to kiss you, Flower Girl,' he said, and she looked up into his ice-blue eyes and his perfect features and nodded.

His kiss tasted exactly of Ben. Of alcohol and cigarettes and arrogance. She let her head be pressed back into the snow and wrapped her arms tight around his back, her head swimming from all the red wine and the thrill of doing something she knew was bad for her.

Marcel only pulled back when they heard the siren of a police car in the background. 'We go, yes? I do not want to be arrested for what I might do next.'

She laughed, pulling her coat tight around her as he stood up and then reached a hand down to help her up.

They walked on a little closer, their shoulders brushing with each step, glancing over at each other and then, as quickly, glancing away. When they saw a pharmacy green cross flash minus four degrees he put his arm around her and pulled her close, rubbing his hand down her arm as if trying to warm her up.

It was late when they got back to her apartment, maybe one o'clock. When she asked, 'Do you want to come up, for coffee?' he didn't answer, just took the key from her gloved hand and unlocked the door, pushing it open for her, and followed her up the stairs.

Rachel felt a pang of guilt to see that Chantal had been there; a bunch of lilies on the turn were lying on the bench by the door next to a jar of strawberry jam.

Marcel picked it up quizzically.

'My friend,' she said. 'She gives me things.'

'I thought you said you had no friends?'

'Well, I—' Rachel started, but he wasn't listening. He pushed the door open and pulled her inside, kicking it shut on the wilting lilies.

As he unbuttoned and pushed off her coat she put her hands on his chest to slow him down, her mind swirling with alcohol. 'Do you want some tea?' she asked, moving towards the kettle.

'Tea?' He looked puzzled. 'Why would I want the tea?'

'To sober up?' She shrugged.

He hung his jacket up and kicked off his boots, then rummaged in his rucksack and pulled out a litre bottle of Armagnac. 'The last thing I want to do, Rachel, is sober up.' He smirked, grabbing a glass and a chipped teacup from the shelf and sloshing them full of booze.

When he handed her the glass he chinked the edge with his cup and said, 'To baking.'

'To baking.' She smiled, taking a tentative sip while he downed his in one and poured them both another slosh.

'To winning,' he said, holding his cup up high like a trophy.

'To winning.' She clinked his in the air and screwed up her face as she drank it down.

He laughed as he poured some more, spilling it over the floor as he trailed between his cup and her glass.

'To the making love,' he said next, blue eyes twinkling in the dim yellow light of the napkin-covered sidelight.

Rachel snorted into her Armagnac and had to wipe it off her face. Marcel was watching her over the rim of his teacup, waiting for her answer before he drank.

She swallowed. Tried not to laugh again and raised the glass in the air. 'To the making love.' She giggled.

'*Bon*,' said Marcel, draining his cup and ambling over to watch as she gulped hers down before sweeping her off her feet and carrying her through the alcove to the hard metal bed.

Next morning she woke when the garbage truck hissed to a halt in the street below. Stretching languidly, she reached across to find an empty bed.

'Marcel?' she said, sitting up and glancing around the flat.

Sensing something wasn't quite right, she looked around for her phone but it wasn't by the bed. Finally she found it still in her bag, alarm unset.

'Shit.' It was eight-thirty. She had thirty minutes to get across Paris to her class. Marcel was nowhere to be seen.

Yanking on her clothes, she glanced outside to see a thick carpet of snow, the heaviest it had been since she'd arrived. People were pushing through it, heads down. Cars were stuck, kids were sliding up the pavements on invisible skateboards.

'Shit.' She pulled on her boots, hopping around on the floor, while trying to look in the mirror. Staring back at her was a white hung-over face, dishevelled hair she had no time to fix and eyes puffy from lack of sleep.

It was only as she was flying down the stairs that it dawned on her Marcel had left her on purpose. That this was game-playing.

What a fool! Hadn't Lacey warned her on the first day?

Clearly Marcel was trying to eliminate the competition by any means possible.

'The little bastard.' She paused, hand on the banister. She wouldn't be surprised if he'd swapped Abby's sugar for salt as well.

Outside the freezing air hit her like cold water and her feet disappeared into the snow. Hauling her bike into the partially gritted road, swerving on the death-trap black ice, she cycled as fast as her frozen legs would pedal her. Wiping the snowy ice from her face as it fell, she pleaded with whoever was listening for her not to be late. She realised how much she not only wanted this, but now wanted to win.

'Mum, if you're listening,' she said up to the foggy white sky, 'help me. Please.'

Chantal's lilies were flopping around in her basket as she pedalled faster. She hadn't wanted to leave them on the step and had been in too much of a hurry to unlock the door and put them inside, but now they were losing petals all over the place. She skidded on the ice and swerved in the thicker snow but as the time ticked away she seemed to be moving slower than ever. The weather was getting worse, the snow falling in heavier flakes so she couldn't see, her tyres sliding in the slush.

'Damn him,' she said out loud. 'Damn *him*.' Exhausted, angry with Marcel but more so with herself for believing he thought her irresistible, she finally stopped when her tyre caught in a snowdrift. Hanging her head over the handlebars, she exhaled with great gulps of despair. Flashing images hit her of her mum serving warm *pain au chocolat* that oozed on the plate when torn open before church on Christmas Day. Of the queues outside the bakery on Christmas Eve. Of what she thought her mum's face might have looked like had she made it through another round, even to the final, maybe—just to beat Marcel! To know that she threw it all away for drunken sex that, from what she could remember, hadn't even been that good.

'Fuck it.' Rachel yanked the bike free but like a stubborn donkey it wasn't going anywhere. She was kicking it out of pure frustration when a car drew up next to her and the window slowly slid down.

'The bicycle, it not your friend?' Philippe leaned over to look out of the passenger window.

Rachel stood back, pushing her hat out of her eyes and patting the bike on the handlebars. 'We're having a slight disagreement.'

He laughed. 'You want a lift?'

'I would love a lift.' She smiled. Locking the bike to the nearest railing, she ran to get in the nicely heated car. 'You've saved my life. I could kiss you.'

As she said it he made a face, bemused, and the air suddenly seemed a little warmer.

'Not actually kiss you, you know, it's just—you know—an expression…of gratitude...'

He kept his face forward, a smile now teasing the corners of his lips.

'Oh, God.' She ran a hand over her face and looked out of the window. 'I'll just shut up.'

'You're late today, no?'

'Yes, I'm really late. Stupidly late.'

'I'm having dinner with him tonight. I'll put in a good word.'

'I fear it might be too late by then.' She checked her watch and sighed. Five minutes—there was no way they'd make it. Then she caught her reflection in the visor mirror and almost shocked herself with her dark puffy circles and glowing white face. She pulled her bobble hat lower.

Philippe wove through the slow-moving traffic as she tapped her fingers on her knees, watching the minute hand tick by.

'I know a short cut, don't worry,' he said, and then, yanking the wheel round, proceeded to drive the wrong way down two one-way streets, up a bus lane and down a cobbled path that she wasn't convinced was made for cars.

When they pulled up to the pâtisserie she was sitting rigid, clinging to her seat.

'*Et voilà*, we are here.'

She looked over at him in his clean-cut smart suit. 'I'm not sure that could legally be called a short cut.'

He laughed. 'You'd better go. You're ten minutes late.'

'Thank you,' she said, and reached over to give him a peck on the cheek. But just as she did he moved his head to look at her and she ended up awkwardly kissing him on the nose.

'Oh.' He pulled back.

'Thanks,' she said again, putting her head down to hide her blushing cheeks and, grabbing her bag, fled from the car.

CHAPTER TEN

'Ah, Ms Rachel, so you decided to join us.' Chef was breaking an egg into a bowl, the yolk caught between his fingers.

'I'm so sorry. It was the snow.' She ran to her work station, uncurling her scarf and shaking the flakes off her hat.

'Look around, everyone else managed to find their way here.' He transferred the yolk to a separate dish while glaring at her. 'I don't like to be interrupted.'

'I know, I'm sorry, it won't happen again.'

'So why let it happen in the first place?' Chef spread his hands wide but was interrupted by a knock on the door.

'Henri, a word.' Philippe pushed it open and was standing in the hallway, beckoning for his brother to step out and join him.

'*Un moment.*' Chef paused mid-tirade, wiping his hands on a tea towel and marching off to join Philippe.

Rachel shut her eyes and took a second to catch her breath.

'Where have you been?' Abby whispered.

She waved her question away. Glancing over her shoulder, she saw Marcel sitting smugly, legs crossed, rolling an egg back and forth on his work surface, a wilted lily lying on the shelf with his pots and pans like a trophy.

She was about to say something when Chef stormed back in. 'OK, let's get on with it.'

'That's it?' Lacey hissed. 'How do you get away with it?'

Rachel didn't look at her.

'Today it is soufflé.'

'Shit,' she said under her breath. Rachel had never really made soufflé. She actively avoided making soufflé. She tried to concentrate extra hard on what Chef was doing but her mind wouldn't focus—it was dancing back and forth between the thrill she had felt sitting next to Philippe on his reckless drive through the backstreets of Paris and Marcel and his traitorous, backstabbing ways. What a fool she had been.

She couldn't stop casting sideways glances in Marcel's direction, determined to make him feel uncomfortable but he wasn't having any of it. Face impeccable, poised, concentrating on every word Chef said. Dressed all scruffy and artfully dishevelled, he was the exact opposite of Philippe with his cashmere suit and confident stride, but she wondered now, remembering the satisfied look on Philippe's face as they'd zoomed up outside the pâtisserie, if maybe both of them had the same glint in their eye—a glint that no good had come from with Marcel as far as Rachel was concerned.

She reminded herself to be more careful; she was here to bake, not to get carried away by good-looking men. If Marcel had had his way she'd have been out of the competition and she was already on thin ice with Chef. Yet when she thought about Philippe she couldn't help but wonder what he had said to stop Chef's anger, and about the fact that whatever he had said, he had said it for her. But as she thought about how that made her feel, an image of the bauble he'd bought on their shopping trip sprang to mind, along with the question of who it was for…

By the time she got round to listening, Chef was pulling a perfect, puffy blue cheese soufflé out of the oven. As everyone gasped at the beauty of it, he said, 'You, this afternoon, will prepare me and my brother a soufflé. *Oui?*' Then he swept out of the room for a cigarette.

Rachel didn't go out for lunch; instead she walked down to the pâtisserie and picked out the largest chocolate éclair there was and rammed it into her mouth right there at the counter. Françoise was laughing because her mouth was so full.

'*J'ai faim,*' she said over the cream.

'Very hungry.' Françoise nodded. '*Un café, aussi?* Very tired too?' she said, pointing to Rachel's face.

Rachel slumped down onto one of the stools. 'Very tired.'

Françoise made her an espresso and popped it down on the marble counter. The dim white milk-glass of the lights took any brightness out of the room, making it perfect for her hung-over eyes. She stared at the wall behind the pastries where there were postcards pinned along of places she assumed customers or friends had been. Perhaps she could run away somewhere hot, leave smug Marcel and the daunting soufflé behind. The high stool she was sitting on was squishy and comfy, the espresso bitter and sharp. She remembered how that morning she had wanted to win the competition to make her mum proud, but just the idea of it now seemed overwhelming, the prizc way out of reach. Perhaps she could have a little nap—the cup clinked into the saucer as she sat back and shut her eyes but she could still hear the clock ticking down the end of her lunch break, so she ended up just ordering another eclair.

Soufflé-making was hard. Rachel had never understood them. Her mum had never understood them. Once baked, twice baked, what was the difference? And were they really baking, anyway?

She was sticking to a really simple three cheese and spinach one with roasted cherry tomatoes and garlic on the side and perhaps a sprinkling of crushed rosemary. Lacey was doing a crab, lobster and clam soufflé with a prawn and fennel bisque on the side and a crispy garlic-infused baguette. George was doing cheese as well but was aiming to make it the highest in the group by fashioning a baking parchment sleeve that would force the mixture to keep growing to practically the height of the oven. Marcel—she didn't even look at what he was doing. Ali had chosen raspberry rice-pudding soufflé with vanilla custard sauce, which he was planning very secretively, and Abby was doing a white chocolate and amaretto one with a sweet lemon and almond curd, which sounded delicious. Rachel gave her a thumbs up before they got started.

As she separated her eggs she could feel the tiredness creeping into her body, and she was coming down fast off the eclair sugar rush. All her determination was seeping out of her in favour of crawling back into bed. But there was the fact that Philippe was tasting and she found herself wanting to impress him with her food.

Ten minutes in, George burnt his butter, which made the whole room smell sweet like cinema popcorn. Ali tipped his whisked egg whites above his head pretending that they might slip out all over him, and when she heard Marcel laugh she gave him a sneer. Then she went back to cutting through her beaten whites with a palette knife but all she seemed to be doing was making her mixture go from light and fluffy to flat and drab. It just seemed too heavy, but it was too late to start again. The smell of her cheese made her feel sick, as did Lacey's bubbling prawn stock.

Tearing her eyes from her solid-looking mixture as it tried to rise in the oven and switching off the grill as her tomatoes bubbled under the heat, Rachel wiped down her surface just praying that her mixture would puff up enough not to be an embarrassment. She only looked up when she saw Abby draw out a white-chocolate stunner. Smooth, fluffy and risen high like a chef's hat, it was the most glorious-looking soufflé she'd ever seen. Dusted from up high with a snowy shower of icing sugar and sprinkled with slices of sugared lemon rind and circled with a vivid yellow curd sauce, it was a definite show-stopper.

As she glanced across at Lacey's individual crab towers that were quite pale and George's burnt crust it was clear that Abby would be the day's winner.

Rachel hardly dared look at hers. Everyone else was putting the finishing touches to theirs. Ali was spooning his custard into a vintage blue and white Cornishware jug. George was looking dubiously at his very forlorn soufflé, blackened like a scorched Leaning Tower of Pisa. Sucking in a breath, she bent down and peeked through the glass of her oven.

There it was—tall and puffy and risen like a skyscraper, with a tear round the edge where the cheese had pulled like crocodile teeth. She did a little clap. Then yanked the door open and drew out her beauty, bronzed on top and glistening with a deep glazed shine.

'Wow,' said Lacey before she could stop herself.

Rachel could only nod, speechless that it had worked. Abby came round to look at it. 'That's amazing.'

'I know, I can't believe it.'

They all stood round gazing at Rachel's cheese tower.

A knock on the door broke the reverie and as Chef went to answer it Rachel pulled off her oven gloves and, turning her back on her prize creation, went in search of a plate.

Philippe walked in, wearing a black cashmere suit, and looked round the room till he spotted Rachel and smiled. She winked back and pointed triumphantly at her soufflé. He did a nod as if humouring her. She raised her eyebrows nodding more, to try and show him how much this risen soufflé meant to her. Even her mum had never been able to make them rise. There was a soufflé curse on her family that had now, finally, been lifted.

Beaming, she looked down to put it on her flowery plate and saw to her horror that it was completely flattened. Dissolved of air and height like a burst balloon. A sunken mush of stringy cheese. An echo of her now deflated heart.

'How?' she whispered.

Glancing around, she noticed that Lacey wouldn't catch her eye. George was fussing with his disaster. Marcel was leaning back against the counter, one brow raised. She made a perplexed face at Abby but she looked down, away from her.

Was it Rachel's imagination or were her cheeks flushed?

'And now we taste.' Chef clapped his hands together and he and Philippe strode forward.

Rachel stared in horror at her sunken mess.

Lacey's, of course, tasted bloody marvellous. Her bisque, Philippe thought, divine. Ali's left them silent; beneath the fluffy top was a cloying mass of sticky rice and raspberry jam that fell from their spoons like baby sick.

Chef snorted when he got to Rachel's. 'Oh, dear, oh, dear.'

Hands clasped behind her back, she looked down, refusing to see the look of sympathy on Philippe's face. 'I don't know what happened. It had risen when I got it out.'

'A likely story, Flower Girl.' Chef grinned and stabbed one edge with his fork, beckoning for Philippe to do the same. 'If you can bear it,' he added.

It was only when Philippe dug his fork in that Rachel saw it—the slice. A cut the size of a Sabatier knife, stabbed into her right-hand side.

She gasped. Someone had murdered her soufflé.

'It is delicious,' said Philippe, surprised.

'*Mais oui*, the girl, she can cook. She is simply a disaster.' Chef licked the last string of cheese off his fork and they walked over to Marcel.

'Delicious,' Philippe said again before leaving, but Rachel could only nod, distracted.

She looked round the room again and she tried to get Abby to look at her so she could mouth what had happened but she wouldn't.

'Abby,' she muttered in the end, but Abby bent down to rummage on her shelf.

And that was when Rachel saw the missing slot on her knife roll. The twelve-inch blade empty. Probably in Abby's sink, slimy with congealed parmesan and Gruyère.

'You!' she whispered.

Abby looked back at her this time, but did a face of pleading innocence before turning away as the men appeared at her station and rhapsodised over her white-chocolate creation.

Rachel stayed in the competition by the skin of her teeth. Luck was on her side as Ali's and George's were both dreadful.

Ali stormed out refusing to talk to anyone after he was dismissed. George stayed and cleared up his table. 'Oh, well.' He shrugged. 'Back to my little business. Dreams of stardom over. Too old anyway.'

Rachel watched his back as he walked over to the coat stand and pulled on his tweed blazer followed by his Peter Storm cagoule.

She wanted to stop him and say it was unfair. That there had been sabotage and cheating. 'You're not too old, George,' she said instead.

'You're very sweet. It was enough for me. I've reached my limit. It's hotting up. If it had been anyone else I'd have said, no, it's time for me to go. I can feel it.' He smiled. 'And you, young lady, need to pull yourself together. You're at the end of your nine lives. You hear me?'

She nodded.

'Good.' He pulled on his flat cap. 'I expect you to win.'

CHAPTER ELEVEN

There were no drinks in the bar that night.

Marcel sloped off almost as soon as Chef left. Abby seemed to be absorbed in a task that prevented her from leaving. Rachel grabbed her bag, pulled on her hat and mittens and stalked out. In the corridor she passed Lacey, who was tapping into her mobile over her bifocals. Neither acknowledged the other. It was competition now. War.

Rachel took a couple of paces outside and then ducked into an alley and waited. The snow was like a sheet shaken from a balcony—a wall of white coating cars in foot-deep white. Kids were pulling sledges down the street while businessmen slipped in leather shoes.

She blew on her hands, white misty breath in the freezing air, and listened to the accordion music drifting out of the pâtisserie as it closed.

When she heard familiar footsteps Rachel stepped out onto the cobbled pavement and said, 'Why did you do it?'

Abby hoisted her bag further up on her shoulder. 'I don't know what you're talking about.'

'Yes, you do. You sabotaged my soufflé. Why would you do that? After I saved you yesterday.'

'Oh, yeah, great, you saved me. Aren't you a star? I heard what he said, Rachel. When he called you back. I waited in the doorway. All good bakers have a signature.'

'So?' she said.

'So he didn't say he couldn't see mine, did he? It was that he saw yours. He thought I had no signature. Well, I do. I do have a signature and I wanted him to taste it.' She wiped her nose with her glove and then thrust her hand in her pocket.

'So show him yours! Make something amazing like you did. That doesn't mean you have to ruin mine.' Rachel couldn't believe it.

Abby scoffed. 'You really think that? You really think he'd have noticed mine after tasting yours?'

'Yes, Abby. Yes, I do. If it was that bloody good. You were meant to be my friend.'

Abby looked away. 'It's a competition.'

'Fuck the competition. It's an excuse.'

'I bake every day, Rachel. Every day I make different pastries, breads, brioche—something. I bake something. I practise and I practise and I'm still not as good as you who doesn't even try.'

'I try,' she said, affronted.

'No, you don't. Not really. It's there in you. You don't have to be here. You could just do it. You have it. I needed this. And yet I'm not good enough. I know I'm not good enough.' Abby scuffed at the snow with her boot, then got out a tissue and blew her nose. 'I know I shouldn't have ruined your soufflé. I knew I shouldn't at the time and I know it more now. I just wanted a taste of it, Rachel. A taste of what you have. Of what Lacey sort of has.'

'A taste of what?'

'Of brilliance.'

Rachel could see the tears in Abby's eyes. She turned her head away.

'I'm sorry, Rachel. I shouldn't have done it. I'll tell Chef.'

'No, don't tell Chef.' Rachel shook her head, still looking at the wall. 'Forget about it. We'll just forget about it,' she said, glancing back.

'I've thrown away a friendship.' Abby wiped her eye.

Rachel sighed. 'No, you haven't. You've just bruised it a bit. I'm sure it'll get better.'

'Thank you.'

'Don't worry about it.' Rachel nodded. 'I've gotta go,' she said and walked away.

Then, hearing Abby stride off in the other direction, Rachel ducked back into the alley and, pulling off her hat, leant her head against the cool bricks. Her heart was thumping in her chest. Her thoughts were whizzing round like crazy. What was this? How could this be happening? It was all just meant to be a bit of fun.

She knew her family had a soufflé curse.

'That was very generous of you.' Philippe appeared in the entrance to the alley. His collar turned up high, hands in his pockets, scarf up to his chin.

'God, you made me jump.' Rachel put her hand over her mouth.

'I heard, from the doorway.'

'Well.' She shrugged. 'Baking does funny things to us all.'

'It was still generously handled. Can I buy you a drink? I don't have long but enough time for one.'

Rachel considered it for a moment, thought over her disastrous day. 'Why not?'

He cocked his head. 'Is that a yes?'

'Yep, that's a yes.'

They didn't go to the bar she went to with the bakers. Instead he led her down a side street to a little place that sat on a crossroads. Tables were splayed out on both pavements around the curve of the building, which stood tall like the Flatiron. In the snowy darkness the windows cast an orangey glow, inviting them inside.

Philippe put his hand on the base of her back as he pulled open the door, guiding her in. She felt the bareness there when he took it away.

In the corner there was a fire blazing and crackling bright, sparks flying up the chimney in a dance. On the bar top sat rows of plump olives, cornichons and salamis and behind that racks and racks of wine piled high to the ceiling. The little wooden tables flickered with candlelight; the cut glasses glinted; a Chihuahua and a Great Dane lay curled by the fire. People were talking loudly, gesticulating wildly, while others read books alone in the corner with a *vin chaud* or played cards.

Rachel glanced round, instantly in love with the place. Philippe beckoned her to a table by the fire and then came back from the bar with a small carafe of red wine.

'Have you smelt it?' she asked as he set it down on the table.

'But of course.'

'OK, I'm going to,' she said, picking the carafe up and holding it up to her nose. 'Wow. It's like erm—'

'The berries.'

'Yeah, blackberries and wood, like a bonfire, you know? That's amazing.'

'I think you will like it,' he said as he took it from her and poured.

'What shall we toast?'

'Soufflés?'

'Urgh, no.' She made a face.

He paused and then said, 'Compassion?'

Rachel blushed. 'What's that in French?'

'Compassion.'

'Oh.' She laughed. 'OK, then. To compassion.'

They clinked glasses and he watched her over the rim of his drink as she took a sip. His big brown eyes seeming to smile at her, as if he was pleased to have her at the table with him, enjoying the wine he had chosen. She glanced away, looking towards the Great Dane that had its legs stretched out long. 'That's the life, isn't it? Bet no one stabs his soufflé.'

'Yes, but it would be very boring, *n'est-ce pas*? Lounging around all day. I would want to do something.'

'I don't know, after the couple of days I've had, I'd take curled up by the fire over anything else.' She sipped her drink; the dog yawned. 'What do you do every day, Philippe?'

'I work in an office.'

She smiled. 'You don't like the office?'

He shrugged. 'It's OK. I have no love for it.'

She was itching to say something about him going back into the kitchen, how of course he would have no love for it when he had such a talent going to waste. 'Why do you do it?' she said instead.

He sat forward, elbows on the table, chin rested in his hands. 'Because I haven't got round to getting out of it.'

'I know that feeling.'

'You do? But you're here.'

'Because I was set up.'

'Set up? I do not know what that means.'

She twirled her coaster and thought about it. 'It means that my friends, they arranged for me to come without me knowing.'

'Nice friends.'

'My thoughts precisely.'

The Chihuahua got up and stretched its legs, did a circle of the Great Dane and then went to lie back down again right up close to the fire, just in front of the other dog's nose. 'They're so cute.' Rachel smiled.

'They stink.' Philippe shrugged.

'Oh, God, the smelling again.' Rachel rolled her eyes.

'You do not find it endearing?'

'Oh, yeah, I'm crazy about it.' She laughed. 'Come on, then, what do I smell of?'

'Lemons,' he said without a moment's hesitation.

'That's my shampoo.'

'And vanilla.'

Rachel paused. 'That must just be me.'

Philippe shrugged. 'Yes, I think so.'

The tension suddenly seemed to have upped a notch, crackling like the fire beside her. She turned her head away, trying not to think of lemon and vanilla and the fact he knew immediately what her individual scent was.

On the rug, the big dog yawned, catching the little dog's tail in its mouth, making the Chihuahua bark and move again, further away this time out of reach.

'No, I do not love the dog,' said Philippe, bringing the conversation back to safer territory.

'You like cats?'

'Why?'

'I think in England we think if you don't like dogs you must like cats. I thought perhaps that was a global thing.'

'I hate cats.'

She snorted into her red wine. 'Good for you.' Then she rested her elbows on the table and her chin in her hands. 'So what are you going to do, then, if you're not a chef and you hate the office?'

'Oh, I don't know, lots of things. I never had the chance to study, you know. Henri got me a job in a kitchen when I left school and that was where I stayed. We both, Henri and I, we had to go straight out, make some money. And then when things they got better we decided that we did not want to work for other people any more and we opened the restaurant.'

'But then you left?'

'*Oui*. I left. I love my brother very much but we should have realised we could not be partners.' He laughed as if the idea were ridiculous. And when she raised a brow for him to explain further he sat back in his seat. 'We had very little growing up. My father, he left when I was maybe seven, and Henri, he was ten. And since then he has been like the father. You know, telling me what to do.'

'I have a friend like that.'

'*Mais oui*, and it is very nice, very caring. I know he looks out for me, but together, so close every day, we kill each other. We were young, doing very well and had too much success too soon I think. We never got to build the place slowly—I think now when I look back that would have been better. I would have liked a little smaller start that people come to gradually and it is successful but not the success that we had. Not that much. Henri, however, he loved the success. He loved the atmosphere and the journalists and the lifestyle. But it was not for me.' He swirled the wine round in his glass and took a sip. 'When we got the Michelin stars, then more people they came but the critics they got harder. They expected more, yes?'

Rachel nodded.

'And the more they expect, the less fun it was for me to cook, to invent, to test and to try new things because if they are not a success then—poof—they write something terrible about us. No, the success it was a curse. It was no fun any more. And one day I realised that I had lost my love for it. It was completely gone.' He glanced at her and gave a sad smile. 'Henri, however, he was at the top and having a great time, so we divide and I leave.' He shrugged a shoulder as if it didn't mean much but it was clear from his tone of voice that it had been a difficult time, one he didn't revisit much.

'But, now…' he sat forward smiling as he spoke, brushing aside the past '…now I would like to open a business that I am in charge of. On my own. Maybe go back and study business—we had no business knowledge and that did not help us. If you start a business you need to know all the little things. Don't leave it to other people. We lost a lot of money leaving it to other people. So that is maybe what I want to do. Study and then start my own company.'

Rachel smiled. 'You could start a perfumery—you could smell things all day?'

'I could.' He laughed. 'I like the sounds of that. A perfumery. Ha. *Très bon.*' Philippe raised his glass to toast the idea with her, his eyes crinkling with amusement.

As Rachel sat back and took another sip of her drink, she added tentatively, 'Or you could start another restaurant. A small one. You know, with a fire and a simple menu.'

He shook his head. 'There will be no more restaurants for me.'

'It's a shame.'

'It's life.'

Rachel watched him as he looked away, avoiding eye contact, and, seeing in him such wasted talent and stubbornness, realised just how easy it was to let the past hold you back, to let a memory dictate your future.

When Philippe looked back at her he said, 'So, this set-up for you to come here. I am still not sure. You are not a baker?'

'Oh, no. I'm a teacher. My mother was the baker.'

He poured more wine. 'And this is how you learnt to bake?'

'Yes. She owned the bakery in the village.'

'Well, that would explain it. Very nice,' he said, stretching his legs out long in front of him. 'Like Henri's?'

'Oh, no, nothing like that.' Rachel was starting to warm up from the fire and, unwinding her scarf, draped it over the chair next to her. 'It was smaller but it was lovely. There was a big main counter that had baskets of croissants and cakes and trays with brownies and things people could try. Do you have brownies here? Do you know what a brownie is?'

'I know what a brownie is.'

'OK, just checking.'

'What else?'

'What else, what?'

'What else did it look like?'

'Oh. Well, there were two little tables and chairs, a bit like these.' She pointed to the chair her scarf was hanging on. Then she paused. 'This is weird.'

'Why?'

'Because I haven't thought about what it looked like for a long time. It's like looking at an old photograph.'

'That's what memories are, *non*? Photographs in your head. It's up to you if you look at them or not.'

'*Mais oui.*' She smiled. 'A photo in my head. I like that. The one I'm looking at now is of my dad, who would usually be sitting at one of the tables. He'd finish work at three and come straight round and read the paper. Or my gran, who was always there, practically every day drinking hot chocolate and eating macaroons. But not like your macaroons. These were macaroon biscuits, like an amaretto with a walnut on the top, as big as your hand.'

'I have no idea, but I am getting the picture.'

Rachel bit her lip, trying to think. 'Oh, there were so many people always coming in for a chat that in the end my mum got fed up being in the back room, so she got the guy over the road to build this extra shelf on the end of the counter, so she could stand there and roll out the dough without missing out on any of the chat. Oh, thanks,' she added as Philippe topped up her wine. 'And another thing, there were these two big ovens out the back that my dad said he'd put me in if I was naughty. That's terrible, isn't it? Like child abuse. I was terrified of them. There was also this huge table where we'd plait the bread and fold the croissants into triangles before school. It was covered in dents from the rolling pin and knife marks and underneath Betsy Johnson had dared me to write my name in silver pen. I spent a lot of time praying to God my mum never found it.'

Philippe laughed and she liked the sound of it, that she'd been the one to make him do it.

'So what was your job?'

'I did everything. But the thing I always did was cut the chocolate for a *pain au chocolat*.'

'That sounds like the best job to me.'

'Oh, it was. Imagine, at eight years old it was one for the croissant and one for me.' She laughed. 'You know, there were these three glass lights—one yellow, one blue and one red—all painted with tiny flowers that hung in a row above the counter. I have them now. In my kitchen. And I bloody hope the Australians staying there don't break them.'

'They are not still in the bakery?'

'No.' She paused. 'It's been closed a long time.'

'Ah. And now you are a teacher.'

Rachel nodded into her wine. Let herself be distracted again by the dogs.

'Why not a baker?'

She shrugged. 'I stopped loving it.'

Philippe made a face. 'Touché,' he said and then raised a brow and added, 'But now you like it again, maybe a little bit.'

She looked up at him, and nodded slowly. His amber eyes were dancing in the firelight. 'Maybe,' she said. 'Would you like another drink? Do you have time?'

'There is a little time.'

She came back from the bar and felt him watching her as she put two little glasses filled to the brim down on the table.

'I'm glad,' he said, 'that my brother has not trodden on your dreams. He has—how do you say it?—very heavy feet.'

She laughed. 'He sure does.' Then after a small pause added, 'He has trodden on your dream.'

'Ah *non*.' Philippe shook his head. 'We both made mistakes, in our own way. We did not want the same thing from our creation. Our ambitions, they were different and we did not know it when we started.'

The Chihuahua trotted over and she put her hand down to stroke it but it buggered off again back to the fire.

Philippe took a sip from the overfull glass of red and asked, 'Why did it close?'

'What?' She looked up from where she was trying to win the dog back.

'The bakery.'

'You ask too many questions. In England men aren't renowned for asking questions.'

'Maybe not in France either. But I'm interested.'

She sat back in her chair, twiddled with the cuffs of her jumper. 'It was lots of things. Lots of little things that built into big things. My mum got ill. We kept having to close. Another chain bakery moved in nearby. It was all those things, and I think we didn't keep a close enough eye on it. Everyone in the village, they helped, they did shifts and it was really lovely, but some were better than others—d'you know what I mean? It was a bit of a disaster actually. It wasn't their fault or anything. It's just they didn't love it like we did. Nor did the staff we had to take on. They didn't have the touch of my mum. People loved her stuff. They still talk about it now. "Oh, do you remember those eclairs, or those cheese scones and that bread?" It's like it was

an institution and it had to be her at the helm. I would
have tried to do it but I was at school and my mum
wouldn't let me. I'd persuade teachers to let me out of
classes early or come in really late because I'd baked
the morning's bread and they'd pretend they hadn't seen
me. People made us food—you know, coming round
with casseroles like they do in films.'

Philippe took a sip of his drink and beckoned for her
to continue.

'In the end Tesco made an offer that at the time we
couldn't refuse.' Rachel realised that it was the first
time in years that she'd told anyone about the bakery.
At the time they'd just put their heads down and got on
with it, but now it felt like a part of her soul that she'd
sold. A part of her mum's soul. 'Tesco, you know, it's
like Carrefour or E.Leclerc. Our friends tried to offer
my dad money to help him out to keep the bakery and
stuff but he wouldn't take it. I think he had enough on
his plate looking after my mum and it was all too much
for him. Tesco paid way above market value and the
money would pay for the best hospitals there were.'

He nodded. 'And that worked?'

'No.'

'Oh.'

'It was so long ago. But you know, all of this—the
smells, the tastes, talking about it—I've hidden it all
away for so long that it's almost a relief. It's like being
given a little bit of it back, you know?'

He paused. 'I can imagine.'

'Thank you.' She smiled at him, not away at the table or her glass but straight at him. He nodded and they were silent for a moment before she said, 'You have really kind eyes.'

He laughed and she blushed, this time looking at the table.

'Hey, Philippe.' The door bashed open and there was Chef Henri. 'I've looked everywhere for you. We're waiting. What you doing?'

Philippe held up a hand and nodded, downing his drink. 'I have to go. I apologise.'

'That's OK.' Rachel smiled.

Chef didn't stop. '*Vite, vite.* We are waiting. Emilie, she is already there.'

'Emilie?' said Rachel.

Philippe paused. 'My wife.'

CHAPTER TWELVE

She stood at the window looking down at the Champs Élysées, at the myriad trees sparkling like beacons lighting the way.

My wife, he'd said. And she'd gasped. An actual audible gasp.

Of course he'd be married. He was a handsome, clever Frenchman. And he was kind. Nothing had happened between them. He'd looked out for her as a friend. He'd coaxed out her secrets and she'd told them to him as a friend. They didn't owe each other anything. She'd slept with Marcel, for goodness' sake, but Philippe was *married.*

It was impossible how much that stung.

Her phone rang.

Jackie.

'Have you won yet?'

'There's still another round.'

'Chances?'

'Slim. There's some dirty fighting.'

'You can fight dirty.'

'I don't know.'

'Oh, come on. I've seen you in the staffroom. What about with Miss Brown?'

Rachel pulled the window closed and went to sit on the hard blue sofa. 'Yeah, but that's for the kids.'

'Well, I hate to break it to you but this is for the kids too. They've made you another banner at Sunday School. They've baked special reindeer biscuits with red noses that little Tommy said you'd talked about. There's even a village fund, Rachel.'

She stopped picking at the thread on one of the cushions. 'What for?'

'I'm not one hundred per cent sure. It's possible it's for a bakery.'

'No way.'

Jackie was silent. 'I'm nodding. I actually do think that's what it's for. Or at least some kind of small caravan with an oven. People miss it.'

'Miss what?'

'Your mum's place.'

Rachel didn't reply, but went back to pulling on the loose cotton and unravelling a strip of cushion embroidery.

'I've sent you something,' said Jackie into the silence.

'What?'

'You'll see. I paid a fucking fortune for it to get there before Christmas Day.'

'Thanks. I think.'

'No probs. What are you doing on Christmas Day?'

Rachel paused, then said, 'Recovering from the final.' And laughed.

'That's the spirit. OK, I'm going. This is costing a fortune. Why is there no Wi-Fi there?'

She looked around the dingy little room. 'If you saw it, you'd understand.'

'That good, eh? Did I not do so well?'

'I'm like Rapunzel at the top of a tower.'

'*Bon*. Well, you'll have to hope some French hunk comes to save you. I'm really going now. Oh, actually that reminds me—Ben asked about you. I said you were seeing a dashing Frenchman.'

'Ha, thanks.'

'OK, bye. Oh and, Rachel… You have to fight. Not necessarily dirty but you have to fight. You'll regret it otherwise.'

'Thanks.'

'*De rien,*' Jackie said and hung up.

Rachel pulled off the loose thread from the cushion and felt suddenly a bit sad that her friend wasn't there in the room with her. It seemed awfully cold all of a sudden. Outside the snow was unceasing. Whopping great flakes like cricket balls were falling past the window, catching on the sill and making an arc across the panels like fake snow in a toy shop.

She thought of Nettleton, of what everyone would be doing. All the kids would be practising for the choir concert, while their parents would be deciding who would bring the mulled wine. People would be stopping each other in the street or as they were walking their dogs and planning what time they'd get to the pub on Christmas Eve. There'd already be queues outside the butcher for turkeys and the fishmonger would be getting ready for lines of people down the pavement in a couple of days.

Rachel found herself actually missing the traditions. Especially the annual Christmas play that she usually rolled her eyes at and refused to be any part of. The others would haul out the moth-eaten Santa suit and the rest of the obscure array of costumes, half of which someone had once pinched from a BBC filming in the village; so Mr Swanson was usually a Regency duke and Jackie, without fail, was a serving wench. Last year they'd brought a donkey on stage, which the minutes of the next parish council meeting had noted as a mistake. She found herself wondering what the story was this year, whether there would be any farmyard animals, who would forget their lines and reduce the cast and audience to tear-filled giggles. One year her dad had played Captain Hook. She wondered if by some miracle he might step forward this year. Would her gran be able to persuade him? Probably not.

She went over to the stove and lit the gas under the kettle, trying not to wonder what her dad was up to and imagining instead the village green and the pond decked in twinkling Christmas lights. Hopefully her gran would get him to the pub at least. He could rarely resist a Whisky Mac. She stood fiddling with the top of the flour bag as she waited for the kettle to boil, pulling the crumpled sides up so they were perfectly straight and then squashing them down again. It was pointless reminiscing, she thought. She was here in Paris, not home. And whatever else was going on she was here to do a job, they'd sent her here, made this all possible, and the least she could do was return home triumphant.

Tea made, she considered finally taking her exhausted body to bed, but, however hard she tried to ignore it, she knew she would lie awake thinking about what Philippe's wife looked like. So, instead, she stayed where she was in the kitchen.

Tomorrow was petits fours. Tiny delicate delights served with coffee. When was the last time she'd practised a macaroon—the bright-coloured French kind with its soft, gooey centre? Or a truffle? How were her chocolate tuiles? Her brandy snaps? Her chocolate ganache hadn't had the shine of Lacey's on the first day. Nor had her crème pâtisserie been as glossy and rich.

Unrolling the flour bag again, she pulled out a set of rusty scales from under the surface and a sieve with great holes as if a mouse had chewed on it. Then glancing at her bare shelves, she pulled on her coat, boots and scarf and ran out of the flat to the twenty-four-hour shop on the corner that mainly sold alcohol, crisps and soup in a can to buy whatever supplies it might have.

Outside the moon was huge in the sky, half obscured by building clouds; it lit the snow on the pavement, making it shine like icing on a cake. The cold was biting, seeping in through the material of her coat, making her hurry towards the fluorescent glow of the corner shop. Inside it was warm and smelt like coffee and sawdust; the guy behind the counter was rolling a cigarette and watching the news. Rachel grabbed a basket and perused the two aisles, bypassing the magazines and greetings cards, and trying to work out what she could use here to bake with. Eventually she filled her basket with bars of chocolate, raspberry jam, a packet of madeleines, milk, sugar and crème de menthe. While debating about some half-rotten apples, Rachel turned to see Chantal at the counter buying a lottery ticket, her coat buttoned up tight and her hat pulled low.

'*Bonsoir, Chantal.*' Rachel waved.

'Ah, *ma petite*.' Chantal smiled at her. 'I was just on my way home and I thought, maybe I will be lucky today,' she said, holding up the lottery ticket, and then glanced inquisitively into Rachel's shopping as she came over to the cash desk and asked, 'You are baking?'

'Practising,' Rachel said. 'Big day tomorrow. But—' she looked at the meagre contents of her basket '—this place doesn't quite have all the stuff that I need.'

Chantal laughed and as Rachel asked her about her day she started rummaging through the collection of bags and straw baskets she had on the floor by her feet, saying, 'I think I can help you. Today was market day and I have too much.'

'Oh, don't be silly.' Rachel waved a hand. 'You have given me far too much already.'

Chantal batted the refusal away. 'I want you to win,' she said as she bent down to search through her shopping, pulling out baguettes and artichokes, spices and wrapped-up cheeses, laying them on the floor until she finally said, *'Ici.'* And pulled out a bunch of brown paper bags, triumphant. Then she handed Rachel a feast of supplies—sugared almonds, candied lemon and orange peel, punnets of fresh fruit and a bulging bag of mixed nuts and raisins all from the market.

About to refuse them, Rachel caught the look of delight in Chantal's eyes just in time and realised finally that she *wanted* to give these things to her. That it gave her pleasure to help her and Rachel should just accept gracefully. 'Thank you,' she said as she looked into each one of the bags. 'Thank you, I think these will actually help me win.'

'Absolument.' Chantal held her hands wide as if to say, of course. And then as Rachel gathered up her purchases and paid the shopkeeper, Chantal looped her arm through hers and walked with her through the snow back to Madame Charles's building where her little car was parked.

As they got to the front door Chantal squeezed Rachel's arm and wished her luck, then held her on the shoulders and kissed her on both cheeks before heading towards the car that was waiting under a blanket of snow. Rachel smiled, watching her as she put her baskets in the boot and then kicked through the heaps of slush in the gutters to start scraping the thin layer of ice from the windscreen. From a distance she looked much older, more fragile, and, Rachel thought, very alone. As she turned away to unlock the front door her eye caught all the little bags of produce that Chantal had given her and she paused with her key in the lock.

'Chantal?' she said, turning back to see her just getting into her beaten-up old car. 'Chantal?' she said again.

'Oui.' The housekeeper looked up, her little gloved hand on the open doorframe.

'Why don't you talk to your daughter?' Rachel asked, walking towards her, the snow cracking crisp under her boots.

Chantal looked momentarily taken aback, started to shake her head instead of answering as if the subject was off limits.

But Rachel walked closer to stand next to the car, and said, 'I'm only asking because it seems that you must really miss her, the way you are taking care of me.'

As she spoke Rachel watched Chantal seem to slump a touch, her shoulders dropping as she exhaled the weight of the world with a sigh and, shutting the car door, came round to stand next to Rachel, brushing some snow off the bonnet so she could lean against it.

'We had a row. A very silly row a long time ago. It was over her boyfriend. Of course, it was about a man.' She shrugged. 'He was useless, mean. Not good enough for her. I say if she marries him then she is making a big mistake. Well—' Chantal patted her gloved hands together to get the snow off the wool '—it of course gets worse and worse and she says they are going to get married and I say that she cannot bring him home and I will not go. I don't know why I said that, I don't know. What a mistake. So she goes away and she marries him and we do not go and we do not talk again.'

Rachel took a step forward and turned so she was leaning up against the car too, brushed the snow from where her back was going to rest and looked across at Chantal, who was dabbing the corners of her eyes with her damp gloves.

'Is she still with this man?' Rachel asked.

'Of course not. He is an idiot. He goes years ago. I was always right about him.'

'But you still don't talk?'

Chantal turned her nose up. 'I have said that I will talk to her if she wants to get in touch with me. But of course she does not.'

Rachel paused, kicked some of the slushy blackened snow at the kerb with her foot. 'Maybe you should just call her?'

Chantal shook her head, the white curls peeking out from underneath her hat bobbing with the movement. 'Ah, *non*. She has the chance to call me.'

Rachel nodded as Chantal pursed her lips and crossed her arms tight across her chest. She blew into her hands and rubbed them together, more to create a pause as she thought of what to say than because she needed warming up. As the clouds drifted darker across the moon Rachel ran her tongue along her bottom lip and then said, 'My mum died a few years ago...'

Chantal made a face of sad surprise and went to say something but Rachel carried on, 'And, you know, it's because of her I know how to bake. She taught me everything. Everything. But when we did bake together we argued all the time—we'd bicker about flavour and ingredients and even what shape half the cakes should be. She was really, really stubborn.'

Rachel raised a brow and shook her head. 'And it was only after she died that I realised that I was really, really stubborn too. I realised it because I also thought she was really, really funny. The funniest person I knew. And she'd say the same about me. Other people probably wouldn't have laughed at our jokes but we thought we were hilarious. I only understood our similarities after she died, when no one made me laugh again quite like she did.' She smiled softly, then swallowed the tiny lump in her throat that talking about her mum always created.

Around them the snow started to swirl lightly in the air, a soft haze falling gently onto the white pavement. It was late but the streets were still busy, people coming home from work or heading out for the night, glancing up to watch the new snowfall, to pull up their hoods and turn up their collars.

Rachel turned to cast a glance at Chantal, who was watching her, her lips tight. 'You are saying that I am stubborn?' Chantal asked. 'Like her?'

Rachel laughed. 'I'm not saying anything. I was just telling you a story.'

Chantal raised her brows and then slowly she smiled. *'Bon.'*

Rachel nodded her head towards the door. 'I'd better go and bake. I have a lot to do.' She pushed herself off from the side of the car and brushed down the back of her coat.

'Yes, you go and bake. Bake to win,' Chantal said before crunching through the snow back round to the driver's side of the car. 'Rachel,' she called just as Rachel was unlocking the big, heavy front door, 'thank you for telling me your story.'

'De rien,' Rachel said with a smile.

Back in her apartment Rachel set to work on making the best petits fours she could come up with. The almonds she decided to crush in a praline that she'd pipe between delicate slices of puff pastry for crisp, flaky *millefeuille* with a chocolate and orange-blossom icing. The leftover almonds she ground into her shortcrust dough, which she rolled into wafer-thin cups and filled with raspberry pâtisserie crème, candied lemon slices and a physalis.

The rest of the lemon became soft Armagnac truffles, from the leftovers of Marcel's bottle, rolled in sparkly sugar, the sharp citrus heavenly alongside the bitterest dark chocolate. And, unable to stop herself, she made some mint chocolate thins that she sprinkled with salted caramel and ate before they had properly cooled.

She worked for hours making perfect inch-square *millefeuille*, powder puffs of meringue dribbled with cranberry coulis, even mini round Christmas puddings that Chef would think revolting but pleased her. She packed them up in a box to save for her dad—always a favourite of his in the past.

Cars were starting to thunder down the Champs Élysées before she finally crawled into bed. But she had four hours of the most blissfully satisfying sleep.

Her only thought when the alarm went off was…

He has a wife.

It was probably a good thing, she thought next. No distractions.

He has a wife.

CHAPTER THIRTEEN

It was the day before Christmas Eve. The day before the final. Lacey, Rachel, Abby and Marcel were still in. Two people would go today.

Rachel had woken up early, walked to her bike in the snow and pushed it most of the way to the pâtisserie, but cycled in the little sections where the grit had melted the thick frosting on the street. She'd had an espresso and an almond croissant with Françoise, who'd wished her luck. Then she passed Chef, who said, 'You have a nice drink with my brother?' with a raised enquiring brow.

'Yes, it was nice, thank you. I hope you had a good dinner,' she replied.

He nodded his head. 'It was good,' he said, then he looked straight at her and she felt the scrutiny of his gaze. 'You should keep your head, keep your focus on the competition. That is why you are here.'

'I know. *I am*,' she replied. 'That's exactly why I'm here now. I have a work station to prep.'

'Don't forget that,' he said with a sneer.

Rachel swallowed back a response and turned to leave. But as she did she felt her hackles rise, felt the unjustness bubble to the surface and spun round to face him. 'What have I done to you? What have I done to make you so annoyed with me? When it comes to your brother, all I've done is have a drink with him— he certainly never told me he was married, for God's sake. And as far as the competition goes the worst I've done is have a couple of flowers embroidered on my top and help out a friend. I'm sorry if you think that's so terrible, but, to be honest, I think that that's all OK. That it brings a bit of compassion into life. A bit of kindness.'

She looked up into his narrowed eyes, watched as he huffed out a breath of displeasure. 'I would prefer never to make it as a baker but to live a life that I was proud of. And to be honest I'm not sure that the two are mutually exclusive. I *am* focused. I have kept my head. I've tried and I am trying. And if you can't see that, well, then I think you're…you're…' She paused, slightly out of breath, searching for a word.

'I'm what?' Chef asked, a brow raised.

'You're not the chef that I thought you were,' she said with a sigh, looking down at her feet, resigned to the fact that her outburst had probably just cost her the competition rather than helped her on her way. 'I have great respect for you, Chef. I think your books are excellent and I wish I'd had the chance to eat in your restaurant, but—' Rachel paused, glanced up to meet his angry gaze '—I will not change myself for you.'

The silence hung in the air between them. Chef glowering at her, Rachel feeling the size of a mouse but pleased with herself for saying something, although walking away might have been the wiser choice. She noticed behind them that Françoise had poked her head through the pâtisserie door and was watching, big-eyed in awe at the confrontation, and now Rachel had finished she was giving her a big thumbs up. Chef still hadn't said anything. The outside door opened and shut slightly as a breeze crept in and the cold air swirled up the stairs and along the corridor, making Rachel shiver.

'I get angry with you—' Chef started then paused. When he carried on he had his hands on his hips and was staring down at her like a schoolteacher. 'I get angry with you because I think that you do not yet use your talent. You frustrate me. *Oui.*'

'I'm trying,' she said, wanting to accompany it with a stamp of her foot.

'Not hard enough,' he said and she realised that she would never win in this conversation; he would always have to have the last word. So instead she decided she would prove it to him in her cooking. Giving a slight shrug of the shoulders, she turned away from him and headed down the corridor to the kitchen, feeling the icy air follow her as she went. It was only as she was nearly at the kitchens that she heard him say, 'My brother's life, it is complicated.'

She paused for a second, felt the muscles in her neck and back tense, and thought about saying nothing, but instead looked back at him over her shoulder and said with as little emotion as she could, 'It really is none of my business. I'm here for the competition, Chef. I'm here to win.' Then she pushed through the swing doors and disappeared into the kitchen.

The room was silent. The stainless-steel work surfaces glinted in the winter sun that was just peeking through the windows. Her confidence was at its best.

'Morning.' Rachel beamed as Lacey strutted in, pausing with surprise at not being the first.

Ten minutes later Marcel breezed in and started to lay out his knives and pots and pans for the day.

She looked around for Abby but there was no sign of her. Chef was on the phone in the corridor. The clock was getting closer to nine. She wondered if Abby'd packed it in, dropped out because of the soufflé disaster. The idea of it made her sad.

At five seconds to nine, Abby burst into the room looking a mess. Haphazard clothing, hair all over the place, white-faced, no make-up—as if she'd just got out of bed.

'Oh, you didn't?' Rachel said under her breath, just catching the glare that Abby gave Marcel.

She snorted into her scarf as she watched Marcel feign his innocent smile while Abby hissed at him, 'You slimy little snake.'

While Chef was still distracted by his phone-call, Abby started making a racket rummaging through the mound of ingredients on her work surface and the shelf next to her, then rattled through drawers and finally went to investigate the fridge before coming out with a jar of cornichons and fishing one out of the jar.

'Marcel?' she whispered and he turned.

'*C'est très petit. Très, très petit. Oui. Comprende?*' she sneered, brandishing her little inch-long pickled cucumber.

Rachel laughed, Lacey looked shocked, while Marcel looked horrified. Abby crunched it between her teeth with a satisfied smile just as Chef strode in.

'You are hungry, Abby?'

'Yes, Chef. I was feeling very unsatisfied. But I'm OK now.'

He nodded. '*Bon.* If we have all had enough to eat, we will begin. *Quatre.* The final four. I am interested to see what you can do. It is time for you all to step up the game, *n'est-ce pas*? Today the final four will make petits fours.' He laughed at the symmetry. 'All day you will make, practise, hone and design and I will watch you either fail or not. *Et voilà*, we will be down to two.'

Rachel was on fire. She didn't look up from her worktop once. Her fingers were dancing over ingredients. Slices of figs dusted with white snow sugar sat on squares of honey-infused filo with brandy syrup and a mascarpone cream. She made cubes of chocolate and pistachio sponge so light they dissolved on the tongue, with a coating of coffee caramel and a layer of chocolate ganache with a shine like a mirror and shavings of gold leaf that fluttered as she moved from one delicacy to the next.

'Christ, no.' A tray of Abby's chocolate-dome marshmallows slipped and she had to catch them in her arms like a juggler, but Rachel didn't turn to look.

Next she made tiny swans from swirls of crumbly hazelnut Viennese biscuit sandwiched with piped lychee and hazelnut cream with white-chocolate necks that dipped into little heads and beaks. Cherries soaked overnight in Armagnac drenched their alcohol into smooth bitter chocolate truffles rolled in chocolate filings and were placed in individual silver filigree cases. A rainbow of macaroons—purple lavender and almond, nutmeg and grapefruit, salted caramel and chocolate, vanilla, almond and blackberry—was laid to rest on baking trays as she whipped up the egg whites for billowy red-berry meringues.

The one time she looked up she saw, through the glass wall, Philippe walking up the stairs. He looked tired, his shirt collar was undone and his hair scruffier than normal. He paused, as if about to turn her way but didn't. She went back to spooning out her quenelles of meringue.

There was a crash to her left, then she heard Marcel shout, *'Merde!'* He'd dropped his tray of macaroons on the floor, the tiny discs rolling about all over the place. Abby gave a snort of laughter. No one went to help.

But when Rachel over-whipped her cream with four minutes to go Abby pushed her bowl over, gesturing for her to take a spoonful, but Rachel shook her head.

'He'd taste your signature,' she said and Abby smiled.

When the time was up Rachel looked down at her delights for the first time with unadulterated pride.

She'd brought with her in a basket some mismatched plates that Chantal had bought from a bric-a-brac sale. They were all different patterns and sizes, some flamboyantly gold-edged, others haphazardly painted with flowers or swirling blue and pink glaze. One had a hunting scene on the front, another fish swimming through reeds.

Each was the perfect stand for her treasures, which sparkled and glistened and winked like diamonds.

She didn't look at anyone else's. It didn't matter about the competition. Hers would speak for themselves.

Chef went straight to Marcel's bench. 'This is all you have? The whole day and this is what you show me?'

'They are here.' Marcel pointed sheepishly to the trays of macaroons in the bin.

'You should spend more time sleeping, *monsieur.* You would be less clumsy, eh?' Chef tasted what was left of the macaroons with a shrug and tore apart his apple and nutmeg financiers, complaining of a stodgy lack of rise.

Moving on to Lacey, he stood for what seemed like hours, taking second bites, rolling round praline slices on his tongue, snapping tuiles that broke with a loud crack. 'They look *magnifique. Magnifique.* The taste...' He kissed his fingers. 'These, though, I am not so sure.'

Rachel peered over to see what he disapproved of— mini banana and maraschino cherry tarte Tatins. She could have told Lacey that he wouldn't want a tarte Tatin messed with.

Rachel looked at Abby, whose hands were shaking as she brushed her hair out of her eyes when Chef strolled over, clearly enjoying himself.

'Tell me,' he said, pointing to Abby's counter.

'Erm, well, these are, um, shortbreads with dark chocolate orange centres and er, these...' Abby took a breath to calm herself down. 'These are apple and blackberry macaroons, finger slices of cherry and amaretti Bakewell, over here are pink grapefruit and lavender bonbons, then sweet sherry and date puff-pastry slices and finally these are mint chocolate eclairs, which I've infused the crème pâtisserie with fresh mint and used an essence in the ganache.'

'*Bon,*' he said after tasting them all.

'That's it?' Abby said, aghast.

He shrugged. 'They are good. *C'est bon.* What more do you want me to say?'

'I don't know. I—' She didn't finish. They all knew that good wasn't good enough.

Rachel could see the tears in her eyes and for a second she wanted to throw hers on the floor and save Abby's place in the competition. She thought of her little kids waiting at home for Mum to win. But then she thought of the little kids waiting for her—3B and their Sunday School banner—and Jackie and the village waiting, willing her to win.

Gliding over to Rachel's counter, Chef paused. He pushed back his thick blond hair and stood against the stainless steel, looking, and finally leant forward, resting his chin in his hand.

'Ooh la la, Flower Girl,' he muttered, before straightening up and spreading his arms wide. 'Finally. Finally we see what you can really do. No more hiding, eh?'

She shook her head. He plucked a Viennese swan between finger and thumb and savoured the flavour on his tongue. Then he followed it with a cherry truffle and closed his eyes, before taking another. Finally he crunched on a macaroon and slapped his hand on the counter.

When he opened his eyes she thought maybe she might have seen a smile.

'*Superbe,*' he whispered. 'Absolutely *superbe.*'

After that there was no question who was in the final.

The words were a formality but he said them all the same. 'Lacey Withers and Rachel Smithson. Tomorrow, you will compete.'

CHAPTER FOURTEEN

Tomorrow was Christmas Eve. The final. The trial meant being at the pâtisserie at four a.m. They would have half the display counter each and they would make the treats for the hungry shoppers who crowded in on the day before Christmas, eyes wide, for the perfect delicacies to box up and take home.

The others—George, Abby, Cheryl, Ali, Tony and Marcel—would stock the shop with bread: baguettes, fruit loaves, soda bread, crisp white rolls etc. The winner was the contestant with the largest queue, the first to sell out and the one to wow Chef Henri and his customers.

Rachel walked out late, having stood absorbing the look of the counter and her new workspace for what seemed like hours. It hadn't stopped snowing. The streets were coated deep and white like icing. Children in mittens were jumping in snowdrifts, their excitement contagious. Snowmen dotted the pavement as far as she could see: some huge with carrot noses and wonky stone buttons, others tiny with little sticks as arms and feet and satsuma slices as mouths. As she shut the door of the shop she heard someone call her name and looked up to see Philippe unlocking his car over the other side of the road, his mobile to his ear.

She didn't stop. Just smiled and walked away leaving his wave in the air. She didn't need any distractions. This, now, was about her.

At home she boiled the kettle and got out her notebook and started planning. Dreaming. Letting her mind drift to locked places. Of peppermint fondants and miniature yule logs. Of chocolate Christmas cake, because her mum hated fruit cake, shaped like a house and roofed with chocolate buttons, the doorknob a silver ball and the windows piped white icing. Of glossy dark chocolate poured into antique silver moulds, with lumps of dried orange and cherry and hazelnuts, then pressed into coloured foil and hung from the tree. Of warm arms wrapped round her as she sneaked a button off the roof of the house or pressed the plastic robin into the Cadbury Flake chimney pot.

At the sound of a quiet knock on the door, she pushed the heels of her hands into her eyes, redid her ponytail and went to answer it. Chantal stood on the doorstep, bags of shopping all up her arms, her winter boots on and coat buttoned up tight.

'I cannot stop but I bring you this.' She turned around and bent to pick up a pot, all her bags sliding forward in a heap. 'Oh, *merde*,' she swore and, dumping the bags, picked up the pot properly and held it out to Rachel.

In it was a branch. Not silver but brown—the colour of its bark. It was pushed into Oasis in a terracotta flower pot and every twig was tied with silver bows.

'For Christmas Eve,' she said.

Rachel stared at it and as she did a lump the size of one of her mini macaroons formed in her throat. This woman had been so nice to her just because she couldn't bear to think of someone like her own daughter living in such a dingy space at Christmas; she had made her flat look like a car-boot sale—but a lovely, colourful one—and given her a bike and been her friend and praised her cooking. And yet this she couldn't take.

'It's beautiful.' Rachel reached out and stroked one of the ribbons. 'But I can't accept it. I'm sorry.'

She could see the look of disappointment on Chantal's face.

'It really is very lovely. I just can't have a Christmas tree.'

Chantal paused. Looked right and left and to her shopping on the floor. 'You don't like Christmas?'

Rachel shook her head.

'Something bad happen at Christmas?'

She nodded. 'It was when my mum died.'

There was a pause. Chantal looked at the branch. 'Well.' She ran her tongue along her bottom lip. 'This is not a Christmas tree,' she said, glancing back up at

Rachel. 'It is a French *brindille*. How do you say in English?'

'A twig?'

'*Oui*. A French twig. For you.' She held it aloft. 'A good luck French twig. For you. Nothing to do with Christmas. Why you think it is Christmas? Does it look like a Christmas tree? *Non*. You see, I bring it for good luck.'

Chantal then put the pot down on the bench outside Rachel's front door and gathered up all her shopping bags. 'It can sit here. Bringing luck,' she said, pushing her bulging bags back up her arm. 'I have to go prepare dinner for *all* my family.'

'For *all* your family?' Rachel questioned, taking in the smile playing on Chantal's lips.

'*Oui*, for *all* the family.' The housekeeper gave a coy little laugh. 'My daughter, she is flying up from Nice.'

'She is? You rang her?' Rachel clapped her hands together, delighted by the rosy blush appearing on Chantal's cheeks.

'I telephoned her, yes. After someone they tell me a story about stubbornness.'

Rachel leaned against the doorframe and allowed herself a moment to feel pleased that she'd broached the subject. 'And she was happy that you had called?'

'Oh, yes,' said Chantal. 'She apologise straight away so then I apologise and then we realise how many Christmases we have wasted. I tell her about you. She is glad her bicycle it has gone to a good home.' She laughed, heaving her bags back up her arms. 'She says thank you very much.' Chantal glanced over at the decorated twig on the bench. 'I am sorry for you that Christmas is not good.' Then she took a step forward, transferred the bags from one arm to the other and reached up and put her cool hand on Rachel's cheek. 'You do your best tomorrow.'

The touch of the old woman's hand on her face and the kindness in her voice was the closest Rachel had got to the memory of her mother, of someone unconditionally looking out for her, spurring her on no matter what, championing her not to win but to do her best.

'I will,' she said.

'*Bon.*' Chantal took a step back and redistributed her bags. 'I have to go. My oysters, they need the ice.'

Rachel nodded, then looked from the housekeeper to the little tree sitting on the bench. 'Thank you, Chantal. For the twig.'

Chantal nodded, looked at the tree herself, the silver ribbons glistening in the light of the bare bulb overhead. 'It is nothing to do with Christmas, remember,' she said with a smile and started to walk away.

'Oh, wait, hang on.' Rachel nipped back inside and came back with a box of the rainbow macaroons she'd made that afternoon. 'Here, for your family.'

Chantal took them, opened the box and whistled. 'They will like these very much.'

'Good luck with your daughter.'

'*Merci,* Rachel. *Au revoir.*' She waved, stuffing the box into one of her bags and disappearing down the stairs.

Rachel looked at the tree and then shut the door and went back inside to carry on with her planning. Then she ate dinner, read her book and got into bed.

At one a.m., when she hadn't slept at all, she got out of bed and went outside into the corridor and picked up the good luck tree. She put it on the table, where she could see it from her bed, and watched the bows winking in the moonlight.

She stared at it till she fell asleep, her heart beating in her ears, and then, what felt like half an hour later, her alarm went off.

She arrived at the pâtisserie just before four. It was still dark, the moon hanging like a bauble in the navy sky. Chef and Françoise were turning on the lights. Lacey was inside, her apron on, her pale hair clipped in a low chignon.

Rachel took a breath. Christmas Eve. She'd come via the church. A tiny one, red rusted brick with a wooden door studded with black nails. It had been open, the choir were practising, and she'd sat at the back for a minute listening. Then when the priest had raised his hand to acknowledge her she'd smiled back but crept away to the side and dropped her Euro into the wooden box to pay for a candle. Hers had been the second to flicker on the plinth. Someone else remembering someone they loved, before her.

'Happy Christmas, Mum,' she'd whispered, placing the candle down and saying a little prayer of hope that all these years later she was still being looked after whatever happened in the afterlife. That she was still looking down and checking on Rachel and would keep watching for ever.

Christmas Eve, Marjorie from the hospice had said the night her mum had died. *At least you know there'll be a big welcoming committee in heaven. They'll all be out, won't they? Celebrating.*

Rachel had laughed suddenly at the memory. The noise louder than she'd expected in the dark little church. The priest had looked up and she'd shaken her head, waving a hand in apology.

'*Que Dieu te bénisse,*' he had said.

She had replied, 'And you also. *Merci.*'

Now she was here at the pâtisserie, standing opposite Lacey. They were both behind big wooden tables, Chef in the middle as if he were counting down a duel.

Abby, Marcel and George had their noses pressed up against the glass from the side room at the back.

Rachel had her apron on. The flowers she'd cut off, restitched.

'Ready?' Chef asked.

Lacey nodded. '*Oui,*' said Rachel.

And he clicked his stopwatch. 'You have four hours. Start to bake. And make it good.'

Rachel began with her praline macaroons, whisking the egg white at the same time for her peppermint swirled meringues. Lacey was chopping something that sounded intriguing. Rachel glanced up to see it was amaretti biscuits. That was her first mistake.

She looked down at her bowl to see that the meringue was over-whipped. Tipping it in the bin, she started again but her carefully noted timings were out. She heard a shout from the back room and looked to see that George had burnt himself, dough was all over the floor, and Abby was running a tea towel under the tap. Was he OK?

Her caramel over-boiled. The smell of burnt sugar filled the air like smoke. Lacey coughed. Rachel felt her palms start to sweat. She fumbled her bowl and it smashed to the floor.

'Clear it up,' said Chef as she was about to leave it and just work around the shards. In the back room she found a brush but no dustpan. The clock was ticking. Finally she found it round the back of a bin and with the bowl pieces swept she started on her tarts. Slices of apple, pear and raisins and a layer of frangipani beneath the apple-blossom-infused crème pâtisserie. But her pastry was cracking.

'Fuck,' she said out loud and saw Lacey smirk.

'One hour gone,' Chef shouted, delighted with his stopwatch.

What did she have to show for one hour's work? Macaroon halves and crumbling shortcrust.

'Calm down,' she whispered to herself. 'Come on, Rachel, just calm down.' She tried to conjure up her mum sitting by her side but it didn't work. There was no Estée Lauder this time.

Lacey was racing ahead.

'Please get a grip. Please,' she told herself but her hands were shaking too much. The sweat on her palms was adding too much moisture to the new pastry.

'Bugger, bugger, bugger.' She stopped, gripped the bench and shut her eyes. What was it she said to little Tommy when his anger took over, when he couldn't calm down? *Go outside and count to ten.*

So she swept her arm across the table, pushing her pastry, her crap caramel, her greasy croissant mix and the remains of her over-whipped meringue into the bin and walked out. She saw Abby tap George on the shoulder and point her way in the reflection of the mirrored door.

Outside the snow was stopping, the sun wasn't anywhere near rising but the sky was lighter. The streetlights caught the remaining flakes and icicles like smatterings of gems. She put her hands over her face and started to count.

'Rachel?'

She peered through her fingers to see Philippe standing there.

'What are you doing here? It's five a.m.'

He shrugged.

'Did your wife like the bauble?' was the only thing she could say.

He shook his head. 'It wasn't for my wife.'

She gave him a look as if to say, *So you've got a number of different fancy women?* Who said fancy women? Her gran. She made a noise, half snort, half laugh. He tipped his head in question.

'I have to go back in,' she said and started to turn towards the door.

'No. I disturbed you, I'll go in. You wait here,' he said, but before moving away he paused. 'I just wanted to get here early enough to see you. To wish you good luck. My brother, he says you have talent. He doesn't say that often and I know he wouldn't tell you himself, but sometimes it helps to know that people believe in you.'

She didn't reply.

'I wanted to thank you for believing in me.' He reached forward and touched her arm. 'I believe in you.'

'This is really inappropriate,' she said, turning away. And he nodded, heading inside and taking the stairs two at a time.

Rachel tipped her head back and looked up to the clouds, then counted to ten, as slowly and calmly as she could. She shut her eyes and tried to think of nothing, but instead images of standing on a box at the bakery counter, jewelled foil chocolate decorations and red-nosed reindeer biscuits danced before her closed lids.

When she opened her eyes, her face upturned to the sky, she watched as a single snowflake fell and landed right on the tip of her nose.

One more chance. For me.

CHAPTER FIFTEEN

Back inside, the room was boiling hot. Lacey was up to her elbows in pastry. Chef eyed Rachel dubiously with a frown.

'Decided to join us, Flower Girl?' he mocked.

But it didn't affect her now she had a secret. He thought she had talent. And that snippet meant more than she'd ever imagined it would. He believed in her.

She felt her nose where the snow had fallen. She thought she could smell perfume. She thought she could hear her gran's laughter as she started again on her shortcrust.

'Yes, Chef,' she said.

'Two hours forty-five minutes,' Chef shouted.

Rachel ripped her neat timing chart off her pad and scrawled a new list. 1. Redo meringues. 2. Redo croissant dough. 3. Scrap all fancy decorations. 4. Scrap swan necks—just do Viennese biscuits.

And it went on to the end of the page. There were no timing charts; it was a free-for-all. Like a Saturday morning in the bakery. She poured all the forest fruits and red berries into a metal pot and started stewing them down for the jam. Then she pushed her raspberries through the sieve for the juices, but it was taking too long so she tipped it upside down and just crushed down some of the lumps with the back of a spoon.

She wiped a raspberry swipe across her forehead. Pulled her hair off her face in an ungainly top knot, accidentally smeared her glasses with flour, and yanked off her jumper, it was so hot. Lacey's table was calm and precise. Rachel's was a mess. There would be no sieving, no delicate folding, no pinching, trimming, pinking, dusting, gold-leafing or piping. If this was going to get done it was going to be rough. But it would taste fabulous. That was all that mattered, surely? Was her good luck branch extravagant? Had the church had frills? No. Her candle had been simple white. Her branch tied only with silver bows.

This felt right. It felt comfortable. It felt like going with her instinct.

This would be village bakery. This would be Christmas fair cake sale. This would be Rachel.

So while Lacey was curling tuiles, cutting petals, painting chocolate onto holly leaves and fashioning spun-sugar bundles, Rachel was rolling, kneading, tasting, boiling. She was making miniature quiche Lorraine with crumbly shortcrust. Tiny Cornish pasties pinched at the top in waves. Crackly cheese spinach pies that burst and oozed together in the oven so were skirted with frills of burnt cheese—the best bits, her gran would say. Her rosemary and tomato Gruyère squares puffed up so high the topping slid off as if it were drunk. Her crème pâtisserie was so wobbly and thick the cranberries almost disappeared. Her croissants were weighed down with almond frangipani so stayed flat like an envelope, moist and dripping with sweet marzipan chocolate. The choux pastry for her Religieuse puffed up in a mishmash of sizes. Her *millefeuille* were overfilled with cream and the layers slapped on too quickly so they leant precariously. Her macaroons were shocking purple from a distracted tap of colouring while checking the slow-cooking meringues. The miniature tarte Tatins had over-browned with thick, glossy apple syrup. Her Sachertortes were slick with apricot jam and the word Sacher illegibly piped over the chocolate icing.

When she moved her cooling meringues to one side while trying to ice her individual vanilla slices at the same time, she dropped the wire rack and they broke like cracks in icebergs. Chef tutted as she began sticking them together with sweet chestnut purée like miniature Eton Mess. And then there were her little Christmas puddings. Solid brown ugly lumps with a sprig of holly in the top. And tiny chocolate sponge houses, each roofed with three chocolate buttons like a teepee.

'Fifteen minutes,' called Chef.

Rachel was sweating, her hair slicked back off her forehead, her apron filthy, her face dusted with flour and raspberry and chocolate, but she was smiling. For the first time in the kitchen. She even winked at Lacey as Lacey placed her delicate gold-leafed macaroons with precision onto a doily at the counter.

Rachel, at the other end of the glass counter, was gulping down the espresso Françoise had put in front of her and piling flat croissants onto a metal tray, dusting them with a generous powder of icing sugar, flaked almonds and grated chocolate in the hope of distracting from the monstrous appearance. Her macaroons she made into a tower that was almost fluorescent. Her pistachio and coffee Religieuse were at the front but their heads kept falling off every time she touched the tray. Her Christmas houses she lined up like a street and the sight of them made her laugh out loud.

'Three minutes.'

Lacey was artfully arranging holly sprigs and mistletoe while Rachel tied silver bows to a branch she'd found outside on the pavement and rammed into the corner of her counter. Then she chopped up pieces of her cheese pies and tarte Tatins for people to taste as they were choosing. Lacey did the same with her hazelnut choux pastry and strawberry buttercream Paris-Brest.

Abby was piling warm baguettes into the racks behind the counter and stopped when she saw Rachel sit back, wiping her hair out of her eyes and sipping her bitter coffee.

'Everything OK?' she whispered.

'Everything is bloody marvellous,' Rachel replied.

The queue outside snaked round the corner. Word had got around and Henri's was still a name that could garner attention. This being a competition meant that people could be part of the choices he made, and they liked that idea. From the inquisitive looks on the faces of customers peering in through the window at Henri as he barked orders and strutted about the place it seemed that the tide was about to turn for the unobtrusive pâtisserie. He could be seen turning round every once in a while to look at the queue, the remains of a smile on his face that he couldn't hide quite quickly enough when he turned back to look at Rachel and Lacey. He had shied away from the spotlight for so long, but from the squaring of his shoulders and the glint in his eye it was clear he'd been missing the attention. Perhaps, thought Rachel, this would no longer be just a little backstreet place where Henri quietly licked his wounds, but instead a hidden gem on the map of Paris. And if she won, she would be working with him as an apprentice. For the first time, as she considered the prize, the idea excited her—the future excited her.

At eight o'clock on the dot the doors were flung open. The click of the espresso machine went non-stop as people peered and picked and pointed.

'Good luck,' Rachel whispered to Lacey, who looked frazzled and exhausted, and for the first time she looked Rachel straight in the eye when she spoke to her.

'Thank you,' she said. 'I want to say good luck to you, but I can't. I'm sorry. I just want it too much.'

Rachel nodded. When she turned back it was to see all the faces crowding round Lacey's half of the counter. They were staring at her delicate creations, pointing for boxes of pistachio, cranberry and chocolate Florentines, cassis and cinnamon truffles, crème de menthe macaroons. Her side however was almost bare; no one was interested in her haphazard creations.

As she stood, feeling a little awkward as more people headed over to Lacey's side, Rachel popped a bit of croissant into her mouth as she waited and to her surprise it was like a Hallelujah chorus on her tongue.

So she yanked one out with her tongs and chopped it up, passing the pieces on a plate over the counter for people to taste.

A little wrinkled hand reached out and took it from her and when Rachel looked up she saw it was Chantal.

'I will hand this down the queue.' She winked. She was dressed in her usual paisley housecoat and fur-lined boots, her shopping bag was nestled in the crook of her arm and her tea-cosy hat was pulled low over her white curls. She popped a bit in her mouth before she turned towards the waiting shoppers and said, 'It is like a little taste of heaven.'

Rachel smiled and watched her as she chatted her way down the queue of customers, pushing the tray of slap-dash croissant pieces at them until they tasted one. She watched their faces transform from disdain and disinterest to sheer delight as they patted each other on the shoulder urging them to sample.

Suddenly her queue was growing. Smaller than Lacey's still but it had potential.

A moustached man with a cane braved a messy meringue and ate it in front of her. *'C'est un triomphe,'* he muttered, kissing his fingers, and as he did a granny with a scruffy white dog in her basket asked for fifteen of them in a box.

Next came a young boy who wanted a chocolate house and when he tried it his mother bought three more for all her children who were watching like baby birds in a nest. A chic woman in fur laughed at Rachel's vibrant macaroons. 'They will go perfectly with my decorations.' She smiled and bought them all.

Rachel was having a whale of a time, drinking espresso, eating her own croissants and laughing with people as they ate her food. The appearance of which was no longer an issue; in fact they were loving it all the more for its ugliness. Someone even commented on her silver ribbon twig and she sold it to them for ten Euros.

Lacey, however, was on fire. Her counter was practically all crumbs. Her stunning brandy cream horns left one man practically on his knees it was so good. Her face was serene as she served; there wasn't a smear of flour on her—in fact Rachel wondered if she'd actually had time to redo her make-up. Her coral lipstick and pale blue eye-shadow looked freshly applied.

Chef was watching from the far corner of the counter. Tasting morsels as they were passed around and occasionally strolling past and taking a cherry truffle or a pistachio Religieuse. But he spent most of the morning just standing and watching. He seemed different though. Rachel wondered whether it was the pleasure of seeing all the customers, shaking people's hands and answering questions about his old restaurant and getting praised for his books, or whether it was pride in them. In what they had achieved and how far they had come—the shelves filled with such spectacular creations. She couldn't be sure but he seemed to be looking at them differently. If she had to put her finger on it she'd say he was seeing them as equals, almost.

At one point Philippe came in; Rachel saw him push open the door of the pâtisserie and glance over to her but she put her head down and rearranged her croissants. She could feel his presence in the shop, walking in front of the counters and admiring the confectionery. She saw his hands through the glass counter, his blunt fingernails as they clenched into a fist as he paused where she was busy unnecessarily piling up pastries and restocking chocolates.

'What flavour are the Religieuse?' she heard him ask.

'Pistachio,' Rachel replied without looking up.

'I'll take four,' he said.

She started to fold up one of the gift boxes but he stopped her. 'Just in a bag,' he murmured. 'They are all for me.'

She raised a brow. 'You might hate them.'

'*Non.* I know they will be excellent.' He smiled softly, his dark eyes watching her as she felt herself start to blush.

Before he could say anything else Chef called him over. As he went to take the bag from her, Rachel found herself wanting to hold onto it too, just for a second, so perhaps their fingers might touch, but she didn't. Philippe nodded, scrunched the top of the bag in his hand, left the Euros on the counter top and went over to join his brother. For the whole time they stood chatting at the side Rachel could sense him. But she didn't look over once.

It was only when Philippe left that Rachel could relax again; she knew the very moment he left the shop and it was as if she could exhale. But her focus had slipped, her mind caught elsewhere. As she stood suddenly a bit flustered she caught Chef watching her and to her surprise, when she caught his eye he didn't frown or glare, he smiled, not too obviously, but just enough, just enough to give her the confidence to put her shoulders back and smile and enjoy this for what it was: her competition. Then Françoise slid past to get more beans for the coffee machine and said about a reindeer biscuit, 'I will steal one of these.'

As she moaned with delight the three old men who sat every day at the counter sipping espresso ordered their own, chuckling at the little red noses.

Rachel found she loved watching them all eat her food, goods that she had baked. However slap-dash and all over the place she'd been, it felt amazing to see the final products being devoured. And she knew she could do better. This had been the first step, the first hurdle; her courage was slowly coming back, and it felt nice. It felt right.

CHAPTER SIXTEEN

Two hours later it was as if vultures had been in. Crumbs lay scattered on silver platters. The racks of baguettes were empty, the confectionery all gone. The only morsel of food left was a truffle that had rolled to the floor and sat in the corner under a table of leaflets and dried flowers. Everything was gone, picked clean.

Rachel and Lacey sat side by side, perched on bar stools next to the counter. George and Abby and all the other contestants hovered by the side of them, all with their hands wrapped around mugs of coffee or herbal tea.

Outside the snow was glistening in the sunlight that was streaming in through the pâtisserie windows. The street was eerily quiet as everyone had left and offices were closing.

'*Ça va, mes petites bakers?*'

'*Oui,*' they said in chorus.

Rachel was exhausted. Lacey looked knackered.

'It has been a good morning, *non*? I am proud.' Chef looked genuinely emotional. 'I do not say this often, so when I do I mean it. Congratulations to you all.'

Rachel was taken aback. *'Merci beaucoup, Chef.'*

Lacey nodded, clearly too tired to even open her mouth to form words. Abby patted Rachel on the back and gave her shoulder a squeeze.

Chef laid his hands flat on the counter. 'I 'ave two bakers in front of me. One the things they make look sensational. She is calm, determined, her food tastes—' he shrugged a shoulder '—*parfait*. Perfect.'

'The other.' He paused, rubbed his chin with his fingers and thought about what to say next. 'The other is a mess. Some things she makes they look… grotesque.'

Abby gasped and stepped forward. George held her back.

'They are untidy, haphazard. *Merde*. They are untrustworthy. They have no timings, no precision, ah no. No regular, reliable precision. And they make some things that are complex but many that are simple, for the children. The food, it is a disaster.' He shook his head, stared down at the dirty floor. 'But,' he said, looking back up at the group. 'But the flavours, they are sensational. The combinations—delightful. I taste and I am in heaven. It is…' He shook his head. 'It is *incroyable*. Some things better maybe than I could have made.'

Abby did an excited little clap and Rachel tried to hold in her smile while George punched her on the arm.

'It is difficult. *Très difficile.* I am in a position that I do not find myself. My 'eart and my 'ead, they are at war.' He laughed to himself. 'So I think who is ready. And I think that one of the people is and the other is not. They have only just begun.'

Chef opened his mouth to carry on speaking but then paused, seemed to take a moment before deciding how best to carry on. Then he took off his glasses and glanced along the row of them, looking at each one of them individually as if for the first time seeing their personalities.

'Someone said to me earlier that they would not change themselves for me. For a competition. And I realised after they said it how much I respected it. I took a wrong path too early—you will understand. I did everything too quickly, too young. I was in too much of a hurry. I did not know what talent I had, and I allowed myself to become confused. I was cooking and baking someone else's style before I had found my own. And this I think is why I am here. Why I am not like the others, on the television. I am not Raymond or Gordon or Marco. I am here because after everything I want just to be me. And I want to have my style, my way. And I do not need the books or the prizes to tell me what that is.' Putting his hands behind his back, he paced in front of them. 'You all have a signature and a style, but some are less loud than others. With practice they will get louder. I have pushed you all to make them as loud as they can be, for now.

'A baker's signature must be strong and confident. And that is what I see in Ms Lacey. And that is why she must win. Because she is ready. She 'as her style. Congratulations, Lacey. You are my winner.'

Chef wiped his eye with his cuff as if perhaps there was a hint of a tear before quickly putting his glasses back on to obscure the evidence.

There was silence in the room for a moment. Rachel waited to feel a sense of overwhelming disappointment but it didn't come. So instead she started clapping and then slowly everyone else joined in and she jumped off her stool and gave Lacey a hug.

'Congrats.' She smiled.

'Thank you.' Lacey was having trouble controlling the tears streaming down her face, as if someone had tipped a bucket over her head. 'I'm so ashamed,' she wept. 'I'm so ashamed I didn't say good luck to you, Rachel.'

'Forget about it.' Rachel waved her away.

'You were tough competition. Well done. I would have liked it if we both could have won.'

Rachel raised a brow. 'No, you wouldn't.'

Lacey laughed and blew her nose. 'No, you're quite right, I wouldn't at all.' It seemed the personality

Lacey'd kept locked tight was finally being allowed out to play.

Everyone gathered round to congratulate her and Rachel stood back, watching. She felt a strange sense of relief come flooding through her and as she breathed out it was as if she hadn't exhaled since four a.m.

'I wanted to choose you.' Chef was suddenly at her side. 'But I couldn't.'

Rachel looked up at him. 'I know. It's good. It was right. You're right. I'm not ready.'

He put his hand on her arm. 'I do see you, Rachel. I see what you have, and that you struggle with it. But you are good. I said once you have a shred of promise, but I was wrong. You have a lot of promise. A lot. And more important you have your own way. Thank you for the reminder.' He smiled and the frown lines in his forehead disappeared. 'Make sure that you do not stop now. I stopped and it let me find what I really wanted. I think this is the same for you. You have stopped and now you start again. And any time you want to come for help or advice you come to me. *Oui.*'

'*Oui.* Thanks, Chef. Not such a tyrant after all, are you?' She bashed him on the shoulder and grinned. 'And any time you want to come to a picturesque English village, you come to me, *oui*?'

'*Mais non.*' He shook his head. 'That will never happen.'

Chef walked away over to Lacey and Abby pulled herself up on the stool next to Rachel. 'You were robbed.'

'No. It was the right choice. I mean, blimey, did you actually see my croissants? Grotesque doesn't even cut it.'

Abby laughed. 'The Grotesque Baker. That's what you could call your shop.'

'That'd have them queuing up!' Rachel raised a brow and shook her head.

'I'll never forgive myself, you know, about the soufflé.'

'I should hope not.'

'I really am sorry.'

Rachel laughed. 'It's fine. Honestly.'

Abby undid her apron and, pulling it off, folded it neatly in her lap, then asked, 'Do you want to come back to the UK with me tonight for Christmas?'

'Ahh, thanks, but no. I'm gonna stay here. Catch up on some sleep. Maybe even do some baking, you never know.'

The bell above the door tinkled as someone walked in and looked around, confused at the lack of stock.

'We are closed,' Chef shouted. 'Go away and come back after New Year.'

Abby snorted. 'He certainly has a way with the customers, doesn't he? Good job probably that you don't have to work with him for a month.' She hopped down off her stool. 'Rachel, I have to say that I don't really like the idea of you being alone for Christmas. If I didn't have the kids I'd—'

'It's fine, honestly.' Rachel thought of the snowflake drifting down to land on the tip of her nose. 'Don't worry. I'm not really alone.'

Abby looked puzzled but knew from the look on Rachel's face it was pointless pushing any further.

Then Chef cut in by yelling, 'Françoise! The champagne.'

CHAPTER SEVENTEEN

Christmas Day Rachel woke up late to church bells ringing. Opening the shutters, she was greeted by a snow-white Champs Élysées and a twinkling avenue of trees. For a few seconds at least it was completely still, no sound of traffic at all.

The box from Jackie had arrived the night before and she'd put it under her Christmas branch.

With tea and a hot almond croissant she untied the bow and pulled off the lid. Inside were lots of crumpled tissue paper and some pine cones, like a real Christmas box. It'd been sprayed with some kind of pine scent that pervaded the whole room. Underneath the pale blue tissue paper was a beautiful, gilt-edged notebook from Jackie. Inside the front cover she'd written, 'Our Star Baker's Notes'. Rachel flicked through the empty pages and imagined herself filling them with all the new recipes and tricks she'd learnt. Putting it to one side, she lifted the next layer of tissue to find a copy of the latest best-seller from her dad and a card from her gran with two baby goats in a box on the front saying she'd adopted 'Pierre and Marie' and they were living happily in a sanctuary in central France, about two hours south of Paris—perhaps she could pop in and see them if she had time. She gave a snort of laughter at the idea of visiting a pair of goats, and propped the card up on the window sill next to her snow-globe.

At the bottom of the box was a crisp white envelope. Croissant in her mouth, Rachel tore it open to find a card signed by practically the whole village; she had to turn it on its side to read all the different messages that had been squeezed onto the paper, all wishing her good luck and best wishes and hoping she came home safely because they missed her. She held it to her chest for a moment and had to wipe her eyes with the cuffs of her jumper.

About to screw up the envelope with the rest of the rubbish, she just caught the edge of something else nestled inside. Pulling it out, she saw it was a photograph of an empty high-street chain bakery. On the back Jackie had scrawled, 'Mrs Norris has said two-year lease, rent-free first year (She's desperado to let it. There's a bright side to the recession!).'

Rachel stared at the picture, holding it as close to her eyes as possible to see every little detail. Then she kissed the image of the bakery and closed her eyes for a second before propping it up on the window sill and standing back to stare at it from a distance.

It was all getting a bit too much; she had to take a small breather and drink her tea, her eyes continually drawn back to the cards and the photo. Never had she wanted to be back home more.

After a couple of minutes she went back to the box and found the last gift. Stuffed in the corner underneath a wodge of tissue was a pile of cut-out snowflakes, each one different, each with one of her pupils' names scrawled on in coloured pencil. Then next to them was an angel, made from a loo roll painted white with silver pipe-cleaners for arms and legs. She turned it over in her hands and smiled at its lopsided face.

The snowflakes concertinaed out when she held them up, joined together at their tips, and she reached up high to hang each end from her empty curtain pole where they bobbed like falling snow. Then she leant over and balanced the angel on the tip of her branch where it sat, skew-whiff, with one wing falling off and little Tommy's name written in block capitals on the back. Its big red smile beaming at her.

Getting dressed and taking a second and third look at her presents, pausing for longest on the photograph, she pulled on her scarf, gloves, hat and boots and headed outside. She took a walk around the silent, empty streets of the city, stared at shop windows dressed for Christmas, had a coffee in a café full of single old men drinking wine and then found herself drawn into a church where she caught the tail end of a carol service and lit some more candles, this time for her dad and Gran as well and one for the whole village. By the time she was sitting on a bench feeding some pigeons and a couple of aggressive crows the remains of a baguette she felt she'd done her Christmas. She'd got through it. And it had been better than the last ones. She was better.

A pigeon cocked its head at her, its spiny footprint trail behind it in the snow.

'Merry Christmas,' she whispered, saying the words for the first time in years. 'You probably don't understand cos you're French. *Joyeux Noël.* But then you probably don't understand that either because you're a bird.'

The pigeon flew away. Rachel pulled her scarf up over her nose as it started to snow again, glistening flakes catching the sunlight like prisms, and walked back to her flat, planning to watch TV for the rest of the afternoon.

Inside her building the staircase was decorated with garlands of green tinsel, red berries and big silver bells. She trailed her fingers through it as she took the stairs, slowly, more tired than she thought from her walk.

'*Mademoiselle? Mademoiselle* Rachel?'

She heard the door of Madame Charles's flat click open behind her as she trudged past.

'*Bonjour, Madame,*' she said, pulling off her hat and clutching it in her hands, slightly concerned that she might be about to hand her a bill for the Internet she'd used. But instead Madame just smiled at her, dark red lipstick-stained lips stretching over whitened teeth.

'*Bonjour*, Rachel. *Joyeux Noël*. You have a good day?'

'*Ah, oui, très bon.*' Their limited language meant that this was the longest conversation they'd had since the first day.

'You are leaving *demain*?' Madame Charles asked. She was wearing her beige polo neck again but had paired it with a cashmere white skirt that skimmed just past her knee and had on a mohair cardigan flecked with gold thread that touched down to the floor. Around the collar it was trimmed with fur that had been dyed dark maroon. Her hair was neatly curled around her head and her glasses hung round her neck on a chain like Lacey's, but Rachel assumed that the diamonds were probably real.

'*Oui*, I go tomorrow. Early. Very early. I'll leave you the key.' She held it up. '*La clé.*'

'*Ah, oui.*' Madame Charles nodded but didn't step back from the doorway. 'Chantal is here,' she said after a moment. 'And I have a few of my friends. Not many, four or five.'

'Oh.' Rachel smiled and nodded, a little awkward. 'That's lovely.'

Madame Charles kept her eyes fixed on her, still smiling encouragingly. Rachel didn't know what else to say and hopped from one foot to the other wondering when would be appropriate to carry on up to her flat.

Just as the silence had gone on for about as long as Rachel could bear, Madame Charles leaned against the wall, took a drag from her cigarette holder and said 'We er…' then paused and Rachel wondered for a moment if she was nervous. 'We would like to invite you inside.'

'Inside?' Rachel couldn't disguise the shock in her voice.

'With us.'

'Oh, no, no, *merci*. It's fine. I don't want to intrude. It's your day. *Non.*'

'Intrude?'

'Erm, I don't know it in French. Maybe, intrusion?'

'*Ah, non, non, non.* We have oysters and champagne. Too much. And salmon, tuna tartare, meringue. Beautiful meringue that Chantal bought. Too much for us.' She smiled and nodded encouragingly.

Rachel glanced from Madame Charles up to her own brown chipped front door and back again. As she was trying to think of a better reason to excuse herself Chantal appeared in the doorway dressed in a russet jumper and matching skirt and tights.

'Rachel! *Entre, entre. Vite. Ici.* You must join in. You must celebrate with us. With me. I have a lovely day with my family on Christmas Eve.'

Distracted for a moment from the invitation to join them, Rachel clapped her hands together with delight. 'It went well with your daughter?'

'Oh, it was *magnifique*. *Magnifique*. We have a time that is—' she held her hands wide '—perfect.'

'I'm so pleased.' Rachel tilted her head to the side and stared at Chantal as if she were her much-adored relative.

'We talk and we hug and then we eat lots and drink lots and the past it stays in the past.' Chantal beamed, her cheeks flushing the same colour as her twinset.

'What is this?' Madame Charles blew out a plume of smoke and looked perplexed between the two of them. 'What has happened?'

'I see my daughter,' Chantal said bashfully.

Madame Charles gasped, transferring her cigarette to the other hand so she could grip Chantal's arm and give it a squeeze, the closeness of the gesture leaving Chantal looking quite taken aback. 'The Christmas,' Madame Charles said through a waft of smoke, 'it has become more to celebrate.'

Rachel, wondering quite how much champagne had already been consumed, took a step backwards up the stairs, already running through her refusal in her head. She was happy for Chantal but it didn't make her want to celebrate.

'Rachel.' Chantal walked a couple of paces closer to her. 'Yesterday I have a wonderful evening with my family and today it is a day to indulge. *Oui*. It is our tradition. It is not Christmas, it is fun, it is a celebration of the year. It is a time to enjoy. I would be very pleased if you were there too. The little oysters are ready.' She laughed, then turned and went back into the flat, coming back out a second later with a crystal flute. 'Champagne?'

'It is because I have no family, Rachel,' Madame Charles added with a flourish. 'Just my cats. So I have my friends. And I would like it if you were here.' Her words made Rachel wonder if perhaps Madame Charles's life wasn't quite as perfect as she had imagined. If she needed to have her housekeeper and lodger over for Christmas Day maybe she was a little alone in this great big perfect apartment? Here Rachel had been in her cramped attic flat thinking Madame was living the high life downstairs when perhaps they had both been as lonely as one another. 'It would be an honour,' Madame Charles continued, the look in her eyes softening. 'I have heard you do very well at the cooking. We have lots of food. Lots of oysters. Please. As my guest.'

Rachel couldn't help a little laugh, feeling suddenly less in awe, less small, and more relaxed in her landlady's presence. Hadn't this been what she'd wanted right from the start? Hadn't she wanted to be embraced into this elegant life of luxury? Hadn't this seemed like the perfect non-Christmas Christmas? And, well, if nothing else it was a chance to snoop around the apartment.

Hopping down the stairs, she said, '*Merci beaucoup*, Madame Charles. It would be a pleasure.'

'*Bien.*' Madame Charles kissed her on both cheeks. 'Welcome.'

Stepping inside was like entering the Snow Queen's castle. White walls, glass tables, pristine cream sofas. In the corner a huge antique gold clock ticked and a crystal chandelier hung low in the centre of the room, watching and winking at them all. It smelt of riches and Diptyque's Verveine candles that she never had enough money to buy and were now flickering in abundance all over the mantelpiece.

Chantal thrust a cut-glass champagne flute into her hand and said, 'Drink, drink. There is plenty.'

CHAPTER EIGHTEEN

It was the loveliest non-Christmas Christmas Rachel had ever had. Madame Charles's friends had been charming—all fascinated to hear what Henri Salernes was like as a person and to quiz her on the rift between the two brothers—the Siamese had stalked haughtily as the friends shucked salty oysters drizzled with lemon and ate gorgeous smoked salmon and duck pâté, cold roast chicken and chicory and walnut salad followed by bitter chocolate tart.

Quite unexpectedly Madame Charles had pulled Rachel and Chantal aside and handed them both a gift wrapped up in red paper with a green bow. 'They are for you both. Do not give me anything. I had these left over, from my assistant when she shopped.'

Unwrapping it to find a stunning cashmere scarf of the palest grey, Rachel had tried to give it back but Madame Charles had waved her away. 'You take it. It is a favour for me.'

As they had thanked her and walked away Chantal had whispered, 'It happens every year. She just buys too much always, just in case.'

Rachel had the scarf wrapped around her now, soft and snug, as she waited for the Eurostar. She had gone back to her flat after the party and baked a tray of less luminous macaroons: hazelnut and white chocolate, violet and blackberry and raspberry and bitter dark chocolate. She had left them in a box tied with ribbon outside Madame Charles's apartment with a note of thanks and the key, which when it came to it she was sad to give back.

Her good luck Christmas branch she'd tucked down the front of her case so it poked out like flotsam on the shore. The bows waggled in the wind of the trains.

As she stood, freezing, on the platform she suddenly heard her name being shouted.

'Rachel. Rachel, *un moment.*'

She turned, her face half concealed in the massive new scarf, and saw Philippe running down the platform.

'I nearly missed you,' he said, panting. He looked different out of his suit, younger, more relaxed dressed in a navy woollen jumper and tatty old jeans.

'How did you get on the platform?'

'I bought a ticket.'

Rachel looked shocked. 'You're not coming with me.'

'No, I know. I just wanted to say goodbye.'

'You paid a hundred and fifty Euros just to say goodbye?'

He was bent over, had his hands resting on his thighs, trying to catch his breath. 'I wanted to talk to you.'

'Don't, Philippe. You have a wife.'

'Yes, I do have a wife but I also don't have a wife.'

'What is she—invisible?' Rachel looked down at her wheely bag and kicked it with her foot.

He stood up straight, shaking his head. 'Listen to me, just for one minute, please.'

She turned back to him, her face pulled further down into the scarf like a tortoise. 'Go on, then.'

'I am married. I married very young and my wife and I have not been right for many years.'

Rachel huffed a disbelieving sigh.

He shrugged. 'Sometimes it is not as simple as it looks, Rachel. Have you been married?'

'No.'

'Well, we have been very unhappy. My wife met someone else last year. When she told me we thought we should try one more time. We went for counselling, we have tried and tried, believe me. But there is nothing worse in the world than being together when you have fallen out of love. I promise, it is the worst feeling. Every day you know you are out of love with each other and nothing will bring it back. It is lonely. I am lonely.' He ran his hand through his hair and laughed. 'We are both lonely. We did not spend yesterday together or the day before.'

Rachel looked down into her scarf; she didn't want to hear it.

'You can think whatever you like about me but I wanted you to know the truth. I could bring Emilie here too and she would tell you the truth. We made a mistake when we were very young and the world, we, have changed. We are both miserable. When I was with you, I wasn't miserable.'

There was a pause; the announcer called her train.

'Listen to me. When I was young it was a mess in my house. Henri, he became the man and he worked and he worked and then he became famous and he leaves. Suddenly there is a bit more money and my mother, she doesn't have to work two, three jobs and I am finished school and I think I need to become a man now, too. And what did I do? I follow in Henri's footsteps into the business and I got married. I think maybe that will make me a man. It was very stupid but I was going to be a famous chef and I was going to work and I was going to be a husband.' He blew out a breath and ran a hand through his hair, looking across at the train. 'I do not try to excuse it, Rachel, I try to tell you how it was, what happened. There was always something that kept us together. When I leave the restaurant it caused a big rift between me and my brother and Emilie, she was there for that, she helped me to make the decision—to do what would make me happy. And then when everything goes wrong for Henri we are there for him, Emilie and I, we take him in, we help him. We have been through a lot. And then it just becomes life. It is what is normal.

Unhappy becomes normal and normal becomes life. But we do not want to be unhappy any longer.'

Rachel glanced up at him, at the narrow eyes and tightness of his lips as if he was trying to force his feelings on her with a look.

'You should have told me,' she said quietly.

'Yes, I should have told you. I told her.'

'What did she say?'

'I think she was relieved. Rachel, we have no children. We made a mistake.'

'Yes, you keep saying that. But you are still married.'

Philippe sighed. 'And we never should have been. But when you are nineteen you do stupid things. Christ, you want a better example, look at this.' He pulled up the edge of his jumper to reveal a tattoo of a scorpion on his lower back.

She tried not to let him see her smile.

'Sometimes you don't find out about your mistakes until it is too late. I like Emilie very much but I do not love her and she does not love me.'

Rachel nodded.

'I like you very much.'

She looked away. 'I like you, too.'

There was another call for passengers to board the train on the platform.

'But—' she bit her lip and turned back to him '— I don't want to be chosen for the wrong reasons. I don't want you to leave her for me. I want you and her to decide what to do for the two of you, to part or try again because it's right for your relationship. I want to be chosen for me. By someone who isn't looking for an escape.'

'I'm not looking for an escape.'

She shook her head. 'I don't think you know that, yet. I don't think you can be certain. Do you think you can really be a hundred per cent certain that I didn't just come along at the right time to make you realise you'd messed up your life?'

He didn't reply, but looked down and scuffed the floor with his Converse.

She glanced down too and smiled. 'You're mad— Converse are really cold. I think they absorb the cold from the floor.'

'Tell me about it.' He laughed. 'I don't even have a coat.'

'Why not?'

'Because I had to get here!'

'Oh.' She laughed.

They stood looking at each other on the platform, the final call booming out for passengers to King's Cross St Pancras.

'You don't even like your job, Philippe.'

'I know.' He nodded, then took a deep breath and she thought maybe he might cry.

Rachel reached forward and squeezed his upper arm. 'Go home and get a coat, and then… Decide what you want from your life. Work out what your dream is. You're wasting your talent at the moment.'

He cocked his head. 'Maybe I should sign up for Henri's next apprenticeship.'

'Worked for me.' She laughed.

He put his hands on her shoulders and said, 'Well, what now? What if I decide that it is you?'

'Well, then, maybe you have coffee with me in six months.'

He snorted a laugh as if that wasn't what he wanted to hear at all but knew that was the only option she was going to give him.

'I've learnt loads this week, Philippe, and one of those things is that if something is right it is always there. You can't run away from it because it follows you.'

'Meet me in six months.'

She rolled her eyes. 'You haven't—'

'I know I will feel the same as I do now. Meet me in six months at the bottom of the Eiffel Tower. Six months from today.' He got his phone out and scrolled through his calendar. 'June twenty-sixth. Midday on June twenty-sixth.'

She rolled her eyes. 'Seriously?'

He nodded.

'Maybe.' She looked dubious.

'I'm putting it in,' he said, tapping on the screen of his iPhone.

'Fine.' She shook her head, disbelieving. 'Now go and sort your life out.'

He pulled the sleeves down on his jumper and blew into his hands. 'OK.'

'OK.'

'It was a pleasure to meet you, Rachel,' he said and, leaning forward, kissed her on both cheeks goodbye. She breathed in deep and smelt that familiar scent of aftershave and soap and skin and closed her eyes, trying to absorb it as if that were the smell of Paris and her whole trip.

'You also.' She smiled and he picked up her bag, the branch waving away out of the top, and put it in the carriage for her. She stepped in after it and he held her hand to help her up.

Just as she was about to walk away down the corridor he said, *'Ah, un moment.'*

Then he jogged back to pick up a white plastic bag he'd left on the platform. 'For you.' He held it up. 'It is a little bashed. Maybe broken. I apologise.'

She looked at the bag and nearly said, 'Aren't we all?' But instead she said, *'Merci beaucoup. Au revoir, Philippe.'*

'Au revoir,' he said. 'Till next time.'

***

Ensconced in her seat, the train pulling out from the station, she reached into the bag and found a plain white box inside. In it sat nestled her bauble. The Russian princess in a carriage with her prince, pulled by bright red horses dancing through the starlit night. She held it up by the ribbon watching as the black lacquered ball twirled around, the princess disappearing away from her, and then she saw down the back it was cracked from top to bottom. As she traced the break with her thumb, it seemed to make her like it all the more.

Sitting back in her seat, she shut her eyes and replayed the whole week in her head, from her first telling off for the flowers to the men at the counter eating her reindeer biscuits. She thought of all her friends, even Marcel who'd apologised to both her and Abby and tried to give them both very friendly goodbye kisses. Lovely George, who'd invited them all up north for a summer reunion. And even Lacey, who was still in Paris; her husband had flown out to meet her, and she'd start her apprenticeship on the second of January. Chef had invited Rachel to join them but she'd declined. She had a home to get back to, which hopefully hadn't been wrecked by the retired Australians, and a village to see. She had her box of mini Christmas puddings to give her dad. She had years to make up for. She had a silver-ribbon-tied branch to lay on her mum's grave to thank her for teaching her to bake.

When her taxi pulled up in the village she was amazed to find a welcoming committee. The Sunday School banner held aloft by all the kids: 'Our Star Baker, Rachel'. The end drooping as little Tommy was waving instead of holding.

Mrs Norris was standing, arms folded across her brown jumper, the keys to the new bakery dangling from between her fingers.

'Woo hoo, well done, Rachel.' Jackie came running forward and gave her a hug. Then peered into the taxi. 'No French hunk.'

'No.' She shook her head. 'I left him at the station.'

'Oh, really.' Jackie snorted. 'I'll bet.'

As the crowd cheered, Rachel searched through all the faces trying to find someone, but as she did little Tommy was suddenly squeezing her tight as he threw himself against her legs and said, 'Will you not be teaching us next year?'

'I don't know, Tommy. I don't think so.' She pushed out her bottom lip in a sad face. 'But you'll be able to come to the shop and eat cookies now, just like I did when I was your age. You can come whenever you want.'

He beamed and ran back to his parents.

'Have you seen my dad?' she asked Jackie.

'I don't think so.' Jackie shook her head, looking a bit sorry for her.

'OK, that's fine. I didn't think he'd be here.'

Rachel took a moment to take in the scene before her. The Christmas tree was as huge as ever, looming at a precarious angle and flashing like a beacon. Lights and bunting had been haphazardly strung between all the branches of the chestnut trees around the green and, in its own way, it looked as beautiful as the Champs

Élysées. The pond was beginning to freeze, the pair of swans waddling on the glassy surface while some of the kids were stamping on the edges trying to make it split. Mr Swanson and his wife had brought Thermos flasks of mulled wine and were serving it out in plastic cups, along with plates of mince pies, any excuse for a little party. And she heard someone say that there would be a cheese board and turkey sandwiches in the pub from seven.

As she stood watching a cloud of perfume enveloped her as suddenly her grandmother was by her side. 'Darling, you look wonderful. I always think the Paris air does wonders for a person.' She winked. 'And the flat's marvellous. One broken plate and a million recommendations for places to go in Melbourne if you're ever in the area.'

'Thank God for that.' Rachel feigned wiping her forehead with relief. 'Is Dad here?'

'Christ, no. He'd never come to this.' Her grandmother looked round her at her luggage. 'What is that monstrous branch?'

'It's a French Christmas tree.'

'I don't think it is, dear. I don't know who told you it was but I think they were pulling your leg.' Julie flicked one of the ribbons with her finger.

CHAPTER NINETEEN

The dark Victorian building that would house the new bakery had previously been an old café that no one had sat in for the last five years. It had served egg sandwiches that curled at the edges and cups of stewed tea in chipped mugs. The waitresses had never smiled and the custard on the apple crumble was fluorescent yellow. When it closed down no one had been surprised or particularly upset. As Rachel stood in the centre of the main room, dust coagulating in the grease on the laminate tables, wallpaper bubbling off the walls, dark cigarette-smoke-stained ceiling covered in cobwebs and cups with rotten milk lining the sink, her heart sank.

Two days before she'd met with the head of Nettleton Primary and handed in her notice, and while she'd felt a pang of sadness that she wouldn't be teaching all her little kids any longer, wouldn't see the fresh batch of hilarious new pupils, she knew that it was time for a fresh challenge. That teaching had been a vocation but this was a dream. And it was made all the easier when her class rammed the double chocolate brownies she'd made into their mouths and demanded that she go away and make more.

But now, standing alone in the darkness, a strip light flickering in the back kitchen and her feet sticking to the dirty floor, she wondered if she'd actually made a massive mistake. Not only was this going to take a lot more doing up than she'd anticipated in her stupid dream-filled head, she was also going to have to spend all the money she had in savings on new ovens and equipment.

The door creaked and she turned to see Jackie walk in, shaking off her umbrella. Outside it was tipping it down, rain in glassy sheets battering the pavement and slicking the tree bark to a dark black.

'Christ, it's worse than I remembered,' Jackie muttered, making a face as her shoes clung to the sticky floor. 'Did you ever eat here?'

Rachel shook her head. 'Never.' She took a couple of tentative steps forward and, looking down, feared that the brown blobs on the floor were mouse droppings. 'I think maybe I was delusional with excitement or still pissed from the champagne last time we had a look around,' she said, looking over her shoulder at Jackie, who had picked an old newspaper up between her finger and thumb and was skimming through dated headlines.

'Yeah, me too,' Jackie said without glancing up. 'I'll tell you one thing, you won't be able to afford those tables and chairs we saw the other day.'

Rachel thought of the glossy magazine she'd been flicking through the day before, cutting out her perfect furniture and sticking it on her mood board. So far she had three Pinterest boards and one giant piece of white card pinned to her living-room wall of ideas for the decor and layout. And it all suddenly seemed like a crazy fantasy.

'Do you think the headmaster will have me back?' Rachel said, scowling as she poked her head into the bathroom to the left of the main room and quickly drawing back in disgust.

'Like a shot.' Jackie laughed then opened a bin bag and swept the entire contents of a table into the rubbish sack so it clattered to the floor. 'Best place for all this junk,' she said, swiping her hands together as if that was that. 'Come on, stop sulking and help me do the rest.'

Rachel knew Jackie was just trying to help, and knew that she was verging on being a bit of a princess, flouncing round her new space only seeing the worst, but as her eyes swept round the dirty cupboards with the doors hanging off and the burnt-out ovens and chip pans that sat slick with old oil she saw her mood boards and all their snazzy minimalist furniture and wallpapers in varying shades of Farrow & Ball grey fizzle into nothing.

The dream suddenly seemed far too big for her.

'It'll be OK,' she heard Jackie say and then felt the weight of her arm as she draped it over her shoulder. 'You just might have to adjust your plans slightly.'

Rachel huffed a laugh. 'Just slightly,' she said. But the doubt had already set in along with a hollow feeling in her chest. 'Jackie, I think it all might be a bit too much.'

'No, don't be daft.'

'Look at it, though. It's a mess. How am I going to pay for it all? I'm going to end up just wiping down these old tables and opening the same crappy café that no one went to five years ago. Shit.' She rubbed her hand over her eyes. 'How did I possibly think I could do this?'

'Because you can,' Jackie pushed.

'Maybe my dad was right.' Rachel kicked an old rat trap with her foot and beneath it a mound of earwigs scuttled away. 'I can't follow in my mum's footsteps. Baking a bit in Paris is one thing. Opening a bakery...I mean, what was I thinking?' She shook her head at Jackie, who made an encouraging face back at her but it lacked her usual persuasion.

The minutes ticked slowly by as they both stood, side by side, listening to the rain clatter on the skylight in the kitchen at the back and watched the branches make shadows on the dirty floor. In the end Jackie said, 'What do you want to do?'

'Go home,' Rachel muttered, on the verge of tears.

With a last despondent look at the derelict space, Jackie flicked off the lights, plunging the bleak view into darkness as they turned to leave. But just as they were about to walk out of the kitchen the main doors swung open and they heard a voice shout. 'OK, then, where do we start?'

'Who's that?' Jackie said, peering round the kitchen door.

'Rachel? Jackie?' another voice called. 'Are you in here?'

'We're here,' Rachel shouted, switching the lights back on so they could see where they were going.

Standing in the doorway, toolbox in hand, was Mr Swanson and behind him all the other members of the PTA. It was like the school nativity all over again. Led by Mrs Pritchard, who was dressed in her decorating dungarees, they all trooped in wearing a variety of old, paint-splattered clothes. At the back, three of the teachers from the school loped in chatting and carrying a cool box of sandwiches and beer, and Rachel's grandmother was outside just beeping her car locked and muddling across the pavement with a giant tea urn.

'Can't let you do this on your own,' said Mr Swanson as Rachel stood open-mouthed watching them pile in. 'It's a bloody shit hole.'

'Bill...language,' said Mrs Pritchard as she deposited her carrier bags on the sticky laminate, made a face of disgust at the filth and then started to lay out dust sheets, covering tables quick as a flash.

Rachel's grandmother pushed her way through to the front and, clattering the tea urn to the floor, gave the place a quick once-over and said, 'It's a bloody shit hole.'

Mr Swanson chuckled to himself as Mrs Pritchard pursed her lips and, ignoring Rachel's grandmother completely, started to chivvy the other PTA members into action. 'We'll have to draw up some kind of plan,' she said. 'We can start by stripping the wallpaper. Bill, you dismantle that revolting counter and the rest of you, well, I suggest you get cleaning.'

The three teachers, who had clearly thought this might be a bit of a jolly that was more beer and fag breaks than on hands and knees scrubbing, made faces like schoolkids behind her back while Mr Swanson started to arm himself with the necessary tools for dismantling.

'I'll just make some tea,' said Rachel's grandmother, tiptoeing through the muck in her French Sole pumps.

Rachel just watched as the flurry of activity started before her. 'I can't believe you're all here,' she said, quite flabbergasted.

'Shows how much people like a good cake,' her grandmother whispered as she walked past to plonk the urn on the countertop.

'Well...thanks, everyone, I'm really touched,' was the best Rachel could come up with, too taken aback with emotion at the support for anything more eloquent.

'It's community, isn't it?' said Mr Swanson, pausing to take a polystyrene cup of tea from Rachel's gran. 'All pulling together in times of crisis.'

'Like the war.' Rachel's grandmother snorted.

'Come on, Bill, chop chop.' Mrs Pritchard had her yellow gloves on and was already yanking off strips of peeling Artexed wallpaper. 'Rachel, darling, we are all here to help you, but I would add we don't have all week so come on, everyone, let's get to it.'

They worked tirelessly all day and half into the night, sawing, bashing, stripping wallpaper, heaving old ovens and fridges out into a van for the tip. The laminate floor was yanked up by Jackie and Rachel's grandmother to reveal, much to their surprise, original Victorian tiles, some chipped and missing but what was there, when washed and scrubbed by Mrs Pritchard, created a beautiful geometric pattern of browns, maroon and cobalt blue. The stunning floor gave them all such a boost that they cracked open the beer and when that was finished the teachers nipped over to the off-licence to buy some white wine, which they drank out of their polystyrene tea cups.

By the end of the day the place looked like a bomb site but the floor sparkled and the walls were stripped and the back kitchen had been almost completely gutted. Most of the crew were getting ready to decamp to the pub, gathering up their stuff and heading out of the door. Rachel and Jackie were slumped in plastic chairs, finishing off the wine, and Mrs Pritchard was giving her floor a final wipe.

'I'll just bash a hole in the ceiling before I go home,' said Mr Swanson, sweat dripping from his brow, his checked shirt filthy from dust and dirt.

'Hang on a minute—what do you mean?' Rachel paused mid sip of wine, wishing it were ice-cold water she was so thirsty and knackered, and stared in horror at the hammer about to be thwacked into the roof.

'It's false. You don't want a false ceiling, do you?' Mr Swanson looked at her, incredulous.

'I don't know what you mean.' Rachel made a face, then looked for support at Jackie, who was equally perplexed.

'He means—' Rachel's grandmother rolled up her sleeves and leant up against a table '—that this isn't the actual ceiling. It's called a drop ceiling. God knows why, but some people want the space to be lower... It was fashionable. Girls, I don't know how you don't know this—it's general knowledge.'

Jackie made a face to suggest that she had absolutely no clue about DIY and felt absolutely no guilt about it, Rachel's grandmother sighed, and Mr Swanson swung the hammer so it crashed through the plasterboard ceiling, shouting, 'Stand back!' as pieces clattered to the ground.

'Oh, my God, look at that.' Rachel's grandmother took a step forward and stared up through the hole.

Rachel came to stand next to her. 'Wow,' she murmured as she tilted her head back to glance up.

Mrs Pritchard stopped looking in horror at the dusty mass of plasterboard on her clean floor, and stared up, open-mouthed.

Through the hole was the real ceiling. Six more feet of height at least and divided into elegant squares by thin wooden beams bevelled at the edges and painted with golden scrolls. Two old chandeliers had been twisted up and hung wonkily from the light fittings so they didn't get in the way. Their glass was filthy and dull and hung forgotten, but held the promise of looking magical. Then around the edge, running from the top of the wall to the base of the actual ceiling, was a stained glass frieze, the pattern obscured with dirt and grime, but in places where the light caught they could just make out squares of brilliant red and yellow and etchings of birds and flowers in the delicate glass.

'Oh, my God,' whispered Rachel, staring up in awe.

Mr Swanson whistled. 'You've got yourself a beauty.'

All the people about to head to the pub paused and turned back to see what all the fuss was about, and soon the whole gang were ripping down the plasterboard so the full glory of the ceiling could be revealed.

Only a few people had said that they could come back the following day and even less for the rest of the week, but after the thrill of their discoveries all but one of the teachers, who said they had a cold but was suspected to be nursing a killer hangover, trooped back in for more the next day. Mr Swanson had brought his ladders, and

Rachel's grandmother and the remaining teachers spent the day scrubbing the stained glass, while a couple of the PTA washed the chandelier glass piece by piece.

Rachel, however, had been up most of the previous night researching the price of the new kitchen plus equipment and, while she was as wowed by the discovery of the ceiling and floor as the rest of them, was becoming more and more terrified by the cost of fitting out the bakery.

'Jackie,' she whispered as the two of them stood in the kitchen at the back looking round the mangled room, wires hanging out all over the place and big patches of grease on the floor where the ovens and fridges had stood. 'I don't know if I'm going to be able to afford it all.'

Jackie scratched her chin. 'What can you pay for?'

'I can pay for the technical stuff. The ovens and all that.'

'Well, that's all you need.' Jackie shrugged.

'But I don't have any counters, or chairs or tables. What will people sit on? How will I paper the walls?'

They both peered back out into the main room, at the walls stripped back to the pale pink plaster.

'I think it looks quite cool like that,' Jackie said with a shrug of the shoulder.

'Are you kidding? It looks a mess.' Rachel slumped back against the doorframe and thought back to her lovely Pinterest boards. Sleek white tables, soft grey carpet, wallpaper painted with tiny hummingbirds, sparkling stainless-steel countertops.

'Rachel.' Jackie put her hands on her hips. 'I hate to say this but look out there,' she said, nodding towards all the people frantically working and cleaning. 'They are doing all this for you. The bloody room itself feels like it's doing what it can to help you—look at the bloody ceiling, for Christ's sake. Now, I'm not saying you're being a spoilt brat...'

'No?' Rachel raised a brow.

'But you are being a bit of a spoilt brat.' Jackie laughed. 'What did Paris teach you?'

'Never leave your soufflé unattended.' Rachel shrugged.

Jackie rolled her eyes. 'Or maybe that you're stubborn and stupid and things don't always go the way you've planned but more often than not turn out for the better because they don't. How about that?'

Rachel pushed herself off from where she leant against the door and, putting her shoulders back, stood up straight, feeling uncomfortable in her own skin, embarrassed that Jackie had called her on her attitude. 'I see what you mean.'

'Do you?'

'I think maybe.' She nodded.

'Like perhaps those Formica tables out there aren't actually that bad. They could look quite retro chic in the right surroundings,' Jackie suggested.

'I can't believe you've just said retro chic,' Rachel scoffed.

'Don't change the subject.'

'OK, yes, I take your point. Perhaps I need a new Pinterest board.'

'Or scrap the board and just see what happens.' Jackie shrugged before turning round and leaving the kitchen, and Rachel on her own, to go out and join the others.

She was right, and Rachel knew it. She had forgotten all the lessons that she had learnt in Paris, living in that little flat. That while Madame Charles's elegant apartment had entranced her, it had been in the scruffy apartment full of Chantal's knick-knacks where she'd ended up feeling most at home, most safe.

Slowly she walked back out into the main room where everyone was working to make the bakery a reality. The remains of the plasterboard had been bagged up and sat on the pavement waiting to go to the tip, the stained glass was beginning to shimmer where it had been cleaned as the sunlight streamed through and the chipped plaster on the walls actually did hold a certain rustic charm.

When she saw one of the teachers lift an old yellow Formica table up ready to cart it out to the pile of junk on the pavement Rachel raised a hand and shouted, 'Hold on a minute.'

He paused and turned to look at her.

'I might keep that,' Rachel said tentatively. 'I think it might actually work…with the right chairs,' she added as she saw Jackie's lips stretch into a smile.

As the teacher put the table back down where he'd found it and stood back to look at it, to try and see it in a different light, Mrs Pritchard paused in her sanding down of the front door and said, 'You know, I have a set of chairs in my garage, nothing special but they're old, possibly antique. Bit battered. You can have them if you want.'

'And, darling,' her grandmother called down from where she was washing the windows up a ladder, 'I have that lovely little table in the hall. It's always got in the way where it is. That would go nicely in here.'

Ten minutes ago Rachel would have declined all the offers, stuck stubbornly to the vision she couldn't afford, but, as Jackie had pointed out, then she would have learnt nothing. Now she realised that the blueprint for the bakery was turning out to be the little flat that overlooked the Champs Élysées, fittingly where she'd learnt to love to bake again. 'Yes, thank you,' she said. 'I'd love anything you have.'

That night, after everyone had gone, Rachel sat with Jackie drinking espressos laced with some Armagnac that Marcel had given her before she'd left Paris.

'So what are you going to call the place?' Jackie asked, taking a sip of her coffee and, finding it under-seasoned, adding another splash of alcohol.

'I don't know.' Rachel shook her head. 'I thought just maybe The Village Bakery.'

'That's rubbish.'

'Well, *you* come up with something better,' Rachel said, wrapping her hand round the warm espresso mug and lifting it up to her nose to smell the Armagnac before tasting it.

'Since when do you smell things like that?' Jackie said, watching her dubiously.

Rachel hadn't even realised she was doing it and looked down at the cup almost with surprise. 'It's important to smell things—especially if you're a chef. Smell, Jackie, is the most sensual of all the senses,' she said with a shrug, repeating the exact words Philippe had said to her.

'Learn that in Paris, did you?' Jackie rolled her eyes. 'So, come on, think of a better name.'

'I'm too tired.'

'Rachel! This is your dream.'

Rachel laughed. 'I know, I know. I just can't think of anything.'

'Have some more Armagnac,' Jackie said, tipping another slug into the espresso cup. 'OK. Right. Let's brainstorm.'

Rachel stood up and went over to get a pad and a pencil, turning off the bright main lights as she did so and flicking on the standard lamp next to a huge wooden mirror that hung on the wall opposite the door. As they started to run through ideas, the low light glowed over their corner of the bakery, the bottle of Armagnac glistened as Jackie kept refilling their cups and sheets of paper were scrunched up and lobbed in the direction of the bin.

'OK, think of something that has meaning for you. Maybe something to do with your mum?' Jackie said, shrugging her shoulders as if that was the best suggestion she had left in her.

'No, I don't want to look backwards. Mum's bakery was hers. This needs to be mine.' The words took Rachel by surprise, but after she said them she suddenly felt a freedom to name it whatever she liked. 'I could call it Love and Lemon Slices,' she said, smiling at the idea. 'Or The Marvellous Macaroon.'

'That's dreadful.' Jackie rolled her eyes. 'Let me think of something…' She was slouching back, had her feet up on the chair in front of her and was cradling her cup in one hand as she shut her eyes and tried to come up with some ideas. 'Oh, God, I can't close my eyes. I actually feel a bit sick from that stuff,' she said, sitting up straighter and pointing to the Armagnac. 'It's lethal. Oh, I have an idea. What about The Parisian Baker?'

'It's nice,' Rachel said, leaning her elbows on the table and resting her chin in her hands. 'But I'm not French, though.'

'I wish I was French. It'd be so romantic.'

'Are you pissed?'

'Maybe.'

Rachel laughed and, lounging back in her chair, tipping it so it rested on only the back two legs, gulped down the rest of her drink. 'It's so bloody difficult. Are you sure I can't just go with The Village Bakery?'

'Absolutely not.' Jackie shook her head. 'I forbid it. Christ, I shouldn't shake my head.'

'Maybe it needs to be something that I make.' Rachel rocked back and forth on her chair as she thought. 'You know, something to do with me.'

'Well, what was your best thing from the competition?'

'My squashed croissants.'

'Well, there you go.'

'I can't call it The Squashed Croissant.'

'Why the hell not?'

CHAPTER TWENTY

By the time the huge gleaming silver ovens had been installed and the glass-fronted fridges slotted into place, The Squashed Croissant bakery was almost complete. In the front a mishmash of different tables and chairs stood on the shiny tiled floor. The yellow Formica table with Mrs Pritchard's antique chairs was next to a metal café table that had been in Mr Swanson's garden and a collection of chairs that Jackie had picked up from the local car-boot sale. Her grandmother's wooden table sat by the window with two big armchairs that Mrs Beedle from the antique shop up the road was getting rid of cheap because she couldn't fit them in the shop. The chandeliers hung low into the room and added a sense of faded grandeur to the place, while the stained glass dazzled in the last of the evening light.

Instead of buying the flash new counter they had refurbished the original one from the café, tongue and grooving the front and painting it a bright cherry red, then adding a top of stainless steel. Her grandmother had surprised her by paying for the glass display units that would house all the delicacies—from thick, gooey custard tarts to dark chocolate cherry truffles and sweet fluffy Victoria sponge. Behind the counter was a second-hand espresso machine that stood in front of a huge mirror lined with shelves for the cups and saucers, glasses, bags of coffee and then big baskets of bread— just like Henri Salernes'. And again, just like Henri's, in front of the counter were three high stools that she hoped her regulars would sit at and chat with her while she served coffee and laid out the freshly baked croissants.

Rachel was exhausted. Delighted but exhausted. She could count the hours of sleep she'd had on one hand. Tomorrow was the grand opening and she'd spent the last few days baking enough cakes to feed the entire village. Her grandmother was there to help her but seemed to taste and chat more than she cooked.

As Rachel's macaroons were cooling on wire racks out the back and her fruit tarts were sitting waiting to be glazed, she'd taken the opportunity to stand for a moment in the centre of the room by herself and just look at it all. To drink in the warmth of the space that now felt almost like home. On the walls she had hung big photos of Paris— of the pâtisserie, the Champs Élysées and the little stalls selling fruits and vegetables in the Marais that she'd visited with Philippe. She had debated about whether or not to hang that last one, but she'd reminded herself that the trip to the Marais had been one of her favourite memories, no matter what the outcome had been between them.

As she stood looking at it now, remembering the smell of the figs and the lavender and the glistening fruit he'd given her in the little bags, she almost didn't hear the bell on the door that tinkled as someone pushed it open.

For a second Rachel had the ridiculous thought that it might be Philippe, come to Nettleton to surprise her on the opening evening of her bakery, so when she saw her father standing on the threshold she tried not to show her disappointment.

They hadn't really spoken since the pre-Paris dinner when he'd told her to bury the baking alongside the memories of her mother. He hadn't come to her homecoming, nor had he called to see how it went. He'd left on a cycling trip to Northern Wales just before New Year without saying when he was coming back.

'Is it OK if I come in?' he said.

'Yes, fine.' She nodded, noticing how he took his handkerchief out of his pocket then put it back again, his movements unsure, nervous.

'Good. Right. Thanks,' he mumbled and took a couple of steps towards her. He was dressed in his usual uniform of mustard-yellow jumper, green cords, brown boat shoes and she felt a pang of nostalgia for the way things used to be. When he'd acted like her dad.

'Rachel, darling, are you going to do these tarts or not?' her grandmother shouted as she came out of the back room and then stopped with a start on seeing Rachel's father. 'About bloody time you showed up,' she said with a raise of her brow.

'Gran—' Rachel held up her hand to make her be quiet.

'No, it's OK.' Her dad shook his head. 'She's quite right,' he said, walking forward another couple of paces, his hands clasped behind his back as he turned to look at the space. Lifting his head, he took in the stained glass and the chandeliers, the huge pictures on the walls, the peeling plaster and the pots of snowdrops on all the tables. Then he scuffed the floor with the toe of his boat shoe and gave a quick nod.

'What do you think?' Rachel said, her voice coming out in more of a whisper than she'd intended.

He didn't say anything.

Rachel bit her lip, holding her breath for his reaction. She felt her gran walk over and her hand slip into hers, cool and comforting.

Her father coughed with the pretence of clearing his throat but seemed to be buying himself some time.

After what seemed like a minute he said, 'I was clearing out the attic. Yesterday. I can't even remember why—I needed something, for my bike.' He ran his tongue over his bottom lip. 'And I found all the boxes of your mother's. All her baking things—tins and, I don't know, rolling pins and whatnot. It's in the car.' He indicated to outside with a nod of his head. 'I thought you might like it. Might be able to use them, I don't know.

Could be too old.' He paused and took in a breath through his nose. 'I think she would have liked you to use them.' He looked around again, breathed in the smell of freshly baked sponge cake. Then he reached into his back pocket and held something out for Rachel. 'I found this as well.'

She reached forward and took the brown envelope he proffered. Inside was a photograph. A little creased and faded but clear enough. A picture of Rachel as a little girl sitting on a huge wooden table, her legs dangling, her hands full of chocolate croissant, while her mum rolled out pastry next to her, both of them laughing at a joke that she could no longer remember.

Rachel felt her breath catch in her throat.

'Your grandmother was right,' her dad said as he twisted his handkerchief round and round with his fingers. 'She would have been proud.'

Rachel glanced up, barely able to look him in the eye, so wanting what he was saying to be genuine.

'I was wrong before. I should never have said what I did. She would have loved this,' he added.

'Too bloody right,' her grandmother scoffed.

Rachel tore her eyes from the picture and stared up at her dad, watching as a smile spread slowly across his face and he said, 'I think the place looks magnificent.' Then, walking over to admire the selection of cakes already on display in the glass counter, added, 'It's about time there was a new bakery.'

CHAPTER TWENTY-ONE

The day of the grand opening of The Squashed Croissant the sun glistened like the dying embers of a fire. There had been a flurry of snow overnight but not enough to have settled, just to coat the pavement like frosting. Now in the hazy sunshine the layer of white was melting to nothing.

Rachel had been up at dawn, the sky still dark, her big coat wrapped tight around her and her hat pulled low as she unlocked the double doors, switched on the lights and started on the bread-baking for the big day, her hands shaking with excitement and nerves as she shaped the loaves.

At seven-thirty, as the baguettes rose to a crisp golden brown in the oven, the croissants puffed and cracked, and light from the little shop shone in the empty square, there was a tap on the door. Drawn out from the back kitchen, Rachel glanced in the mirror and found her face was dotted with flour and her hair was scruffy in the ponytail she'd dragged it into earlier that morning. She tried to make herself look vaguely presentable on her way through to the front.

The man at the door had his back to her; he was moving from one foot to the other, alternating between blowing on his hands and clutching his leather jacket tight around him. His dark hair was long at the back flicking out over his turned-up collar.

She narrowed her eyes, incredulous, then walked over and unbolted the door, opening it enough to be able to poke her head through.

'Ben?' she said, unable to hide the wary surprise in her voice.

He turned, arms spread wide, and greeted her with his infamous half-smile. 'Babe.'

'Oh, good God.' Rachel shook her head. The fact she had barely recognised him before he turned around surprised her. 'What are you doing here?'

'I've missed you,' he said, running his hands through his overlong hair, slicking it back, and then blew into them again. 'Let me in, hon. It's freezing out here.'

He took a step forward assuming she'd open the front door fully but Rachel didn't move.

'I can't,' she said, if anything closing the door a fraction more.

Ben stamped his feet on the step to try and warm himself up, and, hanging his head like a shamed puppy, looked up at her through dark lashes. 'Come on, babe, I'm here in the morning—see, it's getting light. I thought what would it take to get Rachel to see me again, and I knew—it'd be showing up in the morning. The proper morning, you know, not the middle-of-the-night morning.' He laughed to himself. 'Come on,' he said again. 'I'm dying for some food.'

Rachel looked at him, stared at the beautiful eyes, the thick dark hair, the chiselled cheekbones and the stunning, heartbreakingly kissable lips. The ratty leather jacket and the scruffy, worn jeans. The teeth slightly crooked. And she waited.

She waited for the flutter in her chest.

But it wouldn't come. Instead she saw an average drummer in inappropriate clothing.

'Go home, Ben,' she said with a smile. 'And then come back in an hour and a half when I open.'

Ben was momentarily taken aback but covered it quickly, then he crossed his hands over his heart and in a mock-pleading voice whined, 'Babe, you're killing me. I've really missed you. Come on. Come on. Let me make it up to you.' His eyes crinkled at the corners when he smiled at her, making her think of Philippe, and she annoyed herself for wishing that it were him rather than Ben standing on her doorstep. 'Come on, babe, you know you want to let me in.'

Rachel shook her head, realising all of a sudden how far she had come, how far in the past that part of her life was now. 'See you in a couple of hours, Benjamin,' she said, then, taking a step back, closed the door, twisting the lock and walking away across the Victorian tiles back to the kitchen where her loaves were waiting.

Her grandmother and Jackie arrived at eight ready to help her with the preparations. Jackie had three bottles of Dom Perignon stuffed into her bag and her grandmother was all dressed up, the diamonds she kept for special occasions glinting round her neck. As they giggled away excitedly Rachel feared the pair of them might be more of a hindrance than a help.

'Shall we have a toast, Rach?' Jackie held up one of the bottles of champagne.

Rachel was about to nod when she realised there was one more thing she needed to do before she opened the shop. 'Can we wait ten minutes for the champagne?' she said, grabbing her coat from the back of the chair next to her. 'There's just something I need to do.'

Jackie shrugged. 'Yeah, OK. Do you need any help?'

Rachel shook her head. 'No. Thanks, though. I won't be more than five, ten minutes.'

She felt their eyes on her as she reached under the counter, picked up the plastic bag that she'd had stashed there for a while, and jogged out of the door.

Outside it was bitter. The sun was deceptive as the air sparkled with soft rays but the cold sliced like lightning as Rachel dashed down the road. The cobbled streets were starting to come to life, the lights in the other shops flicking on, people scraping ice off their car windscreens, kids wrapped up on the way to school kicking the remains of the snow flurry. Rachel kept her head down and strode past the village hall and away from the square up the road to the church. As she pushed open the wrought-iron gate to the cemetery she could have navigated the route with her eyes closed. Underneath the old oak tree in the far corner and just next to a bush of white winter roses was her mum's grave.

As she approached she noticed fresh flowers that had obviously been laid by her father. He never bought anything from the florist, always made a bunch from whatever was in the garden. Today was holly leaves with red berries and Lenten roses, and next to them a small posy of crocuses, which she assumed her grandmother had brought.

Rachel fumbled around with the bag that she had under her arm and pulled back the plastic to reveal the French Christmas branch that Chantal had given her, the silver ribbons dancing in the sunlight.

'So I've been meaning to bring this to you,' Rachel said, plumping the branches out and straightening the ribbons to make it look its best. 'But it's never felt like the right time. Now though…' She looked around just to check there was no one else around to hear her talking to her mum. 'Now I feel like I can give it to you. It's a French Christmas tree. It might not look like one but it is. Or actually it's a good luck branch…' She laughed as she remembered Chantal bringing it round to her flat. 'You see, I went to Paris for this baking competition. Yes, I know, I said I'd never bake…but, well, you see…'

And Rachel sat down on the tree stump just to the left of her mum's grave and told her all about Paris, about Chantal and Madame Charles, Philippe and Henri, and about every single thing she baked. As she did she felt the weight of years of isolation and anger lift. She talked and talked as the snow around her slowly melted and the sun rose higher until she heard the church bells ring and realised, not only was it time to go back, but it was the first conversation she'd had here when her eyes weren't streaming with tears.

'God, Mum, I was only meant to be ten minutes.' Rachel stood up and dusted off the back of her coat. Then she picked up the branch, looked at it with a smile, and placed it down alongside her dad's flowers. 'Happy belated Christmas,' she said. 'Wish me luck. I have to go and open my bakery now.'

Rachel started to walk away, pulling her sleeves down over her frozen fingers and wrapping her arms tight around her body, but as she took a couple of steps she realised she had one more thing to say and turned back. 'I just wanted to say thank you—thank you for teaching me this—for making me help when I didn't want to, for giving me a passion. I'm sorry I wasted it for so long but I have found it again. And I will do you proud. I promise.'

Scrunching up the plastic bag that the branch had been wrapped in and shoving it in her pocket, Rachel turned and ran from the graveyard as the church bells chimed nine o'clock. Now her eyes were streaming but her lips were smiling, and her coat was flapping open in the cold.

By the time she got back to the bakery there was a queue forming outside already. Red in the face and completely out of breath, Rachel pushed open the door shouting, 'Sorry, sorry, I'm here.'

'Well, it's about bloody time. I'm gasping,' said her grandmother, before popping the cork on another bottle of Dom Perignon.

CHAPTER TWENTY-TWO

The whole of Nettleton was outside. Forming an orderly queue. Rachel's grandmother and Jackie were sozzled and it was only five past nine. The baskets behind the counter were packed with different breads, from crisp baguettes to plump round cottage loaves and fresh white rolls for sandwiches. The counter was full of cakes and chocolates, piles of truffles spilling over, pralines and strawberry creams stacked in pyramids. And then there were the cakes—black forest gateau oozing with cherries, springy Victoria sponge, a beautiful flourless clementine cake were sitting waiting just begging to be sliced. She'd made her trademark macaroons in colours to match the stained-glass ceiling—brilliant reds, bright blues and emerald greens. On the countertop were baskets of croissants and Danish pastries and behind her the coffee machine was bubbling and hissing as Jackie did some overzealous milk frothing.

Rachel had an opening outfit all picked out, but as she'd been so long at her mum's grave she didn't have time to change. Her red spotty dress stayed hanging where it was behind the bathroom door, and instead she got ready to open up still wearing her tatty jeans, faded raspberry T-shirt and white baker's apron that had her name embroidered on the front alongside two little flowers. Checking herself in the mirror, she swiped some of the flour off her cheek and redid her hair.

'Am I OK?' she asked her gran.

'Darling, you're perfect.'

Rachel grinned. 'OK, let's open this place up,' she said, looking over to the window where her art-teacher friend had painted a mural of cakes and flowers and swirls around the edges in all the colours of the rainbow to frame the display. Outside she could see the familiar faces of the people from the village as they waited patiently.

Walking over to the door, she took a deep breath, looked heavenward and gave a wink that she hoped her mum saw, then pulled open the door. 'The Squashed Croissant…' she smiled '…is officially open.'

At the front of the queue was her dad and as everyone clapped he leant forward, gave her a kiss on the cheek, then walked straight past her to take his place on one of the high stools by the counter, ordered a coffee and opened up *The Times*, just as he had done nearly every morning of her youth. And that was where he stayed for the rest of the day.

As the rest of the village piled in Rachel and Jackie were rushed off their feet, cutting slices of cake, serving frothy coffees and wrapping up loaves in brown paper. Her grandmother had propped herself up next to Rachel's dad and was reading the paper over his shoulder, making comments about the state of the world in between chatting to her friends when they came in.

Mrs Pritchard had taken a seat at one of the tables and was telling anyone who would listen that she had discovered the tiled floor, and Mr Swanson kept looking proudly up at the ceiling, admiring his handiwork.

As she was putting warm chocolate croissants into a bag for a customer, Rachel heard Ben's voice drawl, 'Well, look, I'm here.' And she glanced up to see him, still in his leather jacket, lounging against the counter. 'Like you said.'

'That's him.' Rachel's grandmother looked up from the paper.

'Who?' her dad asked.

'Rachel's dreadful boyfriend.'

Ben gave his best lopsided grin.

'He's not my boyfriend,' Rachel said, raising her eyebrows, trying to shut her grandmother up. 'You're not my boyfriend,' she said to Ben.

'I could be though, babe. If you'd let me.' Ben then turned and reached out to shake her father's hand. 'Benjamin Porter, possible future son-in-law.'

'Ignore him, Dad, we are not in a relationship. Jackie, can you serve the people who have just sat at table four?' Rachel shouted.

'I don't like you,' her grandmother said, peering at Ben over her bifocals.

'Sweetheart.' Ben put his hand over his heart as if she'd wounded him. 'Don't knock a man when he's down,' he said, then added, 'At least give me a chance to persuade you otherwise.' After a wink and a flash of his trademark smile, her grandmother, to Rachel's horror, did a little giggle.

'Oh, good God.' Rachel rolled her eyes and turned away from the three of them just in time to see a group of familiar faces burst through the door in a cloud of chatter and laughter.

'Rachel!' she heard them shout. 'We're here!'

Almost unable to believe her eyes, Rachel watched as Abby, George, Ali, Cheryl, Lacey and Tony bustled towards the counter.

'No way! I can't believe you're all here.' Rachel stood, flabbergasted, almost dropping the croissant she was holding with her tongs. She had sent out invitations to everyone that she knew—beautiful postcards that she'd had printed of the chandeliers and stained glass twinkling in the morning light—but she hadn't actually expected anyone to turn up.

'We wouldn't miss this, hon. No chance.' Abby reached over the trays of pastries to pull Rachel into a hug. 'Congratulations. The place looks—' she did a three-sixty and took it all in, from the Paris pictures to the lavishly decorated windows '—awesome.'

'Get some teas on the go, love. I've had a long journey.' George blew out a breath and took a seat on one of the high stools next to where Ben and her father were chatting.

As the others stood around him and oohed and ahhed over the cakes and the decorations, Lacey came up to the counter. Dressed in beige slacks and a turquoise twinset, she looked a lot softer than she had in Paris. She folded her arms across her chest and said to Rachel, in an almost conspiratorial whisper, 'He was a hard taskmaster.'

'Who? Chef?' Rachel paused as she poured the teas.

Lacey nodded. 'Toughest month of my life,' she said with a sigh, lifting her glasses that dangled on their diamanté chain up to her eyes so she could inspect the Danish pastries. 'He nearly killed me. I woke up most days cursing you for not winning.'

Rachel laughed. 'I got off lightly, then,' she said, handing George and Abby their mugs of Earl Grey.

'Three Black Forest for table four, Rachel,' Jackie shouted.

Lacey shook her head. 'I honestly nearly died. I was up at half past three every day. Every day. It was worse than when I had my children. He gave me some good tips, though. I'll email you the best ones.' She looked up at Rachel over the top of her glasses. 'This place is impressive. Well done.'

'Thank you,' Rachel said, cutting great slices from the Black Forest gateau for the group of grannies on table four, somehow the fact that Lacey had said it making her feel even more proud. 'So what are you going to do now you've learnt from the master?'

'Well, would you believe it, but I'm actually going into business with Marcel, of all people.' Lacey gave a snort of laughter. 'My husband and I spent a lot of time with him over the month I was working for Chef and we think we can do something together.' Pushing her glasses up into her hair, she did a wry little smile and said, 'When he's not trying to get someone into bed he's really rather bright and ambitious.'

'Lacey and Marcel are going to conquer the international restaurant business.' Abby leant her elbows on the counter and put her chin in her hands. 'From London to Paris—his Armagnac, her cooking! LOL.' Then she put her hand over her mouth. 'Sorry, I shouldn't say LOL out loud, should I? Too much time with my kids.'

Just then who should slope in but Marcel himself. Cigarette behind his ear, big red woollen scarf wrapped round his neck and a navy-blue car coat hanging half unbuttoned. On his feet were scuffed cowboy boots with his artfully faded jeans tucked into the tops. He'd had his hair cut since Rachel had last seen him and it was cropped neat to his head; at the same time he'd let his dark stubble grow, the look somehow bringing out his eyes and cheekbones so he loped in looking like a Hollywood film star. When he went round the counter and kissed Rachel on both cheeks, grasping her shoulders tight and drawling, 'You are as successful as you are beautiful,' Ben's jaw nearly fell through the floor while every woman in the place flumped up their hair and sneaked a quick look in whatever reflective surface they could find.

Marcel stood back and did a slow, lazy glance around the bakery. 'Very nice.' He nodded. 'Very nice. Our restaurant, Lacey, it should have some of this—' he shrugged '—*je ne sais quoi.*'

Rachel could barely believe the two of them were pairing up; it was such an incongruous duo. But she watched amused and impressed as Lacey took out a pad and started scribbling down Marcel's ideas.

'Oh, Rachel, guess what.' Abby leant over and tapped her on the shoulder to get her attention.

'Three coffees, Rachel,' Jackie shouted.

'Guess what?' Rachel said to Abby, her back to her as she flicked the coffee grinder on and grabbed three cups from the shelf above the machine. The steam billowed out, fogging up her glasses so she had to wipe them on her apron.

'Guess. You won't be able to guess,' Abby said, tapping her fingers on the counter and practically hopping with excitement.

'I'm crap at guessing. Tell me,' Rachel said distractedly as she put her glasses back on and realised she'd pressed the wrong button on the machine. She sighed as she clicked the coffee on and watched the dark liquid pour into the cups while laying teaspoons onto the saucers.

'She's going to be on the TV,' said George, his mouth full of almond croissant.

Rachel turned and made a face, confused.

'He's right.' Abby nodded. 'I'm going on *The Great British Bake Off*,' she said, proudly. 'I'm going to meet Paul Hollywood.'

'You're not?' Rachel scoffed with disbelief as she laid the coffees onto a tray.

'I am, I am, Rachel, and I'm determined that I'm going to win. I've been practising and practising. You wouldn't believe my macaroons nowadays—they shine like I've bloody hairsprayed them. Put yours to shame.' She winked.

Rachel rolled her eyes. 'Are you really? You're not lying?'

Abby shook her head.

'I can't believe you're going to be on the TV,' Rachel said, amazed, then looked over Abby's shoulder for Jackie and, when she couldn't find her, excused herself to serve the coffees to a table of PTA parents.

When she came back Cheryl and Ali were standing to the left of the counter tasting her Victoria sponge and lemon drizzle cake.

'Are you two still baking?' Rachel asked, sweeping her hair out of her eyes, trying to get round them so that she could carry on serving. She could see Jackie laughing with someone and wondered what she was doing when there was a queue building. Just as Cheryl was about to reply to her question Rachel cut her off, calling, 'Jackie...can you—?' She nodded towards the people waiting.

'You're all right, Rachel,' said one of the teachers who was at the head of the queue. 'There's no hurry.'

Rachel raised her brows at Jackie, who made a face back at her to calm down.

When she turned back to Cheryl and Ali, Rachel was shaking her head, frustrated by Jackie's lack of service speed. 'Sorry, guys, I didn't hear your answer. Are you still baking?'

Cheryl gave a shy nod. 'I still do a bit for my family. I don't want to do more than that. I can't take the criticism. I was devastated when I left the competition.'

'Oh, you shouldn't have let Chef get to you.' Rachel frowned.

'He didn't, not really.' She shook her head. 'It was good for me. I feel much braver. But I just want to keep my baking for pleasure. I don't need it tied up with any stress. Do you know what I mean?'

Rachel nodded. 'I do, I understand completely.' She smiled, but turned away, distracted, checking that everyone had what they needed and wiping down the countertop. When she glanced up Cheryl gave her a look that seemed to see right into her.

'You make sure that you do the same, Rachel,' Cheryl said softly. 'Keep it fun.'

'Oh, I will,' Rachel said quickly as she carried on wiping down the counter.

'I think what she's trying to say, darling—' her grandmother came over and draped an arm over her shoulder '—is calm down and enjoy yourself. It's your opening day. You're meant to be having a lovely, jolly time. Your friends are here to see you. No one minds if they have to wait a minute or two for a slice of cake. Now, have a glass of champers.' She thrust a plastic flute into her hand and then said to Ali, 'Who are you, young man?'

'I'm Ali. I like to experiment with flavour combinations.'

Rachel's grandmother snorted. 'Don't we all, darling, don't we all?' she said with a laugh, then added, 'I'm really quite taken with that French chap,' before wandering off in the direction of Marcel.

Rachel took a moment to pause. She felt Cheryl watching her, smiling, as she stopped and took a step back, leant against the counter at the back and watched the bakery in front of her. All the tables were taken and everyone had a slice of cake or a bun and they were chatting and laughing, the noise rising and echoing round the wide open space. The queue at the counter had diminished down to Mrs Beedle from the antique shop down the road, who was deliberating over which was the best cake. Jackie was sipping champagne with Ben, rolling her eyes at his poor chat-up lines, and her father had his nose buried in the paper, a fresh mug of tea steaming on the counter next to him. Then in front of her all her Paris friends were chatting and laughing and catching up and she watched them, still amazed that they'd made the trip to her opening day.

'Abby,' she said, suddenly ashamed that she had been so distracted, 'I don't think I gave your TV appearance enough attention. It's so exciting, and deserves a toast.' Rachel reached into the fridge behind her and took out another bottle of bubbles, popped the cork and, lining up eight mugs, poured them all a cup.

'To Abby,' Rachel said with a smile. 'A future television star. No playing dirty, though!' she added with a laugh.

Abby raised a brow. 'I wouldn't dare. I learnt my lesson.'

They all clinked mugs and just before they took a sip George added, 'I think we should toast Henri as well. Without him all this would be…' He blew out a breath as if to say, nothing.

Abby looked dubious but Rachel nodded. 'I think that's a good idea.'

'To Henri Salernes,' they said in unison, and as they took another gulp the bell above the door chimed and Rachel looked up in horror expecting Henri to walk in, as if by toasting him they might have conjured him up.

But it was only little Tommy coming in with his mum.

She exhaled with relief. As much as she was grateful to Chef, she didn't need him there terrifying her today of all days. She had sent an invitation to the pâtisserie that was addressed jointly to Henri, Françoise and Philippe, but she had heard back from only Françoise who was sorry to say she would be in Bordeaux that week. Rachel was embarrassed to admit that, while she hadn't wanted to send an invite just to Philippe, she was secretly hoping he might walk in through the door. In fact, every time the doorbell went she found herself looking up, nervous that it might be him but pathetically hopeful at the same time.

'Miss Smithson, Miss Smithson.' Tommy legged it up to the counter. 'I'm allowed to have anything I want my mum says,' he shouted, practically pouncing on the counter, his hands and nose pressed against the glass. 'I want one of those cakes with wings.'

'Say please, Tommy.' Mrs Swanson sighed.

'Please,' he said quickly, then with the same breath, 'Oh, look, there's my angel! You've got my angel up there.' Tommy stood back and looked up at the shelf behind Rachel where his home-made angel was perched between the picture of her and her mum that her dad had found, and a black lacquered Christmas bauble with a crack down the back.

As everyone glanced up to admire the cardboard angel Lacey pointed to the Russian bauble and said, 'Isn't that from that shop in Paris?'

Rachel turned to look up; she'd actually intended to take it down before opening, realising how stupid and sentimental it was to have it hanging there, but with everything that had been going on she had forgotten.

'Is that the one the lovely Philippe gave you?' Abby asked with a knowing grin.

'Philippe who?' said Jackie, who was just that moment walking past with a tray of lemon slices.

Rachel blushed scarlet, tried to ignore the look of piqued interest on Jackie's face, and this time actually was saved by the bell, because as the door swung open to her absolute delight in bustled Chantal and Madame Charles.

'Rachel, *ma petite*.' Chantal came straight over to the counter, her camel coat covered in a light dusting of white as outside it had started to snow lightly again.

'I didn't think you'd make it,' Rachel said as she kissed her on both cheeks. 'You said you couldn't come.' Chantal had written Rachel a long letter telling her all about her trips to visit her daughter and meeting her lovely new soon-to-be-son-in-law, but also letting her know that a visit to Nettleton wasn't on the cards for her at the moment as she'd spent so much money going back and forth to Nice.

'I persuade Madame Charles that we take a trip to England. That her life is very busy.' Chantal raised a brow to show that was clearly a lie. 'She needed a holiday. We have been to Hampton Court and Buckingham Palace and guess where we stay?'

'The Ritz?' Rachel said, hazarding a guess based on Madame Charles's Louis Vuitton bag, Chanel jewellery and chic designer coat.

'Ah, *mais oui, mais oui.* It was superb.' Chantal kissed her fingers. '*Très bon.* There are taps in the suite that are gold. I have never seen anything like it.' Then she looked around the bakery, at the knick-knacks that were lined up on the shelf behind Rachel, the mismatched china and the eclectic array of tables and chairs, the snow-globe Blu-Tacked to the till. 'It is like the little flat, *non*?'

'*Oui.*' Rachel laughed. 'I was inspired.'

As the day sloped into evening the party carried on. When the cakes disappeared to crumbs on their stands, Rachel went into the back to whip up whatever she could to keep people satisfied. She hadn't expected the turnout, nor had she thought people would stay long into the evening. All her Paris baking friends hung around chatting and laughing, planning Abby's bakes for the TV and listening as Tony told funny stories about the useless pupils at his school and Lacey recounted more anecdotes about her month with Chef. Madame Charles popped out the front to have a cigarette and was joined by Marcel. When they disappeared for half an hour Rachel worried that

Marcel had had his wicked way with her, but they actually returned with a crate of champagne from the pub, which Madame Charles had put on her gold card.

'To make the evening a little more comfortable,' she said with a wry smile and all the teachers looked absolutely delighted.

Rachel's grandmother was having a little snooze in the corner, readying herself to keep going for the night, while Rachel, helped by Chantal, laid out candles on every table and along the surfaces so, when they dimmed the main chandeliers, the place sparkled like a Christmas tree.

It was only as the church bells struck one a.m. and the last people, Marcel, Rachel's grandmother, Jackie and Abby, left for home—whose home Marcel went to, Rachel wasn't sure—that Rachel finally allowed herself to pronounce the day a success. To lean against the door, her head resting on the glass, look up at the painted ceiling and think, *I did it. I made it.*

And I loved every second of it.

Her only regret was that she had glanced over every time the door had opened it had never been him.

CHAPTER TWENTY-THREE

June 27th

'You didn't go?' Jackie slammed her cup down in its saucer.

Rachel shook her head. 'It was really busy here.' She pointed around the tiny bakery, at the loaves racked up along the shelf behind her and the trays of summer fruit tarts, mint chocolate eclairs, strawberry cream horns and her newly invented cumquat and maraschino cherry truffles, as if to show all the work that had kept her in Nettleton.

'And you only think to tell me about it now. When it's too late?'

'I knew you'd make me go.'

'Too bloody right. Christ Almighty. You fool.'

'She's quite right, you know,' her grandmother shouted from out the back where she was rolling out some filo pastry squares. 'You're a fool, Rachel Smithson.'

'Don't say that,' Rachel said with a grimace, unnecessarily rearranging a tray of hazelnut praline *millefeuille*.

'Oh, give me one of them while you're there.' Jackie tapped the glass counter, pointing at some chocolate tarts topped with fresh-picked summer berries. 'I mean, come on. Christ, everyone makes mistakes. Poor bloke. He married the wrong person. What did you want— fresh out the box? Or did you think there'd be someone better here? Hello. Have you seen an eligible male in Nettleton? Ever?'

Rachel made a face, pulled out a tart and plonked it on a plate. 'Stuff that in your mouth and don't mention this again.'

Her gran walked forward, wiping her hands on a tea towel then checking her hair in a hand mirror. 'Yes, you really are a fool. That's a very good word. Have you learnt nothing? Chances, Rachel, they're for the taking.'

'Yes, yes, I've got it now, thank you. Remember he didn't come to the opening.'

'You didn't invite him!' Jackie almost shouted, exasperated.

'I did.' Rachel sulked.

'A group invite with his brother and the girl who works in the pâtisserie doesn't count. You hardly made him feel special.'

'I wanted to leave it casual.'

Jackie scoffed. 'Casual smashual. You told him you didn't want him until he was sure he knew what he wanted. Maybe it wasn't the right time for him.'

Rachel tried to make herself look busy faffing about with the coffee machine. 'Well, maybe I don't know what I want. Maybe I'm not ready now.'

'Rachel, you've been ready for yonks,' Jackie said round a mouthful of chocolate tart. 'I've never known you to be more ready. You should be in Paris standing under the Eiffel Tower right now, or yesterday or whenever it was. You're an idiot.'

'Oh, it would have just been so romantic.' Her grandmother sighed.

'Shut up,' Rachel said with her hands over her ears. 'Shut up, both of you. Just shut up.' Yanking off her apron, she went outside with the excuse of checking the window display but really she just needed some air.

On the pavement she stood with her hands on her hips and looked up to the powder-blue sky, at the starlings, swooping and diving, and the big candy-floss clouds sliding across each other, then she shut her eyes and counted to ten.

When she opened them again there was a figure walking up the street from the station, jacket slung over his arm, light blue shirt undone at the neck, hair that needed a cut just flicking the edge of his collar.

Rachel watched, her hand shading her eyes from the late morning sunshine as he got closer and closer. She could feel her heart beating in her chest, could hear it in her ears.

He stopped just a foot away. *'Bonjour,'* he said, raking a hand through his hair.

'H-hello,' she stuttered, dropping her hand down to her side.

'You missed a beautiful view from the Eiffel Tower.' His expression was unreadable. 'It looks good in the summer.'

She looked down, toying with the embroidery on the trim of her T-shirt. 'I know. I'm sorry.'

A wisp of cloud inched its way over the sun, dappling the pavement, while the leaves on the avenue of lime trees made patches of shade dance on the street. Rachel didn't know quite what to say, how to make up for the fact she had stood him up.

But then he smiled. *'De rien.* I didn't think you'd be there.'

'No?'

He shook his head. 'Nice bakery.'

'Thanks. Why are you here, then?' she asked, not quite able to look up at him.

'Well, I've made a lot of changes in my life. I no longer sit in an office. My ex-wife is now happily settled with her partner. I'm pretty sure I know what I want in life. My brother is calmer, happier, although he's still waiting for his favourite baker to visit. But it has all taken a little longer than I first expected. When an invite comes for your new bakery I realise that I am not going to come because I do not know yet what it is that I want. And Henri he says, *You should go*, but I think, she doesn't want me there until I am ready. That is what she has said.'

Rachel scuffed her foot against a weed on the pavement, thinking how she'd been waiting for him to walk through the door. How she'd secretly been annoyed when he hadn't turned up. How she had indeed told him that he needed to take the time to work out what he wanted for himself and come to her only when he was ready. How she had completely ignored her own rational advice and jumped straight to the thought that he had rejected her. She kicked the weed a little more, ashamed to look up in case he saw the look in her eye.

'But then you are not at the tower when you say. And I thought—' He looked up and focused on something he clearly wasn't expecting to see. When he paused she glanced to what had caught his eye and saw the Russian Christmas bauble, where she had hung it by the counter, catching the light through the glass. Then he went on, a little more confidently, 'I thought—' a smile spread across his face as he clearly changed tack '—that it was time to take a holiday. See a bit more of the world.'

'And you chose Nettleton?' she said, looking up at him through her fringe, suddenly a little shy.

But then a loud crash dissipated all the tension and Rachel whipped round to see a tray of chocolate mint thins scattered across the floor and her gran pulling herself back from where she'd been practically lying across the counter to get a good look outside. Jackie was pretending to be engrossed in the remains of her summer-berry tart.

She shooed them away and when she looked back Philippe was trying to keep a straight face. 'I chose Nettleton.'

'Why?' she asked, too quickly. 'I mean, there are lots of nice English villages to visit. What made you choose Nettleton?'

'Well, there are a couple of reasons.' He laid his jacket down over the top of his case. 'First I am starting an MBA in London, which I think is maybe forty minutes from here. So it is a close village for what I am doing. And then—' He waited for a second, took a moment to look around at the picturesque little street. 'Then I need to find somewhere to open my restaurant. A little place that will be cosy, not too formal, and I liked the look of this place when I look it up on the Internet. I thought I might take a holiday here and see if it is as good as I think it could be.'

Rachel nodded. 'And you like it now you're here.'

He paused. 'It smells good.'

She laughed. 'It does smell good, you're right.'

Philippe took a step forward. 'There is another reason as well, why I have come here.'

'Oh, yes?'

'It is mainly because someone that was right for me was here and I came to find her.'

'You did?'

'I did.'

It was silent for a second. Philippe rolled the cuffs up on his shirt as the dappled light played on his face. Rachel looked down at the apron she still had clutched in her hand, her name and the flowers embroidered across the top, and then she glanced into the bakery at Jackie, who couldn't hide the fact her eyes had popped out of their sockets. And her gran, who was pretending to wipe down the countertop. Then she looked back up to Philippe, his head angled in question, waiting, his eyes disguising a worry that maybe she might send him away back to Paris. His mouth was almost smiling though; he knew that she wouldn't.

'Would you like to come inside for a coffee and a squashed croissant?' she asked.

'I can think of nothing I'd like more.'

Merry Christmas from
Jenny Oliver

Turn the page for some extra-special
festive treats, just for you...

It's time to make yourself a cup of tea, warm up a mince pie (or two) and have a Christmassy chat with Jenny Oliver

What's your favourite thing about Paris?

I have a friend who moved there years ago and now we try and see her once a year, usually at Christmas. We'll go to all the little shops, stop for coffees at the pavement cafés, eat oysters and drink cheap *vin rouge*. This year they stopped the car on the way home and we didn't know why until we looked out and saw that we were right next to the Eiffel Tower—sparkling and beautiful in the dark. It was really magical and by far my favourite memory.

What is your signature baking dish?

I can make a really good lemon cake. The recipe has been passed down in my family and we're not allowed to share it! LOL. (That's not really in the spirit of Christmas, is it…?)

Have you ever had a complete baking disaster?

Always. But most memorable was my school home economics exam when my pastry crumbled and my patisserie cream didn't set, so when the teacher cut a slice all the poor strawberries slithered off the top into a mush at the bottom of the dish. I don't think I did very well.

If you could eat a particular pastry for the rest of your life, what would it be?

Chocolate croissants. I love them. And actually I quite like a *pain au raisin* and an almond croissant as well, so perhaps that should be all types of croissant. Apart from plain, which I always think are very boring (but realise that actually they're quite nice when I eat them—like vanilla ice cream).

Do you think the key to a man's heart really is through his stomach? Is this how Rachel wins over Philippe?!

Mmm, I think it probably helps. Although it doesn't really work for me, because I love baking sweet things and my husband prefers cheese or an apple!

Do you have any unique talents or hobbies?

I can buy a pretty good gift, I think. (Everyone I've given a present to is probably raising their eyebrows right now.)

What is your work schedule like when you're writing?

Very fast and hectic, with quite a lot of moments of angst-ridden contemplation which have to be talked out in great detail. I also take far too many tea breaks.

What can we expect from you in the future?

I think we'll see Rachel and Philippe again, but there's also loads of other characters and ideas popping up in my head jostling for centre stage.

What has been the best part about writing *The Parisian Christmas Bake Off*?

Definitely researching the food. It was the most incredible excuse to go into some of the most beautiful patisseries, tasting the sugariest cakes and flakiest croissants, watching lots of *Bake Off* on the TV and making all my family remember the recipes that we had grown up with. And then hearing back from people who have read it—that's amazing.

What part did you play in your school nativity play?

Always an angel. One of about twenty in the back row secretly hoping that Mary might get stage fright or break her leg. Once I was part of the night sky, dressed head to toe in navy blue… in retrospect I commend them for convincing us that we were vital to the play.

What are your favourite and least favourite parts of Christmas Day?

I love it all! Without exception. Except when it ends. Although I really like Boxing Day as well—an underrated day of pure relaxation—so I don't mind too much.

What are you hoping for under the tree this year?

Beautifully wrapped presents. It's the expectation more than anything else that still hooks me.

Here are the things I can't wait for this festive season

★ Chestnuts that I leave in the oven too long and that are either too hot, or too burnt to eat

★ The TV movies on that channel dedicated to Christmas miles down the list on my Freeview box

★ My tree that always seems too fat and too short

★ Scoring the Christmas supermarket adverts against one another

★ Wrapping up in my warmest scarf and hat to go Christmas shopping on Oxford Street—imagining it all exciting and bustling with people—and then having to go home because it's just too manic and busy

★ My once yearly ice skating

★ Watching my sister ice that cake. (Maybe this year we'll buy a new robin...)

★ Not buying a new robin—I feel bad for the one-legged one already!

And because I love to make a list...here are my ten things I love about Christmas!

It's pretty hard to narrow this down to just ten, but I'm going to give it a go.

Christmas films. There's a channel that pops up every year that plays nothing but Christmas movies—really bad American ones made just for TV and those are my favourite, but I won't say no to *Scrooged* or *Miracle on 34th Street*. To my shame, I hadn't seen *It's A Wonderful Life* till recently, but I saw it for the first time on the big screen at the BFI, and afterwards stepped out on to the South Bank, where the stalls of the Christmas market were twinkling and everyone was sipping mulled wine and eating hot doughnuts. Now it's a ritual...

Christmas rituals. I love them! I think it's because I'm a massive fan of tradition and not a massive fan of change! Anything I can set in stone as a yearly tradition, I will. And generally it's the expectation that makes me love it rather than the event itself. Like a Christmas shopping day in London—the early coffee and croissant before I start is the best bit...after that I get fed up with the crowds and the too-hot shops! But I still go every year without fail.

Christmas Parties. Nothing like a good canapé and a glass of bubbles, although I wish it were the eighties and everyone wore velvet and diamonds to Christmas soireés.

Christmas shop windows. Selfridges, Harrods, Harvey Nicks. I don't always go in, but just stand outside admiring and thinking what a fun job it would be. Peter Jones has some pretty clever ones already—making reindeer out of Dyson vacuum cleaners and owls out of cutlery... I'll tweet a pic (@JenOliverBooks) so you can see for yourselves.

Christmas presents. I'm probably meant to say the giving of gifts here not the getting, but I really, really like unwrapping presents! Eking it out for as long as possible (something I'm much too old to still be doing) and feeling a bit sad when it's over. I do also love buying people presents—I spend an inordinate amount of time thinking about what will make the perfect gift.

Ice skating. I am not particularly adept at this, but I try and pretend I'm in *The Cutting Edge*.

All my family together—since everyone's got married, moved away or had children, it gets harder and harder for all of us to be in the same room at the same time, but at some point during the festive period this usually happens and I love it. There are inevitably drunken arguments, tantrums (from the adults about who got the better presents!) and bickering over poorly remembered family memories, but for me that's part of the fun.

My upstairs neighbour, who refuses to say hello for the rest of the year, posts a Christmas card with a Ferrero Rocher sellotaped to it through our letterbox.

The Christmas walk. It's cold, dark and everyone's nearly asleep, but someone mentions the walk and we all have to get up, put our new Christmas scarves and gloves on and go for a stroll. We never go further than round the block and spend most of the time peering nosily into other people's windows at their post-Christmas routines and stuffing Quality Streets into our mouths as we walk, but it's another Christmas ritual!

The fact that, as my husband tells me every year in case I forget, the image of Santa Claus we see today—plump, cheerful and dressed in red—seems to owe quite a lot to Coca Cola. (http://www.coca-colacompany.com/stories/coke-lore-santa-claus) Love this or hate it, it's not a conversation topic if you get stuck at one of those Christmas parties where everyone should be wearing velvet and diamonds! ;-)

What are your favourite things about Christmas? Tweet me (@JenOliverBooks) and let us know... I'm always keen for a new ritual.

Merry Christmas, I hope everyone gets what they wish for!

Jen x

Inspired by Rachel and her passion for baking utterly
delicious French patisserie delicacies, here is
Jenny Oliver's guide to Christmas baking—
with a Parisian twist!

The
Parisian Christmas Bake Off
Guide
To
Festive
Feasting

Throw on an apron and whizz up some of these delicious, mouth-watering recipes.

Don't forget to pour yourself a nice drink!

Let the Bake Off begin...

Recipes:

★ Rainbow Macaroons

★ Chocolate Profiteroles

★ Spinach and Feta Filo Pie

★ Henri's Bread

★ Madeleines

★ Candy Cane Squares

★ Coffee Éclairs

★ Berry Kir Royale

Rainbow Macaroons

For me, macaroons = Paris!

Make your own rainbow macaroons with this easy recipe.

- 125g ground almonds
- 200g icing sugar
- 3 free-range egg whites
- 2tbsp caster sugar
- ½tsp cream of tartar
- A pinch of powdered food colouring (choose any colour you would like to get the rainbow macaroons started!)

For the delicious chocolate filling:
- 200g dark chocolate
- 200ml double cream
- 1tsp brandy
- 15g unsalted butter

Method
1. Preheat the oven to 160°C/Gas mark 2.
2. Use a food processor to blend the almonds and icing sugar until they are well combined.
3. Whisk (an electric whisk is completely optional but advisable!) the egg whites until stiff peaks form when the whisk is removed. Then slowly whisk in the cream of tartar and caster sugar until the mixture is smooth.
4. Gently fold in the food colouring (any colour of your choice) and blended almonds and icing sugar until the mixture resembles shaving foam.
5. Now for the fun part! Spoon the macaroon mixture into a piping bag fitted with a 1cm round nozzle. Pipe 5cm circles on to a baking tray (don't forget the greaseproof paper). Sharply tap the bottom of the tray to release any air bubbles from the macaroons. Then set aside for 60 minutes.
6. Bake the macaroons in the oven for 10-15 minutes. Remove

from the oven and carefully peel away the greaseproof paper and set aside to cool.

7. For the scrumptious chocolate filling, heat the double cream and chocolate in a saucepan over a low heat until smooth and well combined. Add the brandy and butter and stir until smooth, then remove from the heat and set aside to cool.

8. Use the gooey filling to sandwich the macaroons together, then chill in the fridge for 30 minutes. Congratulations! You have now made the perfect macaroons!

Chocolate Profiteroles

Become a profiterole fan, just like Rachel. (Honestly, these are *much* easier to make than you think. Give them a go. Ooooh, and post me some!)

For the choux pastry:
- 200ml cold water
- 4tsp caster sugar
- 85g unsalted butter
- 115g plain flour
- pinch of salt
- 3 medium eggs

For the cream filling:
- 600ml double cream
- A handful of orange zest

For the chocolate sauce:
- 100ml water
- 80g caster sugar
- 200g delicious dark chocolate

Method
1. Switch on your oven to 200°C/Gas mark 6.
2. For the choux pastry, place the water, sugar and butter into a saucepan. Heat gently until the butter has melted (try not to burn it). Then pour in the flour and salt.
3. Remove from the heat and beat the mixture until a smooth paste is formed. Transfer to a pretty bowl and leave to cool for approximately 10-15 minutes.
4. Beat in the eggs, a little at a time, until the mixture is smooth.
5. Then, using a piping bag and plain 1cm nozzle, pipe the mixture into small balls in neat lines across a baking sheet.

Handy tip: gently rub the top of each ball with a wet finger.

6. Bake for 25–30 minutes or until golden brown.
7. Now for the tricky part: prick the base of each profiterole with a skewer. Place back on to the baking sheet with the hole in the base facing upwards and pop it back in the oven for 5 minutes.
8. For the delicious filling, lightly whip the cream with the orange zest. When the profiteroles are cold, use a piping bag to pipe fill the profiteroles.
9. For the chocolate sauce, place water and sugar into a saucepan and bring to the boil to make a syrup. Then place the delicious chocolate into a bowl set over the pan. When the chocolate has melted, pour the syrup mixture into the chocolate and stir until smooth.
10. Add the final touch by pouring the chocolate sauce over the profiteroles.
11. Eat them all, then whip up a whole new batch. No one will ever know!

Spinach and Feta Filo Pie

Try this exquisite savoury dish that will melt in your mouth. It (almost) wowed Chef Henri—I hope you love it!

- 2-3tbsp vegetable oil
- 2 onions
- 600g feta cheese
- 450g baby spinach leaves
- 100g pistachios—please remove the shells
- A pinch of salt and freshly ground black pepper
- 150g melted unsalted butter
- 20 sheets of filo pastry

Method
1. Switch the oven to 160°C/Gas mark 2.
2. Heat the oil in a frying pan and add the chopped onions, frying gently until lightly browned.
3. Mix the browned onions, feta, spinach and pistachios in a bowl and season.
4. Grease an ovenproof dish with some melted butter and gently lay a sheet of filo pastry at the bottom, brushing over with melted butter. Repeat this process with another four sheets of filo pastry but leave the top layer of pastry unbuttered.
5. Spread some of the onion, feta and spinach mixture on top of the pastry sheets.
6. Then add five more pastry sheets to the dish in layers.
7. Repeat the process with another five pastry layers and some more onion, feta and spinach mixture.
8. Finish with another five sheets of filo pastry.
9. You now cut a criss-cross pattern into the top layer of pastry and pop it into the oven and bake for 30-40 minutes.

Henri's Bread

Bread is 'the food of generations, it is life' according to Henri. So let's get stuck in with this recipe for *le pain*.

- 500g strong flour
- 15g salt
- 55ml olive oil
- 20g yeast
- 275ml water

Method
1. Preheat your oven to 200°C/Gas mark 6.
2. Combine all of the ingredients into a bowl and knead with your hands and knuckles until the dough is elastic and smooth.
3. Cover with cling film and leave to rise for 1 hour.
4. Mould the dough and place it in a baking tin.
5. Pop it into the oven for 35 minutes.
6. Cool on a wire rack.
7. Get stuck in!

Madeleines

For the perfect tea snacks, these small treats will warm you up this winter. Don't forget to use your madeleine tray.

- 2 eggs
- 100g caster sugar
- 100g plain flour
- 1 lemon for juice and zest
- ¾ tsp baking powder
- 100g butter

Method
1. Turn on your oven to 200°C/Gas mark 6.
2. Whisk the eggs and the sugar into a bowl until it is frothy. Lightly whisk in the remaining ingredients and leave to stand for 20 minutes.
3. Carefully pour the mixture into your madeleine tray (brush the tray with melted butter first).
4. Bake until the mixture has risen a little in the middle and is fully cooked through (around 8-10 minutes).

Candy Cane Squares

Tickle your taste buds with this lovely but simple recipe…

- 900g white chocolate
- 12 candy canes, crushed into pieces
- 1tsp peppermint extract

Method

1. Melt the white chocolate in a bowl over a pot of boiling water.
2. Gently stir the crushed candy cane and peppermint extract into the melted white chocolate.
3. Line a baking tray with greaseproof paper.
4. Spread the mixture evenly on to the tray.
5. Allow it to cool in the fridge until it is firm.
6. Break it into pieces and share with friends. Or, my top tip—put it into a plastic bag and smash into bite-size chunks with a rolling pin. Great for Christmas stress relief.

Coffee Éclairs

Become a star baker by mastering this delicious delight…better known to us as fat fingers!

For the éclairs:
- 50g unsalted butter
- 125ml water
- 75g plain flour
- 2 eggs

For the icing:
- 230g fondant icing sugar
- 2tbsp espresso

Some added extras:
- 75g desiccated coconut
- 425ml double cream
- 1tbsp icing sugar
- ½tsp vanilla extract

Method
1. Turn on the oven to 200°C/Gas mark 6.
2. Line a baking tray with some trusty greaseproof paper.
3. Add 125ml of water and the butter into a saucepan, gently melting the butter.
4. Remove from the heat and add the flour, beating the mixture until it is smooth.
5. Return to the heat for 2 minutes.
6. Remove from the heat again and add the eggs (keep beating them) until you have a smooth consistency.
7. Now for the fun part: spoon the dough into a piping bag and pipe 5cm-long éclairs on to the lined baking tray.

8. Bake in the oven until they are golden brown, then set aside to cool on a wire rack.
9. When finally cooled, make a hole in one end of the éclair.
10. For the icing, mix half of the icing sugar with coffee in a small bowl until it has a spreadable consistency.
11. In another bowl, place the fondant icing with 2tbsp of water and mix until combined.
12. Heat a frying pan to toast the coconut until golden brown.
13. Whip the cream with the icing sugar and vanilla extract.
14. Place the whipped cream into a piping bag fitted with a 1cm nozzle and pipe into the éclairs until they are oozing with cream.
15. Dip half of one side of the éclairs in the coffee icing and the other in the plain icing.
16. Add your finishing touch by sprinkling on the toasted coconut!

You have now made your first show-stopping éclairs!

Berry Kir Royale

When it's all getting too much, it's time to refresh yourself with a truly festive drink! Take a break and relax with the following recipe…

- 300ml rosé champagne
- 100g strawberries
- Ice
- Lime zest

Make a raspberry sauce with:
- A large handful of raspberries
- 2tbsp icing sugar

Method
1. Using a blender, mix the strawberries, ice, lime zest and champagne.
2. For the sauce, juice the raspberries and add the icing sugar.
3. Pour yourself a drink by placing a few raspberries into a glass and top it with the raspberry sauce, followed by the champagne mixture. Enjoy!

Jenny Oliver's next book

THE VINTAGE SUMMER WEDDING

is out now

(Turn the page for a sneak peek…)

THE VINTAGE
SUMMER WEDDING
by Jenny Oliver

CHAPTER ONE

They arrived in the dark in a heatwave. As Anna stepped out of the car, all she could smell was roses. An omen of thick, heavy scent. She remembered being knocked off-kilter by a huge vase of them at the Opera House once — big, luxurious, peach cabbage roses — and shaking her head at her assistant, trying to hide her agitation by saying scathingly, *'Terrible flower. So clichéd. Swap them for stargazers or, if you must, hydrangeas.'*

'Wondered whether you two would ever turn up.' Jeff Mallory, the landlord of the new property, a man with a moustache and a belly that sagged over his dark-green cords, heaved himself out of the cab of a white van.

'Sorry, mate.' Seb strode forward, arm outstretched for a vigorous handshake. 'We would have been here earlier but — '

He left the reason hanging in the air. They both knew it was Anna's fault. Stalling the packing at every conceivable opportunity. Dithering over how clothes had been folded and obsessively wrapping everything in tissue paper, then bubble-wrap, until tea-cups were the size of footballs.

'Not a problem.' Jeff shook his head. 'Just been reading the paper, nice to have a bit of time to myself if I'm honest. Nice little cottage this—you'll love it, just right for a young couple.'

Anna turned her head slowly from the view of the field opposite, the pungent smell of cowpats and hay and something else that she couldn't quite put her finger on that had mingled with the sweet roses and was drawing her back in time like a whiff of an old perfume. She let her eyes trail up from the white front gate, the wild over-grown garden, the twee little porch and the carved wooden sign that she knew would spell out something hideous like Wild Rose Cottage and held in a grimace.

You have to try, Anna.

Seb did all the chatting while she opened the car door and grabbed her handbag.

'It's good to be back.' She heard him say, taking a deep breath of country air. 'Really feels good.'

'Well I never thought I'd see the day.' Jeff ran a hand along the waistband of his trousers, hitching them into a more comfortable position. 'Anna Whitehall back in Nettleton.'

She scratched her neck, feeling the heat prickle against her skin, wondering if by some miracle someone had thought to install air-conditioning in this hellhole. 'Me neither, Mr Mallory,' she said. 'Me neither.' She attempted a smile, felt Seb's eyes on her.

'You know I played you at the village Christmas play the other year.' He nodded like he'd only just remembered. 'Best laugh in the house I got. Dressed in a pink tutu, I had to shout, "I'm never coming back, you fuckers. Up your bum."' He snorted with laughter. 'Brought the house down.'

Sweat trickled down between her shoulder blades as she huffed a fake laugh, 'I'm so pleased I left a legacy.'

'Too right you did.' He moved round to the boot of the car to help Seb with the other cases, hauling them out as his trousers slipped lower. Seb was smiling along, trying to smooth out the creases of tension in the air. 'Whole village has been waiting for you to come back,' Mr Mallory went on, regardless.

Seb wheeled a case past her over the uneven road and let his hand rest for a moment on her shoulder. She wanted to shake it off, not good with public shows of sympathy, trying to keep her poise.

'Well, I'm glad I gave them something to talk about.' *This won't be for ever*, she said to herself, as she gathered some of the plastic bags crammed with stuff out from the back seat.

'Gave?' Jeff laughed, as he hauled another case out the boot.

'Oh, mind that—' She ran round and rescued the dress-bag that was being crumpled under the stack of suitcases he was piling up in the street.

'No past tense about it, Anna. Still giving, sweetheart. Still giving.' He laughed.

She folded the Vera Wang bag over her arm and took a deep breath. That was it, that was the smell that, mingled with the rest. The unmistakable scent of small-town gossip. I bet they loved it, she thought. The great Anna Whitehall fallen from her perch. Rubbing their hands together gleefully, hoping she landed with a painful bump.

Well, she'd made it through worse. She may have promised Seb a year, but she was here for as short a time as she could manage. All she had to do was get a decent new job and, she stroked the velvety skin of the dress-bag, get married. The wedding may no longer be at the exclusive, lavish The Waldegrave and it may not have tiny Swarovski crystals scattered over the tables, a champagne reception, forty-four bedrooms for guests and a Georgian townhouse across the street for the bride and groom, a six-tier Patisserie Gerard chocolate frilled cake and bridesmaids in the palest-grey slub silk, but there was still this bloody gorgeous dress and—she looked up at the cottage, a bare bulb hanging from the kitchen window that Seb had clicked on, and took a shaky breath in—well, no, not much else.

They hauled in bag after bag like cart-horses as the dusk dipped to darkness. When Seb handed over the cash for rent, Anna couldn't watch and, instead, drifted from room to room, flicking on lights and opening windows to try and get rid of the stifling heat. But the air was still like the surface of stagnant water, mosquitoes skating over it like ice, buzzing in every room, their little squashed bodies, after she'd spied them, oozing blood on the paisley Laura Ashley wallpaper similar to the type her granny had had.

Looking out from the upstairs bedroom window, she could see Seb talking with Jeff in the street, their shadows as they laughed. She leant forward, the palms of her hands on the cracked, flaking windowsill, and watched as Jeff waved, clambered into his van and cranked the engine and imagined him pootling off to the King's Head pub, his pint in his own silver tankard waiting for him on the bar and a million eager ears ready for his lowdown.

'So what do you think?' A minute later she heard Seb walk across the creaking floorboards as he came to stand behind her, his hands snaking round her waist, the heat of him engulfing her like a duvet.

'It's fine,' she said, leaning her head back on his shoulder and feeling the rumble in his chest as he laughed.

'Damned with faint praise.'

'No, it's really nice. Very cute.' She turned and almost muffled it into his T-shirt so he might miss the lack of conviction.

'Yeah, I think it'll do. It could be much worse, Anna. I think we'll be OK here. Get a dog, plant some vegetables.'

She bit her lip as her cheek pressed into the cotton of his top, swallowed over the lump in her throat and nodded.

He stroked her hair. 'We'll be OK, Anna. Change is never a bad thing. And you never know, you might love it.'

The very thought led to a great wave of nauseous claustrophobia engulfing her and she had to pull away from him. Going over to the big seventies dressing table, she unclipped her earrings and put them down on the veneer surface; the reflection in the big circular mirror showed Seb's profile—wide eyes gazing out across the fields of wheat that she knew from her quick glance earlier was accented with red as the moonlight picked out the poppies. She couldn't miss the wistful look on his face, the softening of his lips.

She wanted to say, 'One year, Seb. Don't get any dreamy ideas. It's not going to happen.' But she wasn't in any position to lay down the rules. The fact that they currently had nothing was her fault. The dream she had been pushing had broken; now it was Seb's turn to try his. And the feeling was like having her hands cuffed behind her back and her smile painted on her face like a clown.

He turned to look at her. 'Think of it like a holiday,' he said with a half-smile.

She thought of her vacations, two glorious weeks somewhere with an infinity pool, cocktails on the beach, restaurants overlooking the sea, basking in blazing sunshine. Or there was schlepping round Skegness with her dad in the rain as a teenager. At the moment, this was more the latter.

'I'm going to have to shower, I'm too hot,' she said, peeling off her silk tank-top, wondering whether, if she just hung it by the window, the little dots of sweat would dry and not stain.

The bathroom was tiny, the grouting brown, the ceiling cracked where the steam had bubbled the paint. She pulled back the mildewed shower curtain and found herself perplexed.

'Seb!' she called.

'What is it?'

'There's no shower.'

'No shower?'

'No shower.'

He stood in the doorway and laughed, 'You're going to have to learn to bathe.'

'Who doesn't have a shower?' she whispered, biting the tip of her finger, feeling suddenly like a pebble rolling in a wake, her façade teetering.

'Primrose Cottage, honeybun.'

Oh, she knew it was going to be called something dreadful like that.

'Home sweet home.'

CHAPTER TWO

'I lay awake most of the night.' She said this without moving, as if her limbs were tied to the sheet. 'And do you know what I could hear?'

Seb was standing at the end of the bed in just his boxer shorts, drinking a glass of water.

'No, honey, what could you hear?' He raised a brow, waiting for it.

'Nothing.'

'Nothing?'

'Nothing. Not a sound. Just total and utter silence. And do you know what I could see?'

'Let me guess…' He smirked.

'Nothing.' She started to push herself up the bed. 'I could see nothing. It was black. Pitch bloody black. I couldn't even have made it to the bathroom if I'd needed to. I couldn't see my fingers in front of my face.'

'I think that's nice. Cosy.'

'It's like being in a coffin buried underground. Where are the street lights? Where are the cars? What does everyone do after ten o'clock? Does no one go out?' She was so tired she wanted to just bury her head under the pillows. The engulfing darkness of the night had made what was bad seem worse. 'I thought the countryside was meant to be being ruined by motorways and lorries and flight paths.' Seb gulped down the last of his water as she pulled the sheet up towards her chin. 'I didn't hear any bloody planes,' she said. 'At least an animal would have been good. A fox or an owl or something. Anything. A cow mooing would have sufficed.'

'Anna, are you going to get up?' Seb said, going over to a suitcase to pull out a shirt he'd ironed before they'd left the Bermondsey flat. Always prepared for every eventuality, she thought. Some Scout motto or something. She saw him look at his watch as she rolled herself in the sheet and turned away so she could stare at the crack in the wallpaper join. The little leaves didn't match up. She thought about the clean white walls of their old place, the wooden floors she padded across to make a breakfast of yoghurt and plump, juicy blueberries.

'You'll be late for work,' he said, looking down at his buttons as he did them up.

While Seb had landed his dream job of teaching at Nettleton High, getting back to his roots as he put it, Anna was about to begin a new career working in a little antique shop that her dad had pulled in a favour for. If her memory served her correctly, it was a grubby hovel that she had had to sit in as a child while he haggled the price of his wares up before he took her to ballet lessons. It was going to pay her six pounds fifty an hour.

'Come on, get up and we can have coffee in the village before I have to go to school.'

'Do you think there's a Starbucks?' she asked, brow raised.

'You know there isn't a Starbucks.' He rolled his eyes.

'It was a joke!' she said, heaving herself up. 'You have to allow me a joke or two.'

'You have to allow me some semblance of enjoying this.'

'I am!' She put her hand on her chest. 'That's exactly what I'm doing. I'm trying, I promise.'

He didn't look at her, just fumbled around in his suitcase trying to find his tie. She bent down and fished one out of the side pocket of a different bag and went over and hung it round his neck.

She thought about the look on his face when she'd told him that The Waldegrave had gone into administration. That all their money was gone. Everything. That even just the loss of the fifty percent deposit was actually the whole shebang. That she hadn't been exactly truthful about the extent of the cost.

And he had turned to the side for just a fraction of a second, clenching his face up, all the muscles rigid, shut his eyes, taken a breath. Then he'd turned back, eyes open, squeezed her hand in his and said, *'It's OK. It'll be OK.'*

She turned his collar up now and laced the tie underneath, knotting it over, and looked up at him and said,

'I will try harder.'

He shook his head and laughed, 'All I want to do is have coffee with you before my first day of school.'

'And that, my darling,' she said with a smile, hauling the sheet further round her like a toga, squashing the part of her that wanted to sneak back under the covers, and kissing him on the cheek, 'is all I want to do, too!'

He raised a brow like he didn't quite believe her but was happy to go with it.

Driving to the village, Seb had trouble with the narrow lanes, bramble branches flicking into the window as he had to keep swerving into the bushes as Golf GTIs and mud-splattered Land Rovers hurtled past on the other side of the road, beeping his London driving.

'It's a fucking nightmare,' he said, loosening his tie, knuckles gripping the steering wheel. 'You just can't see what's coming.'

'I thought you always said you knew these roads like the back of your hand.' Anna straightened the sun-visor mirror to check her reflection. She'd been told by Mrs Beedle, the antiques shop owner, on the phone to wear something she didn't mind getting mucky in. Anna didn't own anything she minded getting mucky. Her wardrobe had predominantly consisted of Marc Jacob pantsuits, J Brand jeans and key Stella McCartney pieces. The only memory of them now were the piles of jiffy bags that she had stuffed them into and mailed out to the highest eBay bidder. For today's outfit she had settled on a pair of khaki shorts that she had worn on safari three years ago and the most worn of her black tank-tops.

'I did. I think they've planted new hedgerows since my day.'

Anna snorted and pulled her sunglasses down from the top of her head, closing her eyes and trying to imagine herself on some Caribbean beach absorbing the wall of heat, about to dive into the ocean, or settled into the box at the Opera House to watch the dress rehearsal, sipping champagne or a double vodka martini.

'*Et voilà,*' Seb said a minute later, cutting the engine and winding up his window.

She opened her eyes slowly, like a lizard in the desert.

There it was.

Nettleton village.

The sight of it seemed to lodge her heart in her throat. Her brow suddenly speckled with sweat.

'OK?' Seb asked, before he opened the door.

Anna snorted, 'Yeah, yeah, fine.' She unclicked her door and let one tanned leg follow the other to the cobbles. Unfurling herself from their little hatchback, she stretched her back and shoulders and surveyed the scene as if looking back over old photographs. Through the hazy morning mist of heat, she could see all the little shops surrounding the village square, the avenue of lime trees that dripped sticky sap on the pavement and cars, the church at the far end by the pond and the playground, the benches dappled with the shade from the big, wide leaves of the overhanging trees. Across the square was the pharmacy, its green cross flashing and registering the temperature at twenty-seven degrees. She looked at her watch, it was only eight o'clock. The window still had those old bottles of liquid like an apothecary's shop, one red, one green. It could have been her imagination playing tricks on her, but she thought she remembered them from when she was a kid. Next to that was the newsagent, Dowsetts. A bit of A4 paper stuck on the door saying only two schoolchildren at a time. Now that she did remember. Three of them would go in deliberately and cause Mrs Norris apoplexy as they huddled together picking the penny sweets out one at a time and pretending to put them in their pockets. Then, when her friend Hermione locked Mrs Norris in the store cupboard one lunchtime, it earned them a lifetime ban. Did that still stand, she wondered. Would she be turned away if she dared set foot inside? Or was it like prison? Twelve years or less for good behaviour?

Nettleton, she thought, hands on her hips, there it was, all exactly as she remembered it.

Seb came round and draped his arm over her shoulders, giving her an affectionate shake. 'Isn't it lovely?'

She forced a little grin.

They strolled over towards a bakery coffee shop, its yellow-striped awning unwound over red café tables and chairs, a daisy in a jam jar on each.

'Charming,' Seb mused, pointing to the cakes in the window—rows and rows of macaroons all the colour of summer and displayed to look like a sunrise, deep reds into lighter pinks and brilliant oranges fading into acid lemon yellows, their cream bursting out the insides and their surfaces glistening in the shade. Like jewels jostling for space. Behind them were trays of summer-fruit tarts, fresh gooseberries sinking into patisserie cream and stacks of Danish pastries with plump apricots drizzled with icing next to piles of freshly baked croissants, steaming from the oven. There was a small queue of people lined up in the cool, dark interior waiting to buy fresh baguettes and sandwiches. 'Truly charming.'

Anna thought back to when she'd picked the wedding cake in Patisserie Gerard. The slices the chef brought over on little frilled-edged plates and metal two-pronged forks, watching as she placed the delicate vanilla sponge or chocolate sachertorte into her mouth and sighed with the pleasure of it. How he had suggested that she had to have between four and six layers, less was unheard of for weddings at The Waldegrave: two chocolate with a Black-Forest-style cherry that would ooze when cut and soaked through with booze, heavy and dense. Then a light, fluffy little sponge on the top, perhaps in an orange or, he suggested, a clementine. Just slightly sweeter. The guests would be able to tell the difference. They'd definitely be the type to appreciate such delicate flavours.

Then, without warning, her mother's voice popped into her head. *We never had a wedding, Anna, and it was a sign.* Anna didn't see the cakes, just her own reflection as the words carried on. *Pregnant with you, Anna, and standing in some crummy registry office with a couple of witnesses he'd dragged in from outside. I didn't even get a new dress. And in those days you didn't have pregnancy clothes, Anna, not the flashy things you have now. Oh no, I had a big hoop of corduroy pleated around my belly like a traffic cone. There were no photos. Thank*

God. But when I think about it now, I know it was definitely a sign. He wanted to gloss over it. A wedding is more than just a day, Anna. It's a statement of intent.

As Seb pulled out a chair and stretched his legs out in the morning sun, Anna perched on the edge of the one opposite and said, 'My mum rang yesterday.'

He twisted his head round to look at her. 'What did she say?'

'That she'd give us the money to get married. All of it.' Seb sat up straighter. Anna licked her lips and pulled her sunglasses down over her eyes. 'As long as I don't invite Dad.'

Seb spluttered a cough. 'You've got to be kidding me. No way. What did you say?'

She brushed some of the creases from her top. 'I said I'd think about it.'

'Anna, you can't not invite your father.'

'Why not? What difference would it make? At least it'd solve my problems.' She paused. 'Maybe then I wouldn't have to invite yours either.' She snorted at her own little joke, but Seb didn't find it as funny as she'd hoped.

'You can't not invite him.' He raked a hand through his hair. 'I can't start my married life on that kind of threat. She's being a bitch.'

Anna bristled. 'She's not, he just hurt her.'

'It was a long time ago, Anna,' he said.

Anna glanced to the side, away from looking directly at Seb and, in doing so, caught a look at the girl behind the counter.

'Oh God, it's Rachel.' Anna whipped round so fast

her sunglasses fell off her head and landed with a clatter on the metal table.

'What? Who?' He stuck his nose right up against the glass. 'No it's not.'

'It is. You're so obvious.' She pulled him back by the arm.

'Well, what's wrong with it being Rachel? I liked Rachel.'

'Urgh, that's because you were a big old square at school just like her.'

'I don't think people say things like that any more. Not when they're grown up.' He raised a brow like she was one of his pupils.

'God, I bet she's loving this.' Anna said, picking up her glasses and sliding them on to cover her eyes. 'Me back here with my tail between my legs. I bet that means Jackie's somewhere about the place as well.'

'Of course she is, Anna, she's a teacher at the school, she helped me get the job.' Seb shook his head at her like she was mad, as Anna started to breathe in too quickly.

'Oh great, that's all I need. Come on, we have to leave.'

'Anna, stop it. This is ridiculous, you're being ridiculous. You're going to see people you used to know.'

And they'll think, stupid Anna, now it's our turn to laugh at her, she thought. *They'll think, what's Seb doing with her? Have you heard, she lost all their cash? Spending outside her means. Running off to London, we all knew it was doomed. Never made it though, did she? Very few do, it's a tough industry to break into. Did you hear she lost her job as well? Tough times though, isn't it? Or the time to cut loose dead wood?*

'I can't sit here.' She started to push her chair away.

'Anna!' Seb raised his voice just a touch. 'Anna, calm down. Sit down.'

'No, I'll see you later. Have a good first day,' she said, grabbing her bag from where she'd slung it over the back of the chair and marching away in the direction of Vintage Treasure. She heard him sigh but couldn't turn round. She caught sight of her reflection in the window of the old gift shop, Presents 4 You, and tried to regain some of her infamous poise. Her eye caught a T-shirt draped over a stack of gift boxes; on it read *Paris, Milan, New York, Nettleton.* In their dreams, she thought, in their dreams. Who would ever want to end up back here?

'How do you like your tea?' A woman's voice called as soon as the bell over the door of Vintage Treasure chimed.

'I'm fine, thanks.' Anna said, her eyes pained by the catastrophe of objects piled around the place.

'That's not what I asked.'

She heard a clinking of teaspoons and the air-tight pop of the lid coming off a tea caddy, and made a face to herself at the woman's tone.

Contemplating describing her love of lapsang souchong, her dislike of semi-skimmed milk and her tolerance for normal tea as long as it wasn't too strong, she thought it easier to reply, 'I just have it white.'

There was no answer, so Anna carried on her journey into the dingy Aladdin's Cave, just relieved to be out of

the scorching heat and the gossiping voices that seemed
to lace the air. Inside, dust swirled in the beams of sunlight that forced their way through the dirty windows
and shone like spotlights on such delights as a taxidermy
crow, its claw positioned on an egg, a crack across the
left-hand corner of the glass box, a dark-green chaise
longue, the back studded with emerald buttons and a
gold scroll along the black lacquered edges. A looming
Welsh dresser stacked full of plates and cups and a line
of Toby jugs with ugly faces and massive noses.

If there was one thing Anna hated, it was antiques.
Anything that wasn't new, anything with money off,
anything that had to be haggled for or marked down.

All it did was remind her of being wrapped up against
the cold, having her mittens hanging from her coat
sleeves, her dad bundling her up at five in the morning
in the passenger seat of his van, a flask of hot chocolate and a half-stale doughnut wrapped in a napkin that
she ate with shaking hands as he scraped the ice off the
inside and outside of the window of his Ford Transit
before trundling off to Ardingly, Newark or some other
massive antique market. She had inherited her mother's
intolerance of the cold. The fiery Spanish blood that
coursed through her veins wasn't inclined to enjoy shiv-
ering in snow-crisp fields, her fingers losing their feeling, her damp lips freezing in the early morning frost as
she trudged past other people's mouldy, damp crap for
sale on wonky trestle tables.

As she edged her way through the maze of a shop,
a woman bumbled out of the back room with a plate
of gingernuts and two mugs of stewed tea clanking

together, their surfaces advertising various antique markets and fairs.

'I made you one anyway,' she said, pushing her glasses up her nose with her upper arm as she pushed the tea on to the glass counter.

Mrs Beedle. How could Anna have forgotten? Huge, dressed in a smock that could have doubled as a tent, round glasses like an owl, white shirt with a Peter Pan collar, red T-bar shoes like Annie wore in the film, a million bracelets clanging up her wrist and pockets bursting with tape measures, pencils, bits of paper and tissues. Her greying hair pulled back into an *Anne of Green Gables*-style do, the front pushed forward like a mini-beehive and a bun held with kirby grips.

'Anna Whitehall, now look at you.' She leant her bulk against the counter, took out her hanky and wiped her brow. 'Still as much of a pain in the arse as you always were, I imagine.'

'Hello, Mrs Beedle,' she said, running a finger along the brass counter edge.

Mrs Beedle narrowed her eyes as if she could see straight inside her. 'Mmm, yes,' she murmured.

Anna licked her lips under the scrutiny of her gaze.

'Now, remember, I'm doing your father a favour, I don't want you here. Got that?' She took a slurp of tea. 'And why he wants you here, I have no idea.'

Anna didn't say anything, just pushed her shoulders back a bit further.

'To my mind, you're a jumped-up, spoilt brat who's caused more harm than good. But, I'll tolerate you. As long as there's none of your London crap, or' — she picked up a gingernut—'any of that attitude.'

'I'm not sixteen any more, Mrs Beedle,' Anna said with a half-sneer, her hand on her hip.

Mrs Beedle's lip quivered in a mocking smile. 'That's exactly the attitude I'm referring to.' She dunked her biscuit into her tea and sucked some of the liquid off it, before saying, 'So what can you do?'

Anna thought back to the Opera House. She was very good at mingling at parties, casually introducing people; she could calm down an overwrought star with aplomb; she could conjure a masterful quote out of thin air for any production; she could throw a pragmatic response into a heated meeting. And her desk was impeccable, perfect, spotless. A place for everything and everything in its place, her mother would say. 'I'm very organised,' she said in the end.

Mrs Beedle snorted. Then, clicking her fingers in a gesture that meant for Anna to follow, she pulled back the curtain behind her to reveal Anna's worst nightmare. A stockroom filled with stacks and stacks of crap, piled sky-high like the legacy of a dead hoarder.

Anna swallowed. She had imagined spending most of the day sitting behind the desk reading *Grazia*. 'What do I do with it?'

'You organise it.' Mrs Beedle laughed, backing out so that Anna was left alone in the damp-smelling dumping ground and settling herself down in the big orange armchair next to the desk, a thin marmalade cat appearing and twirling through her legs. 'I've been meaning to do it for yonks.'

Anna opened her mouth to say something, but Mrs

Beedle cut her off. 'You know, I think I might actually enjoy this more than I thought I would.'

There had been a time, Anna thought two hours later, as she carefully plucked another horsebrass from a random assortment box and put it into the cardboard box on the shelf she had marked BRASS, that she had had an assistant to do all this type of manual work in her life. In fact, she'd had two. One of them, Kim, she'd rather forget. She had given her her first break and, in return, the ungrateful brat had stolen her contact book and then promptly resigned and was now clawing her way up the ballet world, while Anna was holding what looked like a Mexican death skull between finger and thumb.

Anna had had people to move boxes and post parcels and send emails to the people she'd rather avoid. Her status had defined her. Had made her who she was. She liked the fact she had her own office with her name on the plaque on the door. She liked the fact people came in to ask her advice or crept in in tears and shut the door to bitch about some mean old cow in another department. She liked the signature on the bottom of her email and the fact that she didn't follow most of her Twitter followers back.

She patted the beads of sweat from her face with a folded piece of tissue she'd got from the bathroom and blew her hair out of her eyes. The room had heated up like a furnace and she felt like a rotisserie chicken slowly browning.

She had been somebody. And it didn't matter that at about three o'clock, most days, she had stood in a cubicle in the toilets holding a Kleenex to her eyes after

catching a glimpse of the dancers rehearsing and thinking, *That should have been me*. Before blowing her
nose, telling herself that this was just life, this is what
happens, this feeling is weakness and you're not weak,
Anna Whitehall. Then calling up Seb, all bright-eyed
and smiling voice, asking if he wanted to go for cocktails after work, her treat.

Anna lifted up another brass object: a revolting frame
shaped like a horse-shoe, and thought of her old air-
conditioning unit, her ergonomically designed chair,
the fresh-cut flowers in her office, her snug, new-season
pencil skirt and a crippling pair of beautiful stilettos.

She wanted to grab her old boss by the shoulders
and shout, *Look at me now! Look what you've made me
become, you stupid idiot! Why did you have to scale
down the PR department? Why?*

'Everything all right back there?' Mrs Beedle had
pulled back the curtain and was watching Anna as her
lips moved during her silent tirade. The cat was curled
up under Mrs Beedle's arm, nestled on the plump out-
line of her hip. A wry smile was twitching the woman's
lip as she said, 'Christ, you still stand in third position.'
She shook her head. 'Well I never, you'll be doing pliés
in here next.'

Anna, who hadn't noticed how she was standing,
moved immediately and leant up against the stack behind her.

'Haven't got far, have you?' Mrs Beedle peered at her
work.

Anna frowned. 'I thought I'd done quite a lot. Look!
I have boxes for all the different items. Here—' She

waved her hand along one of the lines of shelves. 'China, figurines, brasses, decorative plates, medals...'

'Maybe,' Mrs Beedle said, with a shrug. 'I'm going for lunch and, as it's so quiet, I'm going to shut the shop and make a couple of deliveries. I'll be back, what? Three-thirty? Four?'

'What should I do?' Anna asked, her forehead beading with sweat, her shorts dusty, her fingers rough with dirt, her Shellac chipping.

'Just carry on as you are. No point stopping now,' Mrs Beedle said and backed out, shaking her head at the marmalade cat. 'She has a lot to learn about work this one, doesn't she? A lot to learn. Always the little princess.'

CHAPTER THREE

'That's it, I fucking hate it here.' Anna was sitting opposite Seb in the King's Head. She could feel the dirt and scum from the shop nestling into her pores.

The pub was as she remembered. Flock wallpaper in red velvet and gold, and a deep-maroon carpet worn threadbare by the end of the bar where the regulars stood. The bar top was dark mahogany, shiny under the low glass lamps and dappled with patches of spilt beer. Silver tankards hung from hooks around the lip of the bar top, swinging below the spirits that were mostly different types of whisky. One side of the room was booth seats and a smattering of round wooden tables. At the back was a dining room that had placemats with hunting scenes or ducks flying.

'Here, drink this, it'll make you feel better.' Seb put a glass of yellow wine down in front of her.

She held it up between finger and thumb, inspected the colour and said, 'I very much doubt it.'

Seb tried to hide a smirk. 'It can't have been that bad.'

'I don't think I can talk about it.' She sighed, taking a sip. Then, unable not to, said, 'She made me clear out the stockroom. Urgh, look at this, sing-along piano tonight.' She picked up a flier that was resting between the mustard and tomato ketchup bottle on their table.

Seb took a sip of his pint and read over the list of songs. '"Knees Up Mother Brown". It's like the good old days.'

Anna took another sip and winced. 'I did a really bad job.'

Seb glanced up. 'Why?'

'Because I didn't want to do it.'

'Anna.' His brow creased. 'You kind of need this job. We seriously don't have any money and if you want a wedding...'

'Sebastian.' She leant forward. 'I get six pounds fifty an hour. Whether I have this job or not, it's not going to cover a wedding. No, I have to get back to London, I have to do some serious looking.'

'Come on. You know there's nothing out there at the moment and the commute will really cost.' He traced the beads of condensation down his glass. 'You're just going to have to get on with it.'

'What if I can't?' she said, and he sighed like he was exasperated with her. The sound took her by surprise; she'd never heard it before. This wasn't the way their relationship worked. Seb adored her. That was their dynamic. It had been since the moment she had walked out of Pret A Manger with her sushi and can of Yoga Bunny and he had walked straight into her, fresh from his interview at Whitechapel Boys' School, fumbled his briefcase and said, 'Wow, God, Anna Whitehall! Didn't expect to bump into you of all people. Wow!'

Really all she wanted now was for him to hate being back as much as she did.

As the fan in the corner of the pub whirred away like it might take off, circulating the stale beer-soaked air, they sat in silence for a second. Murmurs of laughter drifted in from the tables outside the front that Anna hadn't wanted to sit at in case she got bitten by mosquitoes.

'So how was your day?' she said in the end.

Seb held his hands out wide, 'Now she asks!' he said, with a smile. He was good at changing the atmosphere, at not holding a grudge. His aim in life was for everyone to get along, not like Anna, who could cling on to a grudge like nobody's business. But, as usual, she felt herself get sucked into the lines that crinkled around his eyes as he smiled and winked at her across the table.

She rolled her eyes. 'Did you save any poor, badly educated children?'

Seb was back in Nettleton to make a difference. To give back. To do for the new Nettleton generation what their teachers had done for him. Anna could barely remember a teacher, let alone anything good they'd done for her. She could vaguely summon a memory of being whacked with a lacrosse stick accidentally on purpose by Mrs McNamara for calling her a lesbian.

And the satisfaction she'd felt when she'd handed her a note from her ballet teacher exempting her from all school sport because it clashed with her training and the development of her flexibility.

'I made a huge impression,' Seb joked. 'And young minds across the village are rejoicing that I have arrived as head of year.'

A female voice cut in next to them, 'I'm sure they are, Seb, no doubt about it.'

'Jackie, hey, how are you? Come and join us.' Seb edged along his bench seat so Jackie could sit down.

'Anna.' Jackie said by way of greeting, with a distinct lack of emotion.

'Jackie.' Anna replied with similar flatness. Their relationship was such that they'd spent much of their youth circling each other, snogging each other's boyfriends and generally pissing each other off without ever fully acknowledging their mutual dislike.

'So, how are you?' Jackie ran her tongue along her lips, then grinned, 'Never made it to New York, then?'

'No,' Anna winced a smile, cocking her head to one side and then saying sweetly, 'I see you didn't either. Ever make it out of Nettleton?'

Jackie shrugged. 'Everything I need is here.'

Anna blew out a breath in disbelief.

'Whereas you...I mean, what was it we were meant to see? Your name in lights at the Lincoln Center? Wasn't that always the dream?'

Anna pushed a strand of hair out of her eyes. 'I grew too tall to be a dancer.'

Jackie sat back and crossed her legs. 'Shame.'

As the air between them hummed, Seb clapped his hands and said, 'So, what does everyone want to drink?' As Jackie said she'd die for a gin and tonic, Anna hitched her bag on to her shoulder, stood up and said, 'I'll get them.' Just to get away from the table.

She stood, tapping her nails on the bar. *Her name in lights at the Lincoln Center.* It was like a jolt. *New York, Lincoln Center,* her mum had said, holding up an advert listing the New York City Ballet's winter programming in the paper. *If I hadn't got pregnant, that's where I would have been. Imagine being on that stage. Anna, that's the pinnacle.*

When she heard laughter behind her, Anna swung round thinking that it must be about her, but saw instead a couple in the corner enjoying a shared joke. She blew out a breath and tried to relax. But she was like an animal on high alert, poised and ready. At her table Seb and Jackie were looking at something on Jackie's phone and giggling. Anna found herself envying Seb's effortless charm, the ease with which he slipped back into relationships. The way he could be so instantly, unguardedly, involved. Not that she'd ever admit it.

'What's going on?' she asked, as she pushed the tray of drinks on to the table.

'Jackie is educating me on the world of internet dating,' Seb laughed.

'It's nothing,' Jackie waved a hand, 'Just Tinder.'

Anna nodded, not sure what she was talking about but, rather than ask, pretending that she wasn't really that interested. She felt herself doing it on purpose, fitting into the role Jackie expected.

'The website. No?' Jackie said, taking a sip of her gin and tonic, as Anna obviously hadn't been able to hide her blankness as well as she thought. 'Well, I suppose you wouldn't know, not being single. It's meant to be the closest thing to dating in the normal world.' Jackie went on, leaning her elbows on the table, 'You know, you rate people on what they look like, it'd be right up your street, Anna.'

Anna narrowed her eyes.

'Look—' Seb leant forward, Jackie's phone in his hand. 'If you like them, you swipe them into the Yes pile and, if you don't, you swipe them into the No. Isn't it amazing? I just can't believe it exists. It's so ruthless, like some sort of horrible conveyor belt of desperation.'

'Thank you very much, Seb.' Jackie sat back.

'I didn't mean you. I meant them.'

Forgetting her act for a moment, Anna inched her head closer, fascinated, as she watched men appear on screen and Seb swipe them into the No pile as easily as swatting flies.

'Hang on.' Jackie snatched it off him. 'Don't waste my bounty,' she laughed.

Seb leant over her shoulder and said, 'I mean, look at this guy.' He stabbed the shadowy profile picture on the screen, 'Why put that picture up? Why wear a hat and a scarf and take it in the dark? All it does is say I'm fat and/or ugly. Surely that's an immediate no from everyone, because fat, ugly people know the trick because they'd do it themselves, and everyone imagines if they were fat and ugly that's what they would do.

He's a fool.'

Jackie laughed and swiped the shadowy image away.

'He's quite nice, though.' Anna edged closer as a picture of a snowboarder popped up, all tanned, chiselled cheekbones and crazy bleached hair.

'Never fall for the snowboarders or surfers. Believe me, without the get-up they're all pretty average and all they talk about is how great they are.'

'I take it you've been on quite a lot of dates.'

Jackie shrugged. 'A fair few. Before this it was eHarmony and Match. I've done them all.'

Seb crossed his arms over his chest and sat back against the wooden slats of the booth, 'It's interesting, isn't it, the idea of being paired by a computer?'

'I wonder if you two went on something like eHarmony,' Jackie said, without looking up from her swiping, 'whether they'd match you.'

'I doubt it,' Seb guffawed.

Anna tried not to show her shock. 'You don't think?' she asked, as neutrally as she could.

'Oh, come on. You're always going on about how different we are,' he laughed, taking a sip of his pint.

Anna felt her mouth half open, saw Jackie glance up with a wicked look in her eye.

'Well, you are!' Seb said, as if he knew suddenly that he'd said the wrong thing. A slight look of worry on his face.

'Yes.' Anna nodded. 'Yep, I am. Yeah, they'd probably never match us,' she said casually and sat back with her wine, her legs crossed, trying to set her face into a relaxed expression.

Seb looked away from her, back to the phone screen and she felt a chill over her skin despite the stifling humidity. This was a man who used to look at her like she was made of gold, who saw a goodness in her that she barely saw herself, who saw the softness beneath the plating.

She suddenly felt like her dusting of glamour was wearing off.

'Actually, Anna—' Jackie said, handing her phone to Seb. 'I wanted to ask you a favour.'

'A favour?' Anna felt herself stiffen.

Seb paused momentarily and glanced up.

'Well, it's just—' Jackie licked her lips and Anna wondered if she was nervous. Wondered how long she'd been sitting there, laughing and joking, building up to asking whatever it was she was going to ask. 'There's this...this dance group. In the village. They're only little—you know, eight to sixteen. No one's older than sixteen. And well, they always perform in the summer shows and they put on little routines and stuff and everyone really loves it. Well, they've been working towards a *Britain's Got Talent* audition.'

Anna snorted in disbelief at the idea of wanting to go on some hideous ITV show like BGT.

'They're really excited. I mean, really excited. And I know they're not the best but, well, the whole village is kind of behind them.'

They never got behind me, Anna thought, with a feeling not dissimilar to jealousy.

She could tell Seb was listening despite feigning disinterest.

'Anyway,' Jackie shifted uncomfortably in her seat. 'They've been working super, super hard and, well, Mrs Swanson's au pair was teaching them, but her visa ran out a fortnight ago and she hadn't told anyone, so now, well, she left on Wednesday. There's, um, no one to help them.'

'I see.' Anna did a quick nod, rolling her shoulders back. *No way*, she thought, *no way in God's own earth, Jackie, no way. Keep going, but this is never going to happen.*

Someone wedged the front doors open and the sounds from outside got louder, the laughter and chatting, but the heat stayed where it was, like a wobbling great blancmange.

'*You* could do it,' Seb said, jumping into the silence, unable to keep his trap shut.

'I don't think I could, Seb,' Anna glared at him.

'Well, yeah, I mean that was exactly what I was going to ask. You see, it's been me and Mrs McNamara—'

'She's still there?'

Jackie nodded.

Anna blew out a breath of disbelief. 'It's like time literally stood still here.'

'Neither of us are particularly good dancers. I mean, I can hold my own at a party but, you know, I don't exactly know enough to teach them and, well, we all know McNamara's not exactly a lithe mover. I just don't want to let the kids down.'

'I'm sure you don't.' Anna tried to find something to distract herself and rummaged in her bag for her lip gloss. Anna didn't dance. Anna hadn't danced in ten years. She hadn't set foot on a stage, hadn't warmed up, hadn't looked out at the glare of the spotlight or felt the hard floor beneath her feet. Anna's name had never been in lights. 'God, it's so hot. Why does it have to be so goddamn hot?' She could feel Seb watching her.

'Some of them aren't the best kids and it's really good seeing them involved in something—'

'Jackie, I'm really sorry,' Anna cut her off. 'God, it's just insufferably hot.' She pulled her top away from her stomach. 'I'm not going to do it. It's just a definite no.'

'Could you just think about it? We'd pay you?'

'No.' She shook her head again, reaching for the sing-along song sheet to fan herself with. 'All the money in the world and I wouldn't do it.'

'Well, that's not strictly true,' she heard Seb add and shot him a look. 'Actually,' he said, sitting back with a grin on his face, 'You'd be bloody awful teaching kids.'

She narrowed her eyes. He raised a brow. While half of her could sniff out his attempts at reverse psychology in an instant, the other half felt like he was deliberately being mean. Like this was almost her punishment—for hating Nettleton, for spending all their money, for not trying hard enough.

'It's OK.' Jackie shook her head, picking up her gin and tonic and taking a sip. 'I just thought I'd ask.'

Anna rubbed her forehead and felt the heat prickle over her body. Jackie looked away, pretending to glance at the menu chalked up on the blackboard. The fan whirred on above the din of chat in the bar, a low hum beating out the seconds of their silence. Anna watched a fruit fly land in a spilt drop of her white wine and was about to lift her glass to squash it when Seb almost leapt from his seat.

'Holy shit!' he shouted.

'What?' Both Jackie and Anna said at the same time, equally desperate for some distraction after the dance snub.

'It's Smelly Doug.'

Jackie pulled the screen her way. 'God, it is as well. And look, he has a Porsche, he's photographed himself leaning against it. Oh, no.'

'I don't know who you're talking about,' Anna said, confused.

Jackie took another sip of her drink. 'You know, Smelly Doug. Never washed his hair, trousers too short, huge rucksack...?'

Anna only had a vague recollection. 'Was he in the year below us?' Everything to do with school, pre-London, pre-The English Ballet Company School, was a bit of a blur. All she could remember was coming back for a few summers to stay with her dad and despising every minute of it.

'This is fascinating,' Seb said, as he clicked to look at more photos. 'There's one of him in Egypt. Doing that point at the top of the Pyramids.'

'You should go on a date with him, Jackie.' Seb nodded at her over the rim of his pint.

'No way.' Jackie shook her head.

'Go on. It'd be a social experiment. Catch up, see what he's up to. Find out how he could afford a Porsche. It's a fact-finding mission. I'm putting him in your Yeses.'

'Don't you dare,' Jackie laughed. Anna watched them, feeling stupid for feeling left out.

'Too late.' Seb sat back, smug, and Jackie snatched the phone back, incredulous.

As Seb went to take a final gulp of his drink, his eyes dancing with triumph, Anna toyed with a coaster, pretending not to envy their laughter.

Then a shadow fell across the table. And Anna heard a familiar voice drawl, 'Seb, darling, I thought you were going to pop round as soon as you arrived.' Hilary, Seb's mother, was standing at the end of their table, feigning her disgruntlement with a dramatic wave of her hand. But when she then pressed her palm over her crêped cleavage, the pearls looped round her neck bunched up and caught on the buttons of her cream silk blouse, causing her to turn to Seb's father, Roger, for help disentangling herself.

Seb glanced between the two of them, 'Sorry, Mum. Yes, we were going to pop round. Arrived late last night though.'

'Hi, Hilary. Hi, Roger.' Anna stood up as much as the table would allow against her legs.

'Hello, Anne,' Hilary said, not looking up from her tangled pearls.

Anna rolled her eyes internally; she knew she called her the wrong name deliberately. Every time she met Seb's parents, they made her feel like she wasn't good enough for their son. Like he'd trailed his hand in the Nettleton mud one day and pulled out Anna. The list of problems was endless. Her parents' divorce, their messy break-up, her father's job, her mother being Spanish, like her immigrant blood would pollute the famous Davenport gene pool. They must rue the day their lost, London-shell-shocked son had bumped into Anna Whitehall on her lunch break in Covent Garden. They must look back and wonder why they didn't do their weekend orienteering round London rather than the Hampshire countryside. That way Seb would have been savvy and street-wise, not like a lame duck ready and waiting for her fox-like claws to swipe him away. And now, of course, despite getting their precious youngest son back under Nettleton lock and key, the reason behind it had been her fault. Her inability to keep her job. Her fault he left his position at the elite Whitechapel Boys' School. Nothing to do with him hating fucking Whitechapel, all the boys who just put their iPhone headphones in during lessons and said things like, *'My father pays your salary, Sir. Which kind of means he owns you, doesn't it? He paid for that suit you're wearing.'*

'So what's happening with this wedding, then? It's very unusual, this limbo,' Hilary sighed. 'Postponed? Everyone's been ringing me up, asking what it means. People like to be able to make plans, Anne. They have to book hotels. You must understand.'

Anna nodded. 'We are sorting it, Hilary.'

'Well that's all very well for you to say, but it doesn't look like you are. As far as I can see, you have a dress and a hotel that's gone into receivership. And when people ask me what's going on I simply don't know. I know you've lost money, but what about what we gave you?'

Anna could feel herself getting hotter again. Wanting to shoo Jackie away so she didn't witness her humiliation at the hands of Hilary and Roger.

When she'd told Seb how much she'd paid and, as a result, how much she'd lost, the main point he'd kept repeating was: just don't let my mum and dad know.

'It's young people and the value of money, Hilly,' Roger mused. 'I just can't believe you didn't pay for it on a credit card. Everyone knows you pay on credit cards. Instant insurance.'

Anna swallowed. The credit cards she'd kept free to pay off the rest of it, month by month, to siphon off from the salary that she no longer had. 'I've applied to the administrator, I'm doing everything I can.'

Roger snorted. 'As if that will do anything at all. You won't see a penny. You're just a generation who thought they could have, have, have. I blame Labour. All you *Guardian* readers thinking that the world owes you another pair of shoes. What's that woman in that ghastly programme?'

'*Sexy in the City*,' Hilary sighed.

'Yes, just like that. Well, it's come back to bite you.' Roger tapped a cigarette out of a silver case that he always carried in the top pocket of his shirt, put it between his lips but didn't light it, just sucked on the raw tobacco.

Jackie at least had the decency to absorb herself in her phone, Anna noticed, as Hilary leant a hand on the table and said, 'You need to sort it, Anne. Can't fail at your first job as a wife. That wouldn't do at all.'

Tell them to stop, Seb, she thought, as they carried on.

Tell them to stop.

But he said nothing, just looked at his glass.

The conversation swirled on around her until she heard Jackie say, 'I know, I've been trying to persuade her to put her phenomenal talent to use back here in Nettleton. Razzmatazz are heading towards a big *Britain's Got Talent* audition.'

'And Anna—' Hilary frowned, 'You're not doing it?'

'I just—' Anna made a face, glanced at Jackie and thought, *you sly cow*.

'You really should, Anna. I would have thought you'd jump at the chance of extra money. Seb, what do you think?'

Tell them that you think it's a terrible idea. Tell them something, because you know, more than anything, I don't want to dance.

Seb licked his lower lip and said, 'I think it's Anna's decision.'

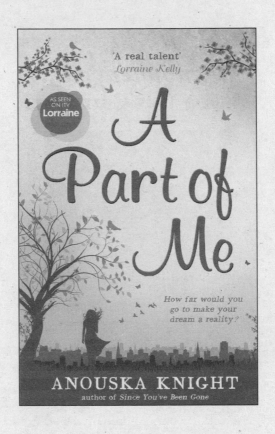

It's a truth universally acknowledged...

...that a single woman teetering on the verge of thirty must be in want of a husband.

Not true for Manhattanite Elizabeth Scott. Instead of planning a walk down the aisle, she's crossing the pond with the only companion she needs—her darling dog, Bliss. Caring for a pack of show dogs in England seems the perfect distraction from the scandal that ruined her career. What she doesn't count on is an unstoppable attraction to billionaire dog breeder Donovan Darcy.

Have you ever wondered what your life would have been like if you'd chosen a different man?

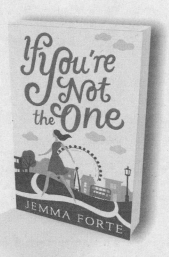

Jennifer Wright is not entirely sure she's happy. Yes, she's got a husband, two lovely children and a nice house, but has she really made the right choice about who to spend the rest of her life with?

When she's knocked down by a car and ends up in a coma, she has the chance to see where her life would have taken her had she stayed with her exes. Maybe looking back will help her to make the biggest decision of her life…